Nobody's Angel

Nobody's Angel

Monique Miller

www.urbanchristianonline.com

Urban Books, LLC
78 East Industry Court
Deer Park, NY 11729

ISBN 13: 978-1-60162-758-2
ISBN 10: 1-60162-758-0

First Printing June 2013
Printed in the United States of America

10 9 8 7 6 5 4 3 2 1

*This is a work of fiction. Any references or similarities
to actual events, real people, living or dead, or to real
locales are intended to give the novel a sense of reality.
Any similarity in other names, characters, places, and
incidents is entirely coincidental.*

Distributed by Kensington Corp.
Submit Wholesale Orders to:
Kensington Publishing Corp.
C/O Penguin Group (USA) Inc.
Attention: Order Processing
405 Murray Hill Parkway
East Rutherford, NJ 07073-2316
Phone: 1-800-526-0275
Fax: 1-800-227-9604

Nobody's Angel

Other Novels by Monique Miller

In Order of Release

Acknowledgments

As always, I want to thank the Lord for giving me this gift and talent for writing. I pray that you continue to give me more stories to share. It has been a blessing to be able to write and I can't believe this is already my sixth novel. It seems like just yesterday I was getting the first one published.

I thank my family. My mom, Ms. Gwendolyn Miller, and my father, Mr. William Miller, for you encouragement and support and mostly for your unconditional love. I love you, Mom and Dad! Also thank you to my sisters and brothers, Denita, Penny, B.J. aka "Will," Christopher and Christina. Penny, you inspire me so very much, please don't ever lose your loving character and godly spirit.

Thank you to Anthony Clark for your encouragement, love, and assistance during the writing of this novel. Mr. and Mrs. Pearson, thank you as well for your help and support during the finishing stages of this novel, it was and is still greatly appreciated.

To the best kids in the world, my daughter Meliah, thank you for your belief in my writing. You inspire me every day to continue sharing my stories with others. To A.J. thank you for the very sweet and loving spirit you possess. You two brighten my days.

I want to acknowledge the WIC Chicks of the Harnett County, NC WIC program. Especially the three NUTS, Annette, Beverly, and LaVonda, who listened to

Acknowledgments

me talk about Morgan's antics. Thank you for listening and letting me bounce ideas off of you. Jennifer, Carla, and Kerri—Morgan is back!

The New Vision Writers Group is one of the best writing groups around and I am proud to be a part. Thank you all for your words of impartation: Jacquelin, Cassandra, Sandy, Suzetta, Karen, Angela, Brian and Titus. See you on the third Saturday.

A special thanks goes out to my agent ShaShana Crichton and my editor Joylynn Ross. You all have been extremely patient in this process and I thank you very, very much!

To all the readers who have followed my novels, I thank you again and again. I hope you'll enjoy this new novel. You'll see some characters from three of my other novels, *Redemption Lake, Quiet As It's Kept,* and *The Marrying Kind.*

Chapter 1

"Get your hands off of me," Morgan said as she snatched her arm away from the man in the suit.

"You are Morgan Tracy, right?" the man was asking her again for the second time.

"Yes, and I want you and your men to get out of my house," Morgan said.

She looked around as a swarm of other men and a couple of women in uniform stormed her house. They had started touching her things, looking in cabinets and through the drawers of her kitchen. "Just what is the meaning of this?"

"Miss, you will need to come with me," the man said.

"I am not going anywhere with you. And don't try to touch me again or I'll have your badge," Morgan said.

She saw one of the women picking up her purse, which sat on her couch. "Take your hands off of my things," Morgan screamed at the woman. She stepped toward the woman to take the purse, but the woman ignored her approach and placed the purse in a bag.

The man stopped her further approach by firmly placing his hand on her shoulder. "You don't want to do that, Ms. Tracy."

"It is Mrs. Tracy," Morgan said.

"Look, lady—and I use the term loosely—you are being arrested for falsely claiming domestic abuse by your estranged husband Mr. Will Tracy. He is pressing charges against you for having him falsely arrested."

"My husband is straight lying. He beat me and now he's got you all here to bully me." Morgan shook her head and wagged her finger in the man's face. "I tell you one thing." She took a deep breath. "Before this day is over, somebody is going to pay for the pain and suffering you all are putting me through."

She looked around at everyone in the room and pointed at them. "Heads are going to roll when I contact the police chief, the mayor, and even the governor about the mental and physical abuse you all are putting me through, I'll tell you that."

Morgan knew she had well made her point as she crossed her arms in defiance. But the man and all of his cronies hadn't even been fazed one bit by what she was saying. It was as if she wasn't even really standing there. The only one really paying her any attention was the man standing in front of her, and he looked bored.

"What's your name again?" Morgan asked. He'd said it and even showed her an official-looking police badge, but she couldn't remember what he'd said.

"Officer Adams." The man sounded as bored as he looked. "Now let's go down to the police department so we can ask you a few more questions."

Morgan stood back on her haunches and rolled her neck. "Maybe you have wax in your ears, but I said I'm not going anywhere with you."

"Barnes and Rodriguez." Officer Adams called two of the other officers over.

"Yes, sir," said the officer with a uniform that said Barnes on it.

"Cuff her so we can take her down to the precinct."

"Yes, sir," the other officer, Rodriguez, said.

Morgan couldn't believe her ears, her eyes, or even the feeling she had in her arms as they were yanked behind her as she was being handcuffed.

"Get off me! Get off me!" Morgan said.

Officer Adams said, "Mr. Tracy has also said that over the past year you have been making attempts to kill him."

Morgan pulled away from the officers once the handcuffs were on her. She'd pulled so hard that she'd almost fallen down. She'd had to stumble forward to prevent falling flat on her face. "Look, my husband can be a little delusional at times. I can explain all of that to you. Just take these handcuffs off of me," Morgan said.

Her temper was really starting the get the best of her and she was trying her very best to keep it in check. Now that they had put handcuffs on her she was having a really hard time trying to keep the little bit of composure she was maintaining.

She could only imagine what she looked like. She had just woken up a few minutes prior to the invasion at her door. A sound outside had drawn her to look out of her window. It was then that she saw police cars parked on the street and in her driveway. In addition, she saw a few cops lurking in her front and side yards.

The pit of her stomach had felt like it had dropped the same as if she had been dipping on a roller coaster at Disney World—only this wasn't Disney World. Right then it actually felt like she was in an episode of *The Twilight Zone*. She wondered if her past had finally caught up with her.

She'd closed her eyes, shut them tight, and hoped when she opened them the scene outside would have disappeared. But when she opened them up, not only had the scene stayed the same, but her doorbell was being rung at the same time. She stood where she was, figuring if she ignored it they would all just go away; that was, until she heard a loud thumping sound ramming her front door.

Taking the steps two at a time she ran down her stairs to see what was going on. When the door crashed open Morgan stood stark still as three police officers streamed into her home with their guns drawn. She'd raised her hands not so much out of surrender, but to make sure the policemen wouldn't have an inkling to shoot her for fear that she had something in her hands to harm them.

The seconds of reflection about the most recent morning events ended when the officer placed his hand on Morgan's head to lead her out of the front door.

She pushed her head back. "Take your hands off of my hair." She could only imagine how she looked now. There hadn't been any time to comb her hair, brush her teeth, put makeup on, or even to put on any regular clothing. At least she had slept in a matching pajama set.

"I am going to tell you one more time to get out of my house." She pulled at the handcuffs behind her back. "Take these handcuffs off of me."

With a look of annoyance, the officer said, "And I am going to tell you again, Ms. Tracy, that we are going to finish our questions downtown at the precinct."

Morgan opened her mouth to say something else but was interrupted by Office Adams. "We will also be investigating the accusations that your husband is giving us about the name you continue to debate with me. He states you are really Ci Ci Jackson, or something to that effect."

Morgan shut her mouth at this statement. Now something clicked for her. She figured it was time to really calm down and think before she uttered another word. It seemed as though her past was finally catching up with her.

One of the other officers led her outside to an await-ing police car. Just as Morgan sat in the seat she looked up. Down the street, parked in one of the neighbor's driveways, she saw what was undeniably her husband Will watching the whole spectacle. Her jaw dropped open as she stared at him.

She knew he had been the one behind getting the police there. And she had to inwardly smile knowing that the man had finally gotten a clue, even though it had taken him two years to do so. Now she would have to see where the cards fell in her situation so that she could play the next hands dealt to her.

"Do you have something to say to that, Ms. Tracy?" Office Adams asked as he got ready to close the car door.

Morgan muttered under her breath, "Don't I have the right to remain silent?" Morgan sneered at the of-ficer. "I want a lawyer."

Chapter 2

"Lookie here. Lookie here. If it ain't Miss Center-fold," said a woman making a beeline straight toward Morgan.

Morgan looked around, wondering who the woman was talking to. She hoped it wasn't her. She hoped that she'd be able to peacefully serve her time at the correctional facility without anyone bothering her. It would be fine with her to spend her time there without having to speak a word to another soul. Then she realized no one else was in her vicinity.

Obviously seeing the confusion in Morgan's face, the woman said, "Yeah, I'm talking to you."

This time Morgan knew without a shadow of doubt that this beady-eyed, buck-toothed, scraggly-haired woman was talking to her. And she didn't have time for it. She was still reeling from being booked and processed into the correctional facility after being sent from the Silvermont City Jail.

She'd been transported on a bus like she was part of some sort of chain gang, except without the chain. They'd herded them in like cattle at first. Then one at a time they were processed. She'd had to give them her vital information, they took her fingerprints, she had to shower and was then given an ID bracelet along with a correctional center–issued outfit. The clothing consisted of a top, pants, and sneakers with Velcro. Then they had her stand and take a picture with an inmate number of 12549 that corresponded with the number on her ID bracelet.

Once processing was over they led her to her cell. It looked like it was about eight by twelve feet. There were two beds, which were situated across from each other. Each side of the room was a mirror image of the other side of the room. Each side had a desk, a mirror that consisted of a shiny metal surface instead of glass, and a bookshelf built on to the wall over the desk. The chair for the desk resembled a short stool, which was bolted to the floor. There would be no relaxing and sitting back at the desk.

There was one toilet that had a sink attached to the back of it. There wasn't a partition to offer privacy for whoever was sitting on the toilet. Morgan's mouth dropped. She wondered if they really expected her to take care of her needs with other eyes watching. Morgan figured it would be her new home until her trial. The thought repulsed her.

One side was bare of everything but a set of sheets and a second correctional facility uniform. The other side was sparsely filled with personal belongings of another woman. While Morgan was glad she wasn't going to have to share a large cell with three or four women, or even a large room filled with a sea of bunk beds of women, it looked as if she was still going to have at least one other person with whom she was going to have to share the tiny space.

She had no curious inkling or anticipation about meeting whoever the other woman was. But she did hope that whoever it was had the common decency to give Morgan as much personal space as possible and she would do the same—unlike the woman who was now staring into Morgan's face and invading her personal space. The heavyset, buxom, scraggly-haired, buck-toothed woman had made her way across the day room and was now close enough that Morgan could see the details on the cross the woman had tattooed on her collarbone, as well as a little pimple that was starting to form on the woman's nose.

Flaring her nostrils, Morgan sneered at the woman. "Do I know you?"

The woman rolled her neck. "No, but I know you." She held up a newspaper of sorts and continued by saying, "Page seventeen, third row and the second one in." Then she pointed at a picture.

Upon a closer look, Morgan realized it was a picture of her. She snatched the paper from the woman. "What is this?"

"*Locked Up Magazine*," the woman said.

Morgan stood and started to pace. "How dare they put my picture in some magazine?"

"Oh Lord have mercy, calm down and get your panties out of a wad. You ain't the only star in this joint. And don't be acting so high and mighty up in here either. Ain't nobody no angel here," the woman said.

Morgan continued to stare at her picture with her name written under it and the crime she'd committed. It was her real name, not the alias she had been using for the past couple of years. She gaped at the picture. She looked like a mess. Her hair was unkempt; she hadn't had time to put on any makeup that morning of the arrest and she'd barely had an hour's worth of sleep.

The photograph only remotely looked like the beautiful woman she had worked so hard to transform herself into over the past years. The name Cecily C. Jackson reminded her of the past she left behind years ago. She'd grown accustomed to the name Morgan, and even though she'd stolen the name and used it for over three years now, the first chance she got she was going to legally change it—mainly her middle name.

The woman snatched the paper back. "Like I said, you ain't the only star in this joint." She flipped a couple of pages back and pointed to another woman. "See this girl here? Miss Candice was arrested for solicitation. And there she is sitting there on that bench over there, reading a book."

Morgan looked at the picture of the woman in the paper and realized that it was indeed the same woman the gap-toothed woman was referring to. Candice's picture didn't look much different from how the woman looked just a few feet away.

The other inmate proceeded to show Morgan a couple more women with their pictures and why they had been arrested. She'd had a stack of the newspaper magazines in her hand. She opened one and grinned. Morgan could see the fillings on a couple of her teeth in the back.

"And can you guess who this is?" the woman asked.

Morgan really couldn't care less who she was going to point to next. She just wanted her to leave her alone so that she could continue sulking in peace about the situation she had gotten herself into. Morgan glanced at the picture in hopes that afterward she would go find someone else to report to with her TMZ-style of gossip reporting.

As soon as Morgan looked at the picture she realized it was Miss Gap-toothed herself. Under the picture it had a name. "Desiree Little. Is that your name?"

"Yep." The woman grinned.

The paper said that Desiree had been arrested for driving with expired tags and for a warrant being out on her for unpaid parking tickets. In the picture the woman looked a little thinner in the face and her hair looked better, not much, but a little better than it did live and in person.

It was hard to believe that it had been a week since the arrest fiasco at Morgan's home. As soon as she was able, the police allowed her to call a lawyer. Since she didn't know of any, she picked one out of the yellow pages of the phone book. And once it was all done, she'd wished her finger had fallen on someone else in her seemingly methodical "Eeny, meeny, miny, moe" style of picking.

Her lawyer hadn't been worth the paper on which his business cards were made. She had been charged with identity theft, and her husband had placed charges against her for his attempted murder.

Desiree looked at Morgan expectantly as if waiting for her to make a comment about her mug shot in the paper.

"Nice picture," Morgan said. Then she added, "You look a little thinner in the picture though." Morgan wondered just how long the woman had been in the correctional facility.

"That's because that was my first mug shot." Desiree pulled another paper from the stack she was holding. "This is my most recent one." She showed her the other paper. "This time they got me for writing a worthless check for $1,800. That's a Class C felony."

Sure enough Morgan could see a better resemblance to the woman who was now sitting in her personal space. "Oh," was all Morgan could say.

As if Morgan couldn't read for herself, the woman extended her hand and said, "Even though it says my name is Desiree, you can call me Tiny."

Desiree, who wanted to be called Tiny, was a big woman and nothing on her body was indeed tiny, except maybe for the little cross tattoo she had. Morgan looked down at the woman's hand and wondered if she was in the Twilight Zone or something. They weren't at some country club talking and networking for some charity. They were locked up in the state correctional facility. She wondered what the heck was up with all the niceties the woman was extending.

Seeing that Desiree wasn't going to put her hand down anytime soon, Morgan extended her hand and gave the woman a limp handshake. "Mor . . ." Morgan started to state the name she'd been going by for the past couple of years, then thought better of it, especially since the name on her mug shot clearly read Cecily C. Jackson.

"More what?" Desiree asked.

"Oh, nothing." Morgan shook her head. "Cecily Jackson."

"Cecily? That's a pretty name," Desiree said.

Morgan's thoughts turned to concern about Desiree. She stared to wonder if the woman was being nice to her in order to try to hit on her. The other inmate was generous with her compliments and it could have only been her imagination, but it seemed as though Desiree was saying her name just a little bit too warmly for her liking.

"What's your middle name? What does the 'C' stand for?" Desiree asked.

The woman was getting way too close and personal for Morgan's taste. And there was no way she was going to tell her that her middle name was Chlamydia, spelled just like the STD. Morgan rolled her eyes as she remembered the first time she found out her middle name was the same as a health disease. Her grandmother, Mama Geraldine as Morgan had called her when she was growing up, had been the one to tell her the story about how proud her mother had been at finding such a pretty name in a magazine at her doctor's office.

Her mother was country, plain and simple, was what Morgan figured. She was too dumb to realize what the word really meant and stood for. Morgan was sure that each and every person from the nurses in the delivery room to the staff at the pediatrician's office had probably laughed at her behind her back for naming her baby such a thing. The conclusions about her mother being plain and simple were solidified over the years as her grandmother often told her other stories about some of the other simple and dumb things her mother had done. The only thing it seemed her mother had been halfway smart about was leaving their little country town and never looking back—that was, except for the fact that she hadn't even looked back long enough to take with her little five-year-old Cecily who she'd abandoned.

After the abandonment by her mother, the only person Morgan had to call a mom was her grandmother, Geraldine. Many of her friends in school actually thought Geraldine was her mother. Even her ex-husband had been under the assumption that Ms. Geraldine was Morgan's mother, and Morgan hadn't corrected him when he had asked her about Morgan's supposedly dead mother.

It was true; Morgan had lied to her husband and told him that her mother was dead. As far as she was concerned her biological mother was dead to her. And, sadly enough, Morgan had no way of knowing if the woman was really alive.

Desiree sat and literally stared Morgan down her throat. Morgan was getting tired of playing nice new girl. "Look, my middle name is none of your business."

The woman sat back. "Oh, well excuse me. I was just trying to make small talk."

"Well, thanks, but no thanks," Morgan said.

"I'll leave you be then. You've got a lot to learn. I was just trying to be nice and welcome you here." Desiree picked up all of her magazines, flipped her hands in a waving manner, and said, "Carry on. I'm gonna pray for you in the meantime."

She clearly heard the sarcasm in the woman's voice. "Keep your prayers to yourself," Morgan mumbled to herself and rolled her eyes. Then louder she said, "Who would want to be welcomed to a place like this? I just want a little privacy."

The woman named Tiny chuckled as she increased the distance.

She had probably laughed because with so many people sitting in the day room, Morgan still was not going to have but so much privacy. Not to mention the fact that there were two guards lurking around and video surveillance cameras in each corner of the big room.

When their break in the day room was over, Morgan welcomed the fact that she could go back to the minimal solace of her room. It wasn't the best place of comfort but at least there she had only one other person to think about being in her personal space.

The first thing she noticed upon walking into the cell was that her roommate's belongings were gone. She breathed a small sigh of relief. If she was lucky, maybe she would have the cell to herself for the rest of the day and night, and even more luck might grant her the chance to have a few more days in what she would consider a private cell of sorts.

Her mattress was not comfortable in the least, completely unlike the mattress she had in her home. But she had slept on much worse in her day and the whole situation she was enduring at the correctional facility now was only bringing back memories she'd kept at bay for years. She had no desire whatsoever to relive and remember them. She looked over at her self-made calendar, focusing on the X marks she'd made on each passing day.

When one of the guards walked by her cell she asked, "Hey, what happened to my roommate?" The question might have sounded like she was actually concerned about the inmate whose name she really didn't remember. Morgan was there to do her time, not make a network of new friends.

"I heard she left on a technicality. Something about her Miranda rights not being told to her when she was arrested," the guard said. He walked off, not paying Morgan any more attention.

It didn't matter; Morgan wasn't paying any more attention to the guard either. Her mind had shifted to the day of her arrest. Had she been read her full Miranda rights? She remembered mentioning something about having her own right to be silent, and the detective smirked at her, closing the door in her face. The more she thought about it, they had indeed failed to give her the full Miranda rights later through booking and arrest. She had demanded to be able to call a lawyer and figured that in the midst of her being uncooperative with the detective and police officers they'd simply forgotten.

She sat up straight on her bunk. Maybe, just maybe, there would be a loophole for her, a technicality as well. She was going to have to get up with her good-for-nothing lawyer. Surely the guy could get this part right. He hadn't even asked her about the Miranda rights statement.

Morgan located her correctional facility—issued phone card, which had ten minutes on it. She waited at the payphone for about ten minutes as another woman sounded like she was talking to her kids and mother. Morgan rolled her eyes as the woman made little cooing noises to a child, and as the woman tearfully hung up the phone when the called ended. When the woman turned around and made eye contact with Morgan, she smiled a bit as she wiped a tear from her eyes. Morgan stared back at her, poker-faced. There was no way she was trying to give the woman some kind of warm and fuzzy smile. *She'd better look elsewhere.*

She brushed by the woman and grabbed the phone before anyone else could jump in front of her. Flipping the calling card over, she dialed the number that she'd committed to memory. When the phone of the lawyer's office was picked up on the other end, she started to speak, not wanting to waste a second more of her tenminute card than she needed to.

To her dismay she realized it was a voice mail recording speaking instead of a live person. Then, to her further dismay, she didn't like what she was hearing on the message. The lawyer was on vacation. As her luck would have it, his vacation had started that very same day. He wouldn't be back for a week.

Once she heard the tone to leave a message, she quickly left her name and information along with a brief message stating that it was urgent that the lawyer call her about a possible technicality in her case. She slammed the phone down on the receiver, as she realized she had used up three of her ten minutes making the call.

Chapter 3

Morgan hadn't had a chance to enjoy her private cell to herself for more than twenty-four hours before they moved Desiree in. From her first moments of moving in, Desiree chatted away and asked a multitude of nosey and probing questions. Morgan had ignored most of the questions, hoping that Desiree would get the hint that she wasn't about to be her gal pal in the slammer.

It seemed as if the next couple of weeks' time seemed to creep by in a recurrent factory-type mode, with not very much excitement and things to do. It was true what she'd heard: that in correctional facilities people got "three hots and a cot," three hot meals and a place to lay your head, and it definitely wasn't any Club Med. The time she was doing was considered soft time, as opposed to the hard time others got with which there were no frills or privileges like going outside on the yard, or watching television in the day room.

Each day was basically the same. In the morning they rose before the crack of dawn for breakfast, then returned to their cell area for supposedly free time, then lunch was served before noon; after, they were given the other supposed time to be a part of some sort of group. They had groups of all kinds. There was a group for postpartum moms with the baby blues. They had classes for people trying to complete their General Equivalency Diploma, also known as the GED. They even had classes for those who wanted to learn a trade like cosmetology. Now her roommate, Desiree, was a completely different story as she seemed to be the correctional facility socialite trying to spread joy and happiness within the gray walls and attending any group gathering that would have her.

Not surprising to Morgan, they even had the preachers, pastors, and clergymen who came in, holding church to try to save the women's souls from the grasp of the devil. Even though Morgan had had no intention of going anywhere near their gatherings, Tiny, with her smooth-talking voice, talked her into going one evening. As it happened the minister from that night had been one from the church she previously attended with her ex-husband Will. Luckily, the minister didn't know her and she didn't know the minister. She was sure word about their marital fiasco had spread through the church, but since she didn't attend that often, hopefully this guy had no idea who she was.

She spent most of the little Bible Study time thinking about getting out of the correctional facility and what she would do once she was finally released. Her thoughts had been interrupted when the minister spoke directly to her, asking her if she was a saved woman. Somewhere from the depths of her soul, Morgan's temper flared; she was sick and tired of so-called holy people trying to help her. As far as she was concerned they were all wolves in sheep's clothing, out to devour her once they had her trust. She stormed out of the meeting and never went back to another one, ignoring the pleas of her cellmate.

She'd guessed overall, from looking at some of the other inmates, Desiree hadn't been that bad of a selection, even though she was a bit of a holy roller of sorts. There were a couple of people with body odor. One woman a couple of doors down from them snored so loudly at night that it seemed as though she were right there in the same cell with them. So she was glad the woman wasn't actually in the same cell. Then there was another woman who walked around not saying a word to anyone, leaving many to speculate about her. The scoop from Desiree was that the woman had been locked up for allegedly trying to kill her husband with a knife. Word had it that the husband was in intensive care and things were touch and go.

Morgan knew there was always more than one side to a story, and either the woman *was* actually trying to kill her husband *or* she might have been defending herself. It all depended on the circumstances. Morgan knew about circumstances all too well. So on the surface of things, it seemed as though Morgan and this particular woman had a few things in common—because situations could bring a person to allegedly do many things. Too often people judged others by mere appearances and what circumstances seemed to actually be. Morgan shook her head to herself.

Desiree let any- and everybody know how good the Lord had been to her and that the Lord was her Savior, but she wasn't a Bible-toting, "thump you over the head" type of holy roller. Not every other sentence or word out of her mouth was about the Lord and how she wanted to help lead each and every person she could to salvation, so Morgan at least respected that much, especially since Tiny respected how adamant Morgan was about not wanting to be converted to complete salvation.

"Miss Centerfold." Morgan heard Desiree calling her by the nickname Desiree had deemed appropriate for her.

Morgan rolled her eyes at Desiree. She did so more so in annoyance than she did for a dislike of the woman. Surprisingly enough Desiree wasn't as bad as she'd first thought she was going to be. Desiree was definitely in the know when it came to knowing the happenings around the facility. But Desiree also knew when and where to draw the line as far as Morgan was concerned. The woman could sense when Morgan felt like talking and when she didn't want to be bothered.

Since she hadn't been in a good mood that morning she figured Desiree was going out on a limb to disturb her now.

"What, Desiree?" Morgan said. She knew Desiree hated to be called by her real name and preferred the nickname Tiny instead.

This time Desiree rolled her own eyes. "Don't call me that."

"Touché," Morgan said.

"Too what? Stop with all that French," Desiree said.

"Just giving it back to you," Morgan said.

Desiree smiled and rolled her eyes again. "Whatever. I've been saying your name, but you didn't seem to hear me. Thought you'd answer quicker to your nickname." Desiree grinned. "And you did."

"What's so important?" Morgan asked.

"Come on." Desiree stood and gestured to Morgan to come.

"Huh?" Morgan asked.

"It's visiting hours," Desiree said.

Morgan settled back on her bunk. "And what difference does that make to me?" Morgan waved her hand in a dismissive nature. "Go ahead and have fun, enjoy the time with your family."

"I am, but you've got a visitor too," Desiree said.

"Huh?"

"Yeah. They called out your name too, for a visitor."

Morgan perked up. "It's about time." She sat forward, slipped on her shoes, and followed Desiree. "My young, redheaded, freckle-faced lawyer could have at least called me to let me know he was coming."

"That's the way it is sometimes," Desiree said.

It was the first time Morgan had ever had a visitor, so she was delayed a slight bit longer than Desiree as she had to have explained the rules set for prisoners with visitors, and agree to adhere to those rules. The rules stated that she wasn't to take anything from the other person, and had to refrain from prolonged contact with the other person as well. She was antsy and agreed to whatever they said, not wanting them to waste any more of the time she could be spending talking with her lawyer. It wasn't like she had any plans of touching him. And she had information to give him, not the other way around.

When she was finally led into the visitors area, she scanned the room as she looked around for her lawyer. She didn't see him. The room was crowded with inmates and their family, friends, and various other loved ones. Desiree sat at a table as she talked with an older woman who looked like an older version of Desiree. She figured it had to be Desiree's mom. Also at the table there were two children: a little girl and boy.

Looking at Desiree and her mom gave Morgan pause. So many moms and daughters looked alike. She could only wonder if she resembled her own mother now that she was a full-grown woman. She had no way of knowing since she could barely remember what her mother even looked like. Her grandmother had long since gotten rid of any pictures of Morgan's mother. The whole scene of mother and daughter and children visiting with a cohesive spirit tugged at the outer edges of her heart—but only at the outer edges. She wouldn't let the thoughts and feelings get any further than that.

She shook off the encroaching thoughts and feelings. As she walked farther into the room she scanned it again. Then she stopped short and gasped, seeing another all-too-familiar face. The face wasn't that of her lawyer either. Sitting alone at a table, and waiting for her to come in, sat Morgan's ex-husband Will. As if someone had doused her with frozen water, she completely stopped dead in her tracks. Morgan had always been the one happy to surprise and shock others, not the other way around. It was obvious her ex was taking glee in what he had done. The smirk on her ex-husband's face revealed that he took delight in being able to catch her off-guard.

Chapter 4

Morgan felt something brush across her leg and she came out of the frozen trance she had been in as she stared at her ex-husband. The brush across her leg had come from one of Desiree's kids. He was running around, pretending like he was an airplane. He wasn't a very good airplane because he was bumping into people and things left and right.

She did her best to regain her composure and stood to her full five feet eight inch height. Self-consciously she touched her unkempt hair, which she had normally been accustomed to being done every week. In addition to her hair being a mess, she hadn't put on any makeup in days to cover the blemishes on her cocoa-colored skin. But it was too late; there was nothing she could do about making herself look presentable right then.

In her mind it didn't really matter much anyway; she figured he'd come there to gloat. With reluctance she stepped over to the table that Will was sitting at. She slid into the chair facing him, the whole time wondering why he had even come in the first place.

"Hello, Ci Ci," Will said.

She wasn't exactly sure, but she thought she heard a bit of sarcasm in his voice. The last time he'd called her Ci Ci she heard not only the sarcasm, but the hurt that accompanied. She heard it in his voice as he confronted her with information about knowing what her real name was.

There was no need telling him she preferred the name Morgan; he already knew that all too well. "Hello, Will." She countered with the same emphasis and tone he'd greeted her with. She wasn't really sure what she was dealing with, still wondering why he'd even come. What did they really have to talk about? She knew where he stood. He was hurt, he'd loved her, and she'd treated his love like an old, worn rag.

They sat for a few moments without either saying a word. Morgan wasn't about to say anything. She wanted him to make the next move, especially since he'd made his first move by coming here to see her in the first place.

With a sigh Will finally spoke. "Why did you do it?"

Oh, now she understood. He was there for some answers. He didn't understand. Maybe he wanted to get back with her, maybe this good ol' church guy was there to ask why she did all that she did and then forgive her. Then they could go on with their lives and finally go to the counseling he so desperately wanted them to go to.

Morgan took a deep breath as she thought about how gullible Will was.

"Just tell me why," Will said again.

Seeing it as a chance to go round two with Will, Morgan decided to apologize and tell him whatever he wanted to hear so he'd drop the charges on her. She'd also try to play the good little wife again, anything to get her out of this place. "Look, I'm sorry, Will. I shouldn't have lied to you about my name." She stopped speaking to gauge his reaction.

"And?"

"And, what?"

"What about how you tried to kill me, Morgan?" Flustered, Will shook his head. "I mean, Ci Ci."

Morgan could clearly see that even Will still wished he had his fairy-tale Morgan back.

"Look, Will, none of that was what it seemed. I wasn't trying to kill you. I . . . I . . ." Morgan couldn't think of what she could say to discount the mountain of evidence and lies she'd already mounted upon herself to make it sound even remotely believable. Was she losing her touch? Had three weeks in the facility doing soft time softened her up?

"Can't lie your way out of this one can you?" Will asked.

"What do you want me to say, Will? I mean really?"

"I want you to tell me why you did what you did to me. I want you to apologize. I want for this whole nightmare to never have happened in the first place," Will said, confiding his wants and thoughts.

"Well. I told you I was sorry. And I can't change the events that have happened. If you can just forgive me then we can act as if none of this ever happened, then we can move on. We can go to counseling and try to patch things up," Morgan said.

As if subconsciously, Will rubbed his forearm. There was still a dark mark there from a wound that had healed after the car accident Will had had less than a year prior—the car accident that Morgan had a hand in deliberately causing, by making it possible for him to lose control of his car while driving.

"Are you crazy?" Will asked.

"What?"

"You heard me. Why in the world would I want you back?" Will asked.

"That is why you are here isn't it? You want me to spill my soul to you so that you can forgive me and we can move on."

"Not even close. True, I want to know why you did all the things you did. But there isn't a snowball's chance in a boiling pot of water that I'd have you back. I might have had the wool pulled over my eyes one time by you, but not again, chick."

Morgan flinched as she realized he wasn't as gullible as she thought. She'd never seen this side of Will. In an offhand kind of way she actually respected him for finally getting a backbone and standing up for himself.

"So why are you here then? Because it isn't like I am going to lay out some long, drawn-out confession about the life and times of Ci Ci Jackson to you. Because, believe me, it would take a whole lot longer than an hour visiting session."

"At least you can own up to Morgan not being your real name," Will said. "That's a start."

"A start? A start for what?"

"I'll bet you were shocked when you saw me sitting in here to come to visit you, weren't you? You are probably wondering why I am even here," Will said.

Morgan didn't answer. She just stared at Will.

"I wondered the same thing, the whole while I was driving over here, as I checked in and throughout the time I've been sitting here, waiting for you to come through that door." He shook his head. "Even though I dislike what you did and how you treated me, I still pray for you. I still pray for your soul."

Morgan rolled her eyes. "Confession is good for the soul right? Is that what you are thinking?"

"It is, Morgan. Believe it or not I don't hate you. And this whole situation has really been laying heavy on my heart. I couldn't let another day go by without coming to talk to you and to let you know that I forgive you for what you've done to me."

Morgan clapped her hands and laughed. "What a great performance, Will. Are you happy? Do you feel good about yourself now that you've forgiven me?"

She noticed one of the guards walking toward them and she toned her actions and laughing down.

"I do, Morgan. I needed to forgive you, because holding in all the hatred I did have for you was only making me sick. I have to let go and let God take care of this. So I am being obedient to what I need to do."

"Oh, so here it goes, are you going to try to save me or something? Bring me to the light?" Morgan asked.

In turn Will asked his own question. "Were you ever saved? At least answer that question for me."

Morgan was ready to get this whole little visiting hour over with. She was done with this whole conversation.

"Yes, Will. I got saved when I was in high school, for all the good it did for me." Morgan rolled her eyes. "See, happy now? I didn't lie about everything."

Will nodded his head, then took a deep breath as he tented his hands in a prayer-type gesture just under his chin. "Morgan, God loves you. And even though you are out of His will right now, you can be redeemed."

Now she'd really had enough. Will had come to try to save her again and she wasn't having anything to do with it. She stood. "Okay, I hear ya. Look, I gotta go." She stepped around her chair.

Will stood as well, understanding that their meeting was over. "Morgan, I don't hate you. I pray for you each night."

Morgan turned to walk away. Then she stopped and turned around. Will was still looking at her as she left. She spoke to him one last time. "Will."

"Yeah." He looked at her with expectation.

"Don't bother coming back here, especially if all you want to talk about is my soul and how I am so loved by God: the only one who can save a wretch like me," Morgan said.

Will stared at her in disbelief. "Is that all?"

"Yeah. There is really nothing else to say," Morgan said.

"This is so sad," Will said as he shook his head.

She started to take steps back toward him. "Stop judging me, Will."

"I'm not judging you. I just think it's sad that throughout this whole conversation, you have not once asked about our son, Isaiah."

Again Morgan found herself stopping dead in her tracks for the second time in less than an hour. She had nothing to say to that. He was right. Not once had she mentioned or asked about their two-year-old son. Not once had she even thought about the boy during their conversation.

"Wow, are you that self-absorbed that you don't even care about your son?" Will asked.

"That's not true. I . . . I . . . ." Morgan stuttered. She felt as if she were having some type of out-of-body experience. It was like she was reading from an emotional script that was supposed to give her direction about the right words she should say—the right words a person who really had emotional ties to their child would.

"Don't worry about it. You don't have to give me any explanations. But for your information Isaiah and I are doing just fine. I've got him in a wonderful daycare. He can count to ten and he even knows most of his colors. He is thriving and I am thriving," Will said.

Morgan turned and backed away. She left without saying another word or looking back at Will.

As she got to the door to leave the visiting area, she heard Will say, "I'll be praying for you."

She couldn't get out of the door fast enough.

Chapter 5

Morgan headed straight to her cell, walking as fast as she could. She had to get away from Will with all his talk about her being redeemed. As far as she was concerned, he didn't know the first thing about redemption and how far a person would have to go to achieve it. All she knew was that the last thing she wanted to look toward was some guiding light that wasn't going to help her. It hadn't helped her in the past, and she had no delusion that she would be helped now either.

She wasn't sure how much time had passed since she'd sought the solitude of her cell; before she knew it, Desiree had returned. She figured Desiree would have a lot of questions about her visitor and, true to her thoughts, Desiree didn't disappoint.

"Ci Ci, who was that good-looking hunk of dark mocha chocolate who came to visit you? Was that your lawyer? I thought you said he was a white guy with red hair and freckles." Desiree talked nonstop. "Shoot, I need to get that man's card. I'm gonna ditch my lawyer for Mr. Dark Chocolate."

Morgan wasn't in the mood to talk and wanted Desiree to stop bombarding her with all of her incessant chatter. All the fire she normally felt had been deflated and she didn't have the energy to banter back and forth with Desiree. The visit from Will had completely taken the wind out of her sails.

"Not now, Tiny," Morgan said.

Morgan figured Desiree had taken the hint that she really didn't want to talk by not only what Morgan said, but also the deflated tone in which she said it, because Desiree instantly stopped talking and sat down on her own bed.

After a few moments, Morgan regained her composure and spoke. "That wasn't my lawyer. That was my husband—well, ex-husband."

Desiree looked up from one of the pictures she was holding of one of her children. Again she must have sensed that Morgan needed time to speak on her own without interruption. Desiree sat quietly so that Morgan could talk freely.

"He was like the last person I would have expected to come visit me. I did some not-so-nice things to him while we were married." Morgan paused as she reflected on the visit from the time she'd set eyes on him until the time when she fled from the visiting room.

"After all I did to him, do you know what he had the nerve to say?" Morgan said.

Desiree shook her head and sat forward. She was all ears.

"He said he forgives me for everything I've done to him." She looked at Desiree. "Can you believe that?"

"Do you think he really meant it?" Desiree asked.

"Yeah. Will is one of the good guys, all into the church and believes in souls being saved. If he said it then he meant it. Will is a good guy," Morgan repeated.

"So I'm a little confused. If he is such a good guy then why did you treat him the way you did?" Desiree asked.

Morgan stared toward the wall, not really looking at it but through it. Without a bit of feeling or remorse, Morgan said, "It's the million dollar question. It seems like everyone wants to know the answer to that." Morgan sighed. "Let's just say that he and I had differences of opinion. He wanted one thing and I wanted other things. And in my mind my wants, needs, and goals came first." Morgan shrugged her shoulders. "A woman wants what a woman wants."

"I know that's right," Desiree said in agreement with her cellmate. "Girl, that man was truly a piece of dark chocolate, but I have to agree with you. If you are not happy then ain't nobody happy. I think that's how that saying goes. Something like that anyway."

"Yeah, something like that," Morgan repeated.

"And, honey, there are even more fish out there in the sea—dark chocolate, milk chocolate, and even white chocolate if your tastes so fancy." Desiree laughed. "And, take it from me, there are men who can overlook the fact that you will be an ex-con."

Morgan cringed at the thought of being deemed an ex-con.

"Girl, if at first you don't succeed, then try, try again," Desiree said.

"Now I have to agree with you on that one," Morgan said. She couldn't wait for her time to be over so she could return to the real world. She still had dreams, goals, and aspirations that she was going to achieve at all costs if need be.

The next week crept by at a snail's pace. Morgan felt as if she was about to go stir-crazy locked up in her cell. She tried to think of any and all avenues that might help her get out of jail. There wasn't anyone she could think of who might help her. As many times as she'd pulled herself up and out of messes she'd gotten herself into, there was nothing smart she could think of doing now.

She realized there might be one last resort. It was the one thing she tried before, but hadn't tried in years. Prayer seemed to work for others, but it hadn't worked for her when she'd tried it in her time of need. God hadn't answered her prayers back then. So now she wondered if He would even hear her now.

She felt she had nothing to lose. Getting down on her knees she knelt in front of the bottom bunk bed. With her hands folded she bowed her head. The positioning was awkward; it seemed to be familiar, yet unfamiliar. It seemed familiar because there was once a time in her life when praying was second nature, but now it was as if she was rusty.

Taking a deep breath she said, "Lord—I mean, dear Lord. You know I am rusty at this. I know it has been a long time, but I hope you haven't forgotten about me. I know I've strayed away from you. I strayed really, really far. But I am still one of your sheep."

She remembered something about a parable in the Bible and one sheep being lost. There was something about a herdsman looking for the one lost sheep even though he had many other sheep. "I am one of your lost sheep. I ask that you find me again. Give me another chance. I'll do my best to do better, I'll do my best to treat people right, and I'll do my best to not tell lies."

Morgan knew what she was saying was a tall order, but she needed a tall order right then. "Lord, I will try my best, I promise." The ending part of the prayer came back to her. It was the part her grandmother taught her to say when sealing the prayer like an envelope to send to the Lord. "In Jesus' name I pray. Amen."

"There, I did it." She didn't feel any better, but she didn't feel any worse either. All she could do was wait now to see if the Lord heard her this time. She didn't hold out too much hope.

She stood and rubbed her knees. The next time she prayed she was going to have to make sure she used a towel or blanket for her knees, because the concrete floor was unforgiving. Now it was back to doing nothing, so she fluffed the pillow on her bed the best she could, and took a nap, because she found sleeping to be the best way to pass the time.

Morgan had a feeling of déjà vu when her cellmate called her name, sporting a grin as wide as a Cheshire cat.

"Oh, Ci Ci. It looks like you have a visitor again today."

That was two weeks in a row. She wondered what Will wanted now. In one instance she wanted to stay right where she was. But in the other instance she wanted to defend her reasons for not asking about Isaiah during their meeting last week. Her reasoning was weak and she knew it. Weak in that it was true what Will had said. She hadn't really thought much about her son. She'd detached even further than she had been to the child when they were all still a family living in the same house.

Subconsciously she stood up from her bed and looked in her murky mirror, doing the best she could to smooth her hair down. Then she did the same with her clothes. She wasn't going to look as much of a mess as she had the previous week. She'd hold her head up high. This time she'd keep her composure as she'd tell him to leave her alone. The relationship she'd had with him had served its purpose for the time being and it was time for her to move on in the best way she possibly could. She'd faced adversity before and gotten through it, and she would get through this.

She took a deep breath before stepping into the room this time; it was time to let the recent past go. She saw many of the same faces of inmates with their family and friends visiting them. Desiree also sat with her mother again and her two little kids. Again she looked around the room for Will, but frowned when she didn't see him. Her frown deepened when her eyes finally landed on a red-haired freckle-faced guy who was also looking around expectantly. Even though the guy made eye contact, he continued to look around.

"What a sorry lawyer," Morgan mumbled under her breath. "He doesn't even recognize me."

She walked toward him, still looking around to see if Will was there as well. After pulling out the chair in front of the lawyer at the table, she sat down, realizing the lawyer was her visitor, not Will. There was a small twinge of disappointment.

"Oh, ah, Cecily Jackson?" The lawyer asked more in question than in a firm greeting.

"Yes," Morgan said.

"Oh, sorry I didn't recognize you," the lawyer said.

He opened up his briefcase as he fumbled and pulled out a folder, pen, and legal pad. "Sorry it took me so long to get back with you. There was a problem with my voice mail while I was on vacation and I just got all of my messages yesterday."

Morgan rolled her eyes, took a deep breath, and tried to remember that even though this guy wasn't the best in the world, he was the only one who could help her right now. "Okay, so I wanted to talk with you about my arrest. They didn't Mirandize me to tell me my rights when they arrested me. So can't this arrest be overturned?"

The lawyer looked at Morgan. "They didn't?" He grinned.

"No, they didn't."

"Well that's good because if need be, I can contest that you were not Mirandized." He nodded his head and jotted down a note on his legal pad.

"What do you mean, if need be? You need to contest it so I can get out of here."

The lawyer held his hand up. "Hold on a moment, Ms. Jackson. I have good news for you."

"Good news?" Morgan asked.

"Yes." The lawyer flipped through some pages in Morgan's file and pulled off a pink message note that was paper clipped to another page.

Morgan sat up in her seat as she wondered what kind of good news the guy had for her.

"Stacked among the messages I missed after my vacation was a message from your husband's . . . well, ex-husband's . . . well, you know what I mean . . . from his lawyer."

Morgan couldn't really call Will her husband or her ex-husband since she had used a false name to get married to him in the first place. This made the whole situation about how to refer to him a bit of a challenge, for all concerned. To keep it simple, she'd probably just continue to say ex-husband to people. There was no need in her mind to explain her business to others.

"I got a call from Mr. Tracy's lawyer saying that Mr. Tracy wants to drop all charges he's filed against you."

Morgan's head dropped while her mouth simultaneously dropped wide open in disbelief. "Are you serious?"

"Yes." The lawyer looked at his watch. "The only bad thing is that it is Friday afternoon. I may not be able to get up with his lawyer for everything to be run through the proper channels before close of business today. Plus, like I said, if need be I may not be able to file that you were not Mirandized by the close of business today either. So you might have to stay here for a few more days until we can hopefully get things resolved on Monday."

She was still stuck on the lawyer's good news, and again she asked, "Are you serious?"

"Yes, if I can get it worked out you should be out of here on Monday or Tuesday at the very latest."

Morgan couldn't believe her ears. She couldn't believe her luck. Her ex was actually dropping the charges. She guessed she shouldn't be so surprised at this. He was always such a standup guy. He probably did so out of the goodness of his heart.

She shook her head thinking about what a complete and utter weak wimp he was. What did she ever really see in him other than the fat check he was bringing home each month before he got laid off from his job? She'd never forgive anyone who had done all the things she'd done to him.

"I'll try to get up with Mr. Tracy's lawyer before close of business today, but don't hold out any hopes that things will be resolved by then. Just prepare yourself for Monday," the lawyer said. "In the meantime is there anything you need?"

"Nope, all I need is for you to do whatever needs to be done to get me out of here."

"I'm on it, Ms. Jackson." He stood and gathered the file and legal pad. He placed them back in his briefcase.

Morgan stood as well.

The lawyer extended his hand. "Have a good weekend."

Morgan firmly shook the extended hand. "With the news you've brought me today, I'll be sure to have a wonderful weekend."

With that the lawyer excused himself and left the visitors area.

Morgan did a 360-degree turn around the room, looking at all the women who could only dream about when they would be released. That morning she was one of those women. But this afternoon she was only a phone call and a few signatures from being free again.

She wanted to jump up and down and scream out that she was about to be released. But she kept her composure. She wasn't going to say a thing to anyone, not even Desiree. If word got out that she was leaving soon, some of the more trifling inmates might get jealous and try to make her last few days miserable.

She realized the Lord had actually heard her and He had answered her prayer. He was giving her another chance and this time she would do things right. Once she returned to her cell, she tore a piece of paper out of a notebook and started writing down a list of things she needed to do after her release. Number one would be to find somewhere to live. Number two would be to visit her storage unit. Number three would be to find a job. Number four was to legally change her name. And number five—while it was last was not the least in importance—number five would be to find a new husband. Morgan's goal was to accomplish everything on her list, by whatever means necessary.

Chapter 6

Morgan awoke from a fitful sleep. Her dreams were filled with memories of being locked up in the correctional facility and memories of the past when she lived in the little house with her grandmother in the little town of Warsaw. She was unable to escape from the correctional facility in her dreams and she was unable to escape from Warsaw. Every time she got to the outskirts of the town she was sucked back in, to the traffic light that was located at the center of town.

She was tangled in the sheets she lay in and it took her a couple of tries to untangle herself. When she did, she headed toward the bathroom in the suite she'd been living in at the hotel and splashed cold water onto her face. The splashing of cold water helped her to fully wake up. She had no desire to lie back down to fall into the same dream cycle again.

The clock on the hotel's nightstand indicated that it was only six thirty-four in the morning. She guessed her body had gotten accustomed to being up at six and eating breakfast at seven while she was incarcerated. Eating wasn't on her mind, but starting on her list of things to do was on her mind. She'd read an article once that stated that successful people were morning people, and ever since then she'd made it a point to be an early riser, like the proverbial early bird getting the worm.

For the past couple of days she'd stayed at a hotel. The goodness of Will's heart wasn't about to let her stay in a house that she now legally had no rights to stay in. Many of her things were still in the home they'd shared, and Morgan wasn't about to call him to see if she could retrieve any of them. Besides, she had all the basic necessities tucked away in a storage unit she'd gotten as soon as Will had gotten laid off of his job. At the time, things had started getting tight, and she wasn't about to lose everything she'd worked so hard to acquire with Will just because he wasn't able to find any more work.

In addition to getting a storage unit to store items in, she had started working overtime, and while she used most of her paycheck to pay the bills, she stashed away money for herself as well. She also literally put money away in a gold bubble mailing envelope in her storage unit. At her last count she had been able to squirrel away a little over $7,000. There was no telling when a rainy day might come and now she was glad she'd been thinking along those lines, because the clouds and storms had come the day the police knocked on her door to arrest her.

Morgan smiled to herself. The clouds were now clearing. She had a plan. The plan had worked for her in the past, and she had no doubt the same plan would work for her now as well. This time she'd be even savvier about how she handled things. And this time she'd try a different angle. She'd try telling the truth, which was an uncomfortable thought. She wouldn't necessarily have to tell the whole truth, but figured a little truth would still take her a longer way.

After brushing her teeth and taking a quick shower, Morgan slipped on the jogging suit she'd purchased just a couple of nights before from Target. Her credit cards still worked and she had a couple of thousand dollars in her checking account still.

She slipped on socks and the pair of nondescript sneakers she'd also purchased from the retail chain. For the past couple of years she'd shopped at higher-end retail stores, but now she knew she'd have to watch her pennies until she landed a job and a new husband.

Even though she didn't like being in the financial situation she was currently in, Morgan had been in much worse situations in her life—much worse. This was only a temporary situation, and temporary could be endured, especially when there were goals that would lead her to a light at the end of her seemingly dark tunnel.

On her list of things to do, finding a job and finding somewhere to live were closely related, and one would be contingent upon the other one. She also needed to make a trip to her storage unit to get the other money she had and to inventory the things she'd also put in there just in case she needed them one day.

There was often a dread that she'd be found out. It was as if she was always looking over her shoulder to make sure no one found out about the persona she'd taken on along with the name she'd stolen and started using as her own. Things had caught up with her. Now her ex-husband was living in their home. And her son was living with his dad.

Isaiah was probably better off with his father. Will was a good guy. He'd make sure Isaiah had any and everything his heart desired: clothing, shelter, food, and mainly the love she just could not provide for him. Will didn't have to worry about her trying to take Isaiah from him. That was the furthest thing from her mind, and somewhere deep down she figured Will wasn't too worried about the possibility of her trying to take his son from him. She shook her head as if to shake any thoughts about Will and Isaiah out. It was time for her to move on with her life. She couldn't continue to dwell in the past—it wouldn't do any good.

The first order of business that day would be to get her hair and nails done. It seemed like ages since she'd been to the beauty salon and she was tired of looking more similar to the old Ci Ci Jackson before she became the new and improved Morgan. The second order of business would be to apply to have her name changed. Instead of Cecily C. Jackson, she'd have it changed to Cecily M. Jackson. She liked the name Morgan and wanted to keep it. The name suited her. It was time to get her affairs in order.

The third thing she needed to do was to find a place to live. At the rate she was going at the hotel, a week's stay would be enough for a month's worth of rent somewhere else. The goal was to have a key to an apartment in hand by the end of the day. Once she secured a key, she'd make a trip to her storage unit and pick up a few things for her new place.

"Here you are, Ms. Jackson," said Brad, who was Morgan's new leasing agent.

Morgan shook his hand. He then proceeded to hand her the keys to her new apartment and mailbox.

"Thanks, Brad," Morgan said.

Brad was a young guy, about twenty years old, Morgan figured. He had dark brown medium-length hair, which fell slightly in his face whenever he turned his head too quickly. He was tanned and looked as if he made trips to frequent either the beach or the tanning bed.

Morgan also figured the guy had a thing for African American women because every time she batted her eyes at him or laughed and touched his arm playfully she could see him blush a bit under his tanned cheeks. The lighthearted laughing she was doing was all in a ploy to help make sure Brad approved her application for renting the apartment.

Since her name change wouldn't be legal for another couple of weeks, Morgan had reverted to using her birth name to rent the apartment, since she couldn't legally use the name Morgan Tracy. She'd held her breath at first while waiting for Brad to return with the decision from the company about whether the application was approved on her real name and her real social security number. She'd breathed a sigh of relief when he returned with a cheesy grin on his face and a welcome packet in hand for her.

He'd also done some flirting of his own throughout the whole process, and while he was a really cute guy, he was younger than she was and made about $75,000 or so less than what she needed him to make for her to even consider going out on a date with him.

Love didn't pay bills, and love wouldn't afford her the life she really wanted. Besides, love was all overrated anyway. She thought of the saying about loving the one you're with, so why couldn't a person find someone and then fall in love with them, or their money, later? Or at least give the appearance that she was in love. As far as she was concerned, love didn't have a space to live in her heart anymore—it was dramatically overrated.

Morgan looked at her watch. She needed to cut this short. "Thanks, Brad. I'd love to chat with you further, but I've really got to get going." She smiled and winked at him. "You know, gotta get the moving company set up and all."

"Oh, yes, ma'am. I do understand," Brad said.

Such the gentleman, Morgan thought, *using his verbal Southern hospitality.*

"If you have any other questions or there is anything else I can help you with, don't hesitate to ask," Brad said.

"Will do, Brad."

Morgan left the leasing office and headed to the storage unit across town where her belongings were being stored. Once again she breathed a sigh of relief as she wasn't really sure about how the submission of the application was going to fare. But the more she thought about it, she guessed she shouldn't be too surprised.

Even though she had not really used her legal birth name in a while, the few times she had used it, she'd never used it in any ill-gotten ways, nor did anything to put her credit in negative jeopardy. Either the complex might have said that she didn't have enough credit or they might have said that she wasn't showing any activity on her credit report for over two years, but in the end neither of those two things mattered. And if nothing else, luck was again on her side—first being released from the correctional facility and now being approved for an apartment lease.

She smiled to herself. The day was going absolutely wonderful. Her hair and nails looked immaculate, soon she'd be dropping the STD as her middle name, and she now had a new place to call home. Once she got the little incidentals out of the way, she could focus on what would really make her happy—finding a new man to have and to hold, until death do they part.

Chapter 7

The door to the storage unit creaked and shrieked as Morgan pulled on to roll it up and open. It was dusk outside and there was a bit of a chill in the air. The weather in late September could be funny—some days still warm and others with a chill. Not to mention occasional problems in North Carolina of hurricanes during hurricane season.

There wasn't an affixed light in the unit, but Morgan had a flashlight available. There were many nights when she'd visited the storage unit to put things in there, nights when Will thought she was at work making extra money. She was like a squirrel preparing for winter.

As she thought about it, it seemed like she'd been putting things away for a rainy day her whole life. It first started as a child. She would hide food away during the lean times when her mother often disappeared for days on end. It looked as if the squirreling away of things had paid off. Her forethought was now going to help her get through the next few days and weeks.

She located the flashlight and pushed the button to click it on. The light shined bright. She set it on a box located in the center of the unit. It was a good-sized unit and she'd stored things in there in a U shape so that she could easily get to them and not feel claustrophobic at the same time.

As she looked around, she realized there was more than she remembered. A couple of trips in her car wouldn't suffice in moving everything. She was going to have to rent a truck to move the things. She didn't think she really needed professional movers. In volume there was much: a lot of boxes, a lamp, a small microwave, a thirteen-inch flat-screen digital television, and a small, lightweight Netbook computer. There weren't any big items. The mattress she'd be using was a queen size but it was inflatable. She hadn't stored a sofa or love seat, just a lightweight butterfly lounge chair she'd be using for lounging. She could move everything herself and save some money in the process.

She wasn't broke, but she knew she'd have to be frugal—something else she wasn't a stranger to doing. She'd stretch her dollars as far as they needed to go. Morgan had played her cards right before with Will and if she played them just right again, she'd be sitting pretty in due time.

Looking around she located the box she labeled with the words PERSONAL HYGIENE ITEMS. All of the boxes were labeled, which served two purposes. First, she could easily find whatever she needed quickly. Secondly, so that if anyone broke into her unit, they'd also find pretty much what was labeled in each of the boxes, except for the personal items box. In that box, tucked in another personal hygiene box, Morgan had hidden the gold bubble mailing envelope with the cash she'd been putting to the side.

It had been a huge risk putting the money in the unit, especially if there had been a fire, but what fun was life without a few risks? Besides the chances of there being a fire in the storage units were slim to none. She'd never heard of a fire at a storage unit before in her life. And as luck had it, she still hadn't heard of one.

After opening the first box, she opened the other box, and tucked inside she found the envelope. She quickly tucked it into the waistband of her pants and pulled her top over the envelope and waistband to conceal it. When she was in the locked safety of her new apartment she'd pull it back out and count the exact amount of the contents.

She located some of the various items she would need immediately, like her lamp and the multi-function portable folding table purchased on Amazon.com. She pulled the boxes that held her inflatable mattress, the stand for the mattress, her sheets and a pillow, coffee maker, the personal hygiene box, and another box with clothing. After she had those items, she found a few more necessities and packed them into the trunk, back seat, and passenger side front seat of her car.

By the time she finished, it was just past eight-thirty at night. She patted her side, making sure the envelope had not slipped, closed the storage room door, and placed the padlocks back on it. Within the hour she'd arrived back at her new apartment and had unloaded the car. It had also only taken her another thirty minutes to set up her bed, lounge chair, and lamp. The rest she'd unload in the morning. In her pajamas Morgan sat in the lounge chair and patted her hands together in a satisfactory wiping motion. It had been an awesomely productive day and she couldn't wait to embark on the next day and the other days ahead.

By the end of the week, Morgan had unloaded everything but a couple of boxes of winter clothing, a set of flannel bed linen, a couple extra blankets, and many of her kitchen items. When it got colder she'd switch out warm wear for her colder weather wear and pull out the other sheets and blankets if needed. As for the kitchen items, she had no intention of making anything more than cups of fresh-brewed coffee, and warming up leftovers in the microwave.

For the next days and weeks, other than eating and sleeping Morgan would be focusing on two things: working as much as possible to put some money away, and finding a new man so that in the future she wouldn't have to work so hard. It was going to be a bit tricky working so much. The more she worked the less time she'd have to actually be on the prowl, but if she was going to keep up the same appearances she kept when she'd hooked Will a couple of years prior, she'd need some funds to at least show the image that she had a little bit of money of her own.

She'd learned over the years that men wanted more than just a pretty face and a smile, especially if the man was on the right track professionally. They wanted someone who could hold her own, while also appreciating the fact that she had a good, strong man on her arm. Men wanted a woman who carried herself well when she was out and about and a woman who would also take care of her feminine duties at home. Morgan knew she could be all that and more. She could fit into whatever mold she needed as long as in the end she obtained her own goals. And if the man continued to stay on the same lines she was thinking about, then wonderful, and if he didn't then Morgan would have to make whatever adjustments she'd need to in order to make sure she remained satisfied. If only Will had done what she wanted and needed him to do, she wouldn't be back out on the dating scene again.

"Ms. Jackson."

Hearing the woman sitting across the desk calling her name, Morgan was pulled out of her thoughts. It was the hiring agent who was interviewing her for a job. The interview was for a position as a sales supervisor at one of her favorite department stores.

"Yes, Ms. Westfield."

"Your job application as well as the resume you've brought with the additional references looks very promising. And I must say that the friendliness you showed to the customer who was trying to find the shoe department was very impressive," Ms. Westfield said.

Ms. Westfield was a short, pudgy woman who had amber-colored eyes. She looked as if she might be either Hispanic or was possibly biracial. Her hair, which came to her shoulders, was wavy with tight curls.

"Thank you," Morgan said.

The interview was now being wrapped up. Earlier, as Morgan and Ms. Westfield had done a tour of the areas that Morgan would be working if she was hired, Morgan jumped at the opportunity to help an elderly woman find the shoe section. As soon as Morgan had seen the elderly woman amble around, Morgan's intuition told her the woman was lost and confused, so she excused herself from Ms. Westfield for a second and with a warm, friendly manner she spoke with the woman and gave her easy directions and pointed her in the way she should go.

Morgan wasn't going to be working anywhere near the shoes, but she knew the store like the back of her hand. And she wanted to make sure the woman saw her friendliness, enthusiasm to help customers, and also that the woman realized the knowledge Morgan possessed about the retail chain.

She'd dressed up for the interview wearing a black-and-white pinstriped suit and a pair of black high-heel shoes, she had her hair pulled up in a bun, and had exchanged her flaming red nail polish for a more subdued and nauseating shade of beige. Morgan knew it was one thing for someone to look at a black-and-white application, but it was a far better thing for the hiring agent to see Morgan's abilities live and in person.

"I can see that you will do well with our customers." The woman chuckled. "And I also realize you probably didn't even need a tour."

Morgan laughed as well. "No, I know this store inside and out. But it did give me an opportunity to see some of the latest lines of clothing that have been recently released."

The woman tilted her head and looked at Morgan with appraising approval. She looked back down at the application before her. As she stood she said, "Is your cell phone number the best number to reach you?"

Morgan stood as well. "Yes." She extended her hand and gave the woman a firm handshake. "Thank you for your time and consideration."

"It's been a pleasure." The woman smiled. "We'll be making our decision within the week."

Morgan was pretty sure that from the woman's response and demeanor the job would be hers. But she fished for a more definitive answer. "How will you notify people?"

"We send out e-mails to those who did not get the position. And we call the people who we want to offer positions." The woman clutched the application in her hand and read off Morgan's cell phone number again.

"Yep, that's the right number," Morgan said. She was pretty sure this meant the woman was going to call her.

"Good," the woman said. "Within the week."

With the woman's last statement, Morgan was 99.5 percent sure the job was hers.

After leaving the store Morgan decided to treat herself. She went to the Bonefish Grill. She had a taste for their tender Bang Bang Shrimp with its spicy, creamy sauce. In her opinion she deserved it, because so far she'd had a banging kind of month and an especially banging couple of days. Things were really taking shape for her.

Since Silvermont didn't have a Bonefish Grill, Morgan had driven to the one in Raleigh, North Carolina. It was a bit of a drive, but it gave her time to think while getting some fresh air. She relaxed and pulled the hairpins out of her bun, allowing it to fall on her shoulders in body wave curls. The temperature was perfect, allowing her to let the windows down a couple of inches while she drove.

When she got to the restaurant it was close to five o'clock in the evening. There were already people waiting to be seated. She was hungry but knew her stomach could wait the ten or fifteen minutes until she was seated.

About twelve minutes later, she was seated. As she waited for the waitress, she took the time as an opportunity to practice scoping out men. She was a little rusty, since the last time she'd been on hunting expedition had been months before she'd finally met Will. She smiled to herself as she thought about it.

As Morgan rifled through exercise DVDs, she smelled the scent of a man's cologne, then saw movement from the corner of her eye. The person moving past her was tall, dark, and extremely handsome. Upon looking up she'd done a slight double take as she thought the guy resembled Corey Reynolds, one of the detectives from her favorite TV show, The Closer, *who acted alongside Kyra Sedgwick.*

She realized it wasn't Corey, and the guy actually looked better than Corey if that was even possible. The guy looked around as if he was looking for something in particular. He glanced her way as if trying to see if she worked there, but he quickly looked elsewhere. That day she had looked nothing like an employee of any store. She'd been in her apartment most of the day, first starting off with an old workout DVD, then spending a couple hours cleaning. She looked a mess. Her outfit consisted of jogging pants, a sweatshirt, and a pair of old sneakers. She'd pulled her hair back into a ponytail and hadn't bothered to put her contacts in, so she was wearing her eyeglasses with the thick lenses. To top matters off, she hadn't put on a bit of makeup—no foundation, no lip gloss, or even ChapStick.

So she hadn't felt right speaking to him at all, or even smiling in his direction. She could have kicked herself for leaving the apartment the way she had. Here was this fine-looking piece of dark chocolate, smelling like he'd just stepped out of a Stetson cologne commercial and she looked like an adult version of a ragamuffin—with scruffy-looking clothing, and messy hair.

She turned back toward the DVDs, acting as if she didn't have a care in the world, and certainly hadn't noticed him at all. Then when he turned and headed toward customer service, she turned and tilted her head in order to watch him stride away. Once he was out of sight she nodded her head, and mumbled under her breath, "If I could only turn back the hands of time."

If she could go back to the time when she'd decided to walk out not caring how she looked, she'd stop and make the effort to take a shower, comb her hair, put

her contacts in, put on some makeup and decent cloth-
ing. She continued to mumble, "You only have one
chance to make a first impression."

After finding a couple of DVDs she could use for car-
dio workouts and toning workouts, Morgan headed
toward the checkout. She waited in line and continued
to mentally kick herself for being so careless. Once she
got into the car she shook her head again and said,
"You only have one chance to make a first impression."

She cranked the ignition and looked up through the
windshield. That's when she saw the same handsome
guy talking on his cell phone in his own car. She sat
stark still as if any movement from her would alert
him to her presence. A few moments later the guy
clicked his phone off and pulled his car backward in
reverse.

Morgan got a bright idea. She whispered to herself,
"Who says you only get one chance to make a first
impression?"

Like the guy had done, she also put her car into re-
verse and pulled out of her space. Then she proceeded
to follow him out of the parking lot to the traffic light.
When he turned right she did also, trying to stay as
close as possible. There wasn't anything on her agenda
that afternoon, she had over a half tank of gas, and un-
less he crossed the state line into Virginia, she had all
the time in the world to follow him to his next destina-
tion. She hoped with any luck that he was headed home
and she would soon see.

Morgan felt a slight tap on her shoulder, pulling her
out of her trip back down memory lane. She was now all
too aware of the sound of clinking glasses, people talking, and the smell of seafood, which wafted through the
air.

She looked up to see a man gazing down at her, with
a grin showing a mouth full of pearly white teeth.

Chapter 8

The man staring down at her said, "Excuse me, miss. You dropped your napkin." He smiled and handed it to her.

She took it from him. "Thank you."

"You looked like you were pretty deep in thought. I didn't want to disturb you, but didn't want you to think I was just standing here staring you down either." He smiled again, showing his gleaming white teeth.

Morgan smiled back. It looked as if he was appraising her as he gazed down. And she was okay with that because she was appraising him right back.

He wore a light yellow Polo shirt with a pair of khaki pants. He had a bald head and was wearing a pair of thin black glasses that framed his face nicely. The whole look made him look like a decent, innocent, laid-back guy. She wondered if he really possessed all of those wholesome qualities.

Extending his hand, the man said, "Hi. My name is Charles."

Morgan tilted her head and extended her hand to shake his. Instead of offering her name she said, "Charles huh? You're a little forward aren't you?"

Charles smiled, showing his pearly white teeth again. "No, not forward—just a gentleman who sees a fine-looking lady in front of him. Now I had two choices. I could have given you the napkin and walked away, or I could continue to stand here and offer my name to strike up a further conversation. I chose the latter, as you can see."

Morgan nodded her head. "Ah."

"Is anyone sitting here?" The guy indicated the empty seat on the other side of Morgan's table for two.

The waiter walked up. "Sir, will you be joining us?" The waiter also indicated the same chair that Charles had indicated.

Speaking to the waiter Charles said, "That depends on what Miss . . ." His voice trailed off a bit as he looked down at Morgan, who had not yet told him what her name was. Then he continued, "That depends on what the lady wants."

Morgan gestured her hand toward the seat as she looked at Charles. Then she said to the waiter, "Yes, he'll be joining me."

"Okay, very well," the waiter said in a professional and polite voice. "I'll need to grab another set of utensils and a menu. I'll be right back." He left to get the items.

Charles pulled the seat out and comfortably sat down in it.

Morgan waited until he was fully comfortable and said, "So, Charles, how often do you frequent restaurants and hit on women?"

"Oh, no, no. You've got it all wrong. I just happened to be here and I was sitting at the bar. I was going to order takeout actually when I saw you sitting over here. I wanted to find a reason to speak and then I saw you drop your napkin and the rest is history." He smiled. "I don't see why both of us should eat alone."

Morgan eyed his left-hand ring finger. "So, Charles, are you married?"

Charles's eyes widened. "Now look who's being forward."

"Like you, I don't believe in beating around the bush. It can make things a lot easier in the long run," Morgan said.

The waiter returned and handed Charles a menu and laid out a set of utensils. He also placed two glasses of water down for the two of them. "I'll give you both a few minutes to decide on what you want. I'll be back in a few."

Charles nodded his head in agreement. Morgan smiled to indicate that the waiter's suggestion would be fine.

After a moment, Morgan repeated her question. "So, are you married?"

Charles took a sip of his water. "My, my, inquiring minds want to know."

"I sure do. I don't need your wife to walk up in here and mistake this friendly little dinner for something it is not," Morgan said. She wanted to make herself very clear.

"No worries. I am not married." He lifted his left hand and faced it outward as he wiggled his fingers to indicate that it was ring free.

"Ah, not wearing a ring doesn't mean you aren't married. It just means that you aren't wearing a ring," Morgan said.

Charles chuckled. "Again, let me put your fears to rest, so that I state this and so there is no shadow of doubt. I am not married. I have not hidden a ring somewhere so that it will make it look like I am not married. I am a happily single man."

Morgan nodded her head, hearing what he was saying. For the moment she would give him the benefit of the doubt and move forward with having a pleasant conversation with a nice-looking and very nice-dressing guy.

"So what about you?" He looked at her ring finger.

"I'm not married either," Morgan said. Then she added, "I don't have a ring hidden anywhere either."

"Good, then we can sit back, relax, and enjoy this beautiful evening while getting our bellies a little full."

Morgan picked up her glass of water and held it up to Charles. "I'll toast to that."

They clinked glasses, then both looked back at their menus. Morgan decided to get the Bang Bang Shrimp she'd come there to get and Charles ordered the longfin tilapia. As they waited for their food they continued to talk.

"Now that we've toasted and all, can I at least get a name?" Charles asked.

"Oh, sorry about that, my name is Morgan."

"Well it is nice to meet you, Morgan, and thank you for agreeing to let me sit with you for dinner."

Morgan smiled and took a quick glance at her watch. "So, Charles, what do you do?" Morgan wanted to cut to the chase even more. Maybe on this first night out, she'd get lucky and her search for the next new man will have ended before it started. Maybe fate was finally throwing her a hand in the right direction.

"I'm a teacher. I teach middle school math and I also teach GED classes at night at the community college."

Morgan smiled, hoping it didn't look too much like a grimace. "You're a teacher, huh?"

Charles's face lit up. "Yes. I love teaching. Kids are like sponges and many of the adults in my GED classes are sponges as well."

Morgan continued to smile and nod her head. She even added a couple of "Umm humph's" in to feign interest in what Charles was talking about. She wasn't interested in the least. Even though the guy wasn't bad on the eyes, he would be bad on her pocket. He was a mere middle school teacher and obviously had to work a part-time job to make ends meet.

She figured the dinner they were eating was probably going to set him back, especially if he paid for her meal. She figured he just might, especially since he'd been so forward in introducing himself—and especially since he was probably trying to do his best to impress her. If he had just waited to talk about his chosen profession at the end of their meal then maybe she could have held on to the illusion that this man might just be the next Mr. Right.

As it was, she was now going to have to make small talk with him while trying to get through their meal. He talked nonstop almost until their food arrived. Morgan contributed to the conversation here and there by basically repeating some of the things he'd already said, and each time she did, it seemed to spur Charles on to elaborate even more.

When he finally got tired of talking about himself, Charles asked, "So, Morgan, what do you do?"

She had no interest at that point to try to impress Charles, but in the same instance she didn't want to tell him she'd recently gotten out of a women's correctional facility and was unemployed. So she made something up that would hopefully not be too far from the truth in a couple of days.

"I am a manager at a retail store," Morgan said. She didn't offer any more.

"A retail store, huh? Which one?"

Morgan looked around to see if the waiter was anywhere near to bringing their food to the table. "Now, Charles, I know we've known each other for a good . . ." She cut off her own sentence and looked at her watch. Then she continued, "Twenty-two minutes, but I am not going to just simply lay out all of my personal information to you. I mean you could be a serial killer or something. You could find out where I work and stalk me or something."

Charles laughed out so loud that people at a couple of the neighboring tables looked over at him. Noticing, he put his hand up, nodded his head in an apology, and picked his cloth napkin up to wipe his mouth.

"You must watch a lot of Lifetime television." Charles said. "What, do you think I am the type of person who might scour all the Macy's, Belk, and Sears stores in the Raleigh-Durham area to find you?"

Morgan uttered a slight chuckle as a small mirroring of the laugh he'd done a moment before. "No. I guess not."

He really didn't look like someone who would do what he'd just suggested, unlike her; she was the type of person to do just that very thing—and more if need be. She liked the movies on Lifetime and figured Charles needed to watch a few more or he might just find himself in a Lifetime scenario-like predicament if he wasn't careful one day.

She continued, just in case he was really that type of guy. "I am a manager at Walmart."

"Walmart, huh?" Charles asked.

The way he had asked, it seemed as if Charles was being a bit condescending. It was as if he didn't think highly of her because she wasn't working in some type of profession that called for a college degree. She didn't like his air of condescension one bit. She'd chosen Walmart because there were so many in the area that if he did look for her he'd have a hard time finding her. She figured he wouldn't go anywhere near the malls trying to track her down after they parted.

Before she could comment on his visible reaction, the waiter returned with steaming plates of food that made Morgan's mouth water. So instead of commenting on his reaction to what she had said about where she worked, she picked up her fork.

They dug into their plates and barely said two words to each other for the first couple of minutes. Then they proceeded with more small talk until both of their plates were sufficiently cleaned. A few times during their conversation, Charles's phone vibrated in his pocket. The first two times he ignored it, acting as if it wasn't buzzing. The third time he pulled it out of his pocket and checked to see who the caller was. Then the fourth and fifth time he ignored it again.

As they waited for the check, Morgan grew more and more tired of hearing Charles talk about himself and all of the boring things he wanted to talk about. She was also tired of listening to the sad pickup lines he was using as he continually tried to flirt with her. Every few sentences or so, he would interject comments about how pretty he thought she was, and what beautiful hair she had. The vibrating phone in his pocket was getting on her nerves. After each time it buzzed, Charles tried to nonchalantly look at his watch to check the time. She couldn't wait to get out of there.

By the time the waiter brought the check, Charles seemed anxious and antsy like he was about ready to jump out of his seat. Morgan figured the calls were from a woman—possibly a wife, who wanted to know his whereabouts. He took the bill from the waiter's hand and just as she thought he would, Charles paid for both their dinners.

"So, Morgan. What are your plans for the rest of the evening?"

She figured he probably had some kind of ulterior motive in mind, especially since he had been trying to set up some kind of after-dinner rendezvous with all his pathetic attempts to entice her with his lame pickup lines.

"I'm going to head on home." Morgan faked a yawn. "I've got to get up early in the morning."

Charles frowned. "The night is still early and it doesn't have to end here. We could enjoy this wonderful late summer night and take a walk somewhere." He changed his frown into another pearly-white-teeth-showing, pleading grin.

It was Morgan who frowned now. She'd been nice not saying a thing about all the phone calls and the numerous times he'd looked at his watch, but she couldn't hold her frustration in anymore.

"Look, Charles. Thank you for buying dinner, but we are both grown adults here. And you know as well as I do that you want more than just an evening stroll." She could feel her neck rolling as she spoke. "And you know good and well that there is some woman, probably your wife, who keeps blowing your phone up. You'd better call her, especially since you've been looking at your watch every couple of minutes."

Charles tilted his head as if he had no idea what she was talking about. "Now, Morgan. I told you I am a happily single man. My phone keeps buzzing but it is an unknown number." He pulled the phone back out of his pocket and turned the vibration off. "Sorry about that distraction. Now we won't be distracted anymore."

Morgan couldn't believe the man's nerve. She wasn't born yesterday and she wasn't anybody's fool. But it looked as if this guy wanted to play her for a fool, so taking a different approach she took a deep breath and said, "Charles, I hear you."

She paused and smiled sheepishly. "You are a really nice guy and I'd love to spend a little more time with you but I am really tired. Maybe we could hook up another day."

Charles perked up as he started to believe that Morgan was really as gullible as he thought. "Now that sounds good to me," he said. He actually also looked a little relieved. Morgan figured it was because he now had a free pass to get back home to the little wifey.

"So why don't you give me your number and I'll give you a call," Morgan said. She stood to indicate that she was also ready to leave.

Charles frowned again and stood as well. "Are you really going to call me? Or are you just trying to appease me so we can part ways, then you can throw my number in the trash?"

Morgan stepped up close to Charles within his personal space. She looked directly into his eyes. "Now now, Charles. I am not one to play games." She placed her index finger on his nose and tapped it lightly." She continued to speak. "That is unless someone puts the ball in my court."

Charles placed his hand on Morgan's arm. "Sweetheart, I promise you I am not a brother who plays games."

She stepped back. "Okay then. I'll be sure to call you."

Charles smiled. He looked at his watch again. "Okay. I'll be waiting for your call." He pulled his keys out of his pocket and gestured for her to walk ahead of him as they headed to the front door.

Once they were outside, Charles said, "You take care now. Talk to you soon."

"Okay," Morgan said.

With that he turned and headed toward his car.

"Figures," Morgan said to herself aloud. She looked down at her own watch. The night wasn't that late. She didn't have anywhere to be in the morning. A feeling of nostalgia came over her. It had been awhile since she'd been on the hunt. The last time she started one was when she followed Will out of the sporting goods store to see if she could find out more about the man smelling of the good Stetson cologne.

She tilted her head as she watched Charles as he walked over to his light blue Toyota Camry. "I wonder just how rusty I am." After pulling her own keys out of her purse, she quickly headed to her own car. She was pretty sure Charles hadn't paid any attention to which direction she'd gone in. And he obviously didn't care since he had not even had the decency to walk her to the car. He hadn't cared a bit about her safety, but then what had she really expected?

Something just didn't sit right with her and she had three choices—she could either go home and never call the guy, she could go home and call the guy but wonder if he was really telling her the truth about himself, or she could get in her car and follow the Camry.

She quickly decided to get in her car and follow the Camry. Charles wasn't looking at his watch so often and acting antsy for no reason. Her gut told her he wasn't being truthful with her and she'd bet a hundred dollars that the guy was going straight home to a wife.

Chapter 9

By the time she got her car started and pulled out of the parking space, she'd almost lost him. He'd pulled out of the restaurant's parking lot and on to the main street. She'd yielded at the stop sign, glad there wasn't any traffic coming. Charles was pretty close to breaking the speed limit, and Morgan had to pick up even more speed to be able to catch up with him to be a couple of car lengths behind him.

She followed him down streets on to the interstate and then back on to a few city streets until they hit a residential area. Speed limit signs indicated the need for a slow speed and Charles was adhering to the signs. Morgan slowed her speed as well in hopes to not alert Charles that he had a tagalong behind him.

While following him Morgan again thought about the first time she'd done this very same kind of following maneuver with Will. That day after she drove out of the Play It Again Sports store she'd followed him to a gas station, where he filled up his car with gas; then she proceeded to follow him to the post office, where she watched him enter with a package to be mailed.

Once he finished at the post office Morgan then followed him to an apartment complex, where he checked his mail at a bank of mailboxes; and then he proceeded to park in a parking space, exit his car, and then enter an apartment on the second floor in building number 900. From the vantage from where Morgan strategically parked her car at the complex to watch him, she saw him ascend the stairs to the second floor. Then she watched him open the door to one of the apartments.

After he'd been in for a few minutes and she saw that he might not be coming back out anytime soon, she drove back over to the bank of mailboxes where he'd checked his mail. She'd been watching him when he'd checked his mailbox and remembered which one he checked. Once she was close enough to them she was able to see the number on the mailbox. The number was 912. It stood to reason that he lived at apartment number 912.

She pulled a pen out of her purse and located the receipt from the sports store. Then she wrote down the guy's apartment number as well as the car's make, model, and license plate number so she'd have it for future reference. Now she knew where the handsome guy lived; that was only part of the battle. Next she wanted to find out his name and anything else she'd be able to use to make a second first impression on him.

With the small bits of information she possessed, Morgan knew she'd be able to find out quite a bit of information on the man. And with more information she could set up the perfect scenario to meet him again in person. She vowed to herself that when he saw her for a second time, he'd be hard pressed not to notice her, because she would come correct—with her hair, nails, and makeup done. She'd be sure to wear the most alluring perfume she owned and she would be wearing a banging outfit that would be sure to turn any man's head.

So after she left the man's apartment she headed to her own. She wanted to get online so that she could take the pieces of information she had and see if it would lead her to more pieces of the puzzle of who her mystery man actually was.

For the second time that evening, Charles had pulled her out of her trip back into memories of the past as his brake lights brightened. He turned his signal on and turned into the driveway of a two-story, one-car-garage home.

In the window of one of the rooms upstairs, Morgan saw someone pull the shades open then close them. A couple of seconds later the light in that room turned off. She drove on down the street and turned around to drive back by. As she turned she saw a porch light come on as Charles was putting his key into the door. When she did make it back in passing the home, Morgan saw a woman standing just in the door with a head scarf on as she was holding what looked like a crying child in her arms.

Morgan continued to drive by, not wanting Charles to realize that the same car that was behind him on his street was now doubling back. She smirked to herself, then said, "Charles, it seems as if you were lying to me after all."

Morgan was a patient woman. She drove farther down the street and parked between two houses on the side street. After turning the ignition off she sat and waited almost forty-five minutes for all the lights in the home to turn off. Then she got out of her car and walked down to the mailbox that was situated in front of the home. If she was lucky then maybe neither Charles nor his significant other had remembered to check the mail for the day.

Luck was on her side. In the mailbox were a few pieces of mail—a couple of official pieces and a couple more pieces of junk mail. She kept one of the pieces of junk mail and replaced the other mail in the box. Even though she wanted to dial the digits for his cell phone as soon as she saw Charles with the woman, she waited.

Morgan wanted to make sure Charles really learned his lesson about toying with a woman's emotions.

As soon as she got back into her car, Morgan looked more closely at the piece of mail in her hand. The name on it was Mr. Michael C. Beatty. She figured the C stood for Charles but would confirm it further. The address on the mail was 1795 Dillahunt Street. Morgan used a search engine on her smart phone to do a reverse address search for 1795 Dillahunt Street.

Modern technology always came in so very handy. She'd used the very same technology a few years prior when she did her research to find out more about Will. Back then she'd had to go all the way home to log into the computer to do the same search she was now more quickly able to do on her handy smart phone.

Within seconds the phone provided her with the information she needed. According to the Web site, the home belonged to a Michael Charles Beatty and Natasha Smith Beatty. "Bingo," Morgan said aloud to herself.

She started her car and drove back home. Within an hour of her getting home, Morgan had found out more information about Mr. Michael Charles Beatty and even his wife. Both of them had social networking sites that were not restricted. On the sites she was able to determine that Charles was a teacher and his wife was a librarian. There was information about where they were from, where they both went to school, and even more information along with pictures like a timeline of their lives, which included their two children, M.J. and Makenna.

Morgan wondered why in the world so many people put so much information about their personal lives on the Internet. They might as well put a note on their front doors to tell people, "The door is unlocked and you can come right on in." The pictures for both of them had not only their names, but captions that depicted what was going on in the pictures as well as tags to go with their family's and friends' corresponding pictures.

From the pictures Morgan was able to figure out what daycare the children attended, as well as the church the family attended. The more information she found the more she smiled to herself. She still had the knack for gleaning information by just starting with nothing much.

Even though it looked as if Mr. Michael Charles Beatty wasn't going to be a promising prospect for her next husband, it was nice to know she hadn't lost her touch over the last couple of years. If she could get this much information from a total stranger in the span of just a few hours, then she knew she could do even more wonders working with someone who gave even more information on their own more freely.

At around 4:05 in the morning, when Morgan figured Mr. Charles was snug in his bed with his wife, she picked up her cell phone, pushed the buttons needed to block her cell phone number on the receiving end of the call, then dialed the number Charles had given her.

The phone rang a few times and then the voice mail picked up. Then after about five minutes she dialed the number again, and then again a few minutes after that. On her fourth try she heard Charles's annoyed and groggy voice on the other end.

"Hello?" Charles asked in a whispering tone.

"Hey, Mike," Morgan said in an upbeat voice. She figured if his first name was Michael, his friends and family most likely called him Mike as a name of endearment as well.

"Yeah. Who is this?" He continued to whisper as he asked in confusion as if trying to figure out which one of his friends was calling him in the wee hours of the morning.

"Oh, Mike, I am hurt. You have forgotten my voice already?" Morgan said, playing with him.

"Hold on," he said.

In the background it sounded as if he was moving to get up. She heard a door creak and other sounds that sounded as if he might be descending the stairs. Then he continued in a louder voice. "Now who is this and why are you calling me at four o'clock in the morning?"

"Charles," Morgan said.

"Huh?" he asked.

Morgan could hear the confusion in his tone. Most likely the people who called him Mike or Michael didn't call him by his middle name.

Then, as if a light turned on in his head with recognition, he asked, "Morgan? Is that you?"

"Yep," Morgan replied.

"Ah, uh, what's . . ." His voice trailed off. Then he continued, "Why did you call me Mike? I never told you my name was Mike. You had me a little confused."

Morgan chuckled within. "I am sure you are more than a little confused. You must have confused me with some woman who wanted to play games. I told you I don't like to play games, but you wanted to put the ball in my court anyway."

"Look, Morgan. First of all, you don't need to be calling me in the wee hours of the morning. And—"

Morgan cut him off. "No, you look, Michael Charles Beatty who lives at 1795 Dillahunt Street with his wife named Natasha Smith Beatty."

Morgan heard a slight gasp on the other end of the line. She figured this Mike was trying to figure out how she knew any of the things she'd just spouted off to him. She was sure he was fully awake now.

She continued, "You need to listen to me."

"What . . . How . . . Why—" he started to say, but Morgan cut him off again.

"You have a very nice house, and M.J. and Makenna are just as cute as they can be."

There was now silence on the other end of the line. Morgan was sure the guy was reeling by now, fully confused by all the information she was throwing at him.

Finally he spoke. "Who are you? How do you know so much about me? What do you want?"

"The better question you should be asking yourself is why you decided to lie to me and play games? I know all about you, even down to the amount of money you have in your checking and savings accounts."

"What the—" Charles started to say, but Morgan cut him off again.

"Stop with all the questions. I'll bet you the next time you decide to play with a woman's emotions you'll think twice about it. If you know what is good for you then you'll go back to bed after this call, snuggle up with your wife, and treat her like she is the best thing that has ever happened to you. If I were you I'd also stop cheating on your wife, because if I find out you've been up to no good I'll be back to make your life an absolute living nightmare," Morgan said.

"I . . . I . . ." he stuttered.

"Save it. I don't want to hear anything you have to say. Men who cheat on their wives are the scum of the earth. Now do what I said and have a good night— what's left of it anyway."

Morgan hung up the phone. She was sure he was probably sitting there with his mouth agape, staring at the phone. He had no idea what had just happened, and for the rest of the night, the upcoming days, weeks, and months to come, he would be wondering.

She knew the guy might try to cheat on his wife again, but he'd think long and hard before that ever happened. After all the information she divulged to him in the phone conversation, he probably thought she knew more than she did. He was probably wondering if someone put her up to getting all the information. He might have even thought she was a private detective or something, especially when she told him she knew how much he had in his bank accounts.

Morgan didn't know anything about his bank accounts, not that she couldn't find out with a great deal more of intense searching, but she had no desire to spend one more second, much less a minute, on Mr. Michael Charles Beatty. She had done her job. In her own strange kind of way she'd helped Charles's wife out.

For a moment she felt vindicated about what she had done to Michael Charles Beatty. Then her thoughts drifted back to over a decade before to her very first marriage. She wished someone would have been thoughtful enough to have done the same for her and helped her with the cheating and conniving husband she'd had.

Chapter 10

Morgan dressed in another conservative suit, a pair of two-inch yet comfortable pumps, and applied a touch of makeup. Today, instead of putting her hair up into a bun she pulled it into a ponytail, clamping it with a butterfly-shaped clip. As she looked at herself in the mirror she knew she still exuded the persona of a woman who was in charge, but also looked good at the same time.

It was her third week at work at her new job as a sales supervisor. Just as she thought, the powers that be were impressed with her job application, the resume she'd provided in addition to the application, and especially the display she showed of being people-friendly and already very knowledgeable about the store for which she was applying.

Since her first day she hadn't disappointed in being the model employee. Throughout her training and shadowing of another supervisor she continued to shine. She was even told that at the rate she was going, she would probably be in line to be a store manager in the future. Her hard work was a means to an end. She wanted to save as much as possible to make it look as if she was the caliber and type of woman who would be the perfect companion and future wife of a wealthy executive or entrepreneur.

While she worked hard each and every day to make money and to show those she worked for that she was a hard worker, the ultimate goal was to hook a new husband. A husband who would give her a life that would afford her all the things she wanted. Once she secured that relationship she wouldn't have a need to work.

Once she got to work she was informed that there were a couple of employees who had called off work in the shoe section and they needed her to help in that area. Morgan didn't mind because, except for the children's section, the rest of the store was pretty much her playground. Not only could she shop and get a discount while doing so, but they were actually paying her to be able to see everything firsthand when the new lines of clothing came off the delivery trucks.

"Excuse me, miss."

Morgan heard a man's voice calling toward her. She looked toward where the voice was coming from. A man stood holding a boy's sneaker. He smiled at her.

"Yes, sir. How can I help you?"

"Do you have this shoe in a size three and a size five?"

Morgan looked at the man quizzically, wondering why he needed two sizes that were not one size apart. Then as she looked past him she realized the reason why. She saw two little boys sitting next to a woman who, Morgan figured, must have been the mother.

"I think one wears a three and the other one wears a five," the man said. He looked toward his wife for confirmation.

"Yeah. I think so too," the woman said.

Morgan took the shoe from the man. "Let me check. We got these in a few days ago, so I think the chances are good that we have these in both sizes."

"Thank you," the man said.

"Yes, thank you," the wife said.

As Morgan walked toward the stockroom of shoes she saw the little boys both grab their father's legs as if trying to keep him from walking. The dad played with the boys, pretending to try to walk. As he did it was as if he had cement for shoes. While the parents laughed at the boys' antics, the boys giggled at the same time.

Morgan rolled her eyes to herself. The whole scene was nauseating. She figured they were the kind of family with the idealistic 2.5 kids, a white picket fence around their home, and a dog, and probably even a cat named Fluffy. They were dressed alike, all wearing white shirts and blue jeans. They looked like a family ready to be models for a portrait studio.

After locating the shoes she returned to the family. She forced a smile as she said, "Yep, just as I thought. Here are both shoes." Then she handed them to the father.

The boys sat down next to their mother. And then both parents took a child and tried the shoes on to see if they fit.

"How does that feel, Cameron?" the father asked his son.

The boy hopped around in his shoes. "They feel good, Daddy."

"How about you, Jayden? How do your shoes feel?" the mother asked the other boy.

He took a few steps, walking forward then returning to his mom. "They feel all right."

"What do you think, Travis? Do you like these better than this pair?" the wife said. She held up another shoe in a different style and color.

"I like these, Beryl. I think the boys will get better wear out of them. The last pair we got them in this brand worked out great until they grew out of them," the man named Travis said.

"We'll take these two pair," the woman named Beryl said.

They took the shoes off of the boys and the boys started to chase each other as they ran around in their socks.

"Oh, honey, I wanted to go by the men's section to get another dress shirt," Travis said to his wife.

They both looked toward Morgan. "Do we have to pay for these here or can we pay for them in the men's section?" the wife asked.

"You can pay for them in the men's section if you'd like," Morgan said.

"Okay, thanks. We didn't know if you got commission or something for helping us. We didn't want to slight you," the wife said.

"Oh, no need to worry about that," Morgan said.

She was ready for them to leave—glad they were finished in the shoe section. In the seconds it took them to talk about where items could be paid for, the boys had already knocked down three shoes set on tables as displays. At the rate they were going, the whole shoe department might have shoes lying on the floor like fallen dominoes.

"Come here, boys," Travis said.

The boys returned to their parents for their old shoes to be put back on. After they were finished, the family, even the two little boys, thanked Morgan again for her help. For anyone else the sight of an all-American black family would have warmed their heart. All it did for Morgan was make her bitter.

They probably never had a rough day in their perfect little marriage. The father probably was the type to work hard bringing home the bacon, while the wife probably stayed at home, cooking, cleaning, baking cookies, and homeschooling their children. All of them probably went on family camping vacations and trips to the amusement park. She could just see them now, laughing and playing while roasting marshmallows over an open fire.

Morgan shook her head, with a twinge of jealousy. She could have had all that and more but the marriage to her first husband, named Frank, back in her hometown of Warsaw, North Carolina shattered that dream. She had married young, had three children, it seemed like before the ink in their marriage certificate could dry, and three weeks after her youngest son had been born, Ci Ci found out her husband had been cheating on her the whole time.

Frank left her for the other woman. With no job, no education further than her high school diploma, and with no money, he'd left her penniless and with three mouths to feed. When she'd said "I do" to him at the justice of the peace, she had meant for it to be forever. Little did she know that his dreams were not the same as her dreams.

From the day Frank walked out of the door on her, things had gone into a spiral downspin. It seemed like all in a matter of days she lost her husband, then her three sons, and then her extended family. Without having a job and means to take care of her sons, they went without a lot of things.

One day someone from social services came and knocked on her door. The woman from social services said that there had been a report made on her about her children being neglected. That particular day the boys hadn't had a bath in a few days, and her kitchen only had a Kool-Aid pitcher filled with only tap water, she had a couple of dry boxes of stale cereal, and a package of tortillas she'd been provided by the WIC office, the supplemental program to assist families with nutritional foods.

She had let a month's worth of WIC food vouchers expire due to a lack of transportation to be able to get to the grocery store. The only person she had on whom she could depend was her grandmother, but the marriage to Frank had soured the grandmother-granddaughter relationship. Her grandmother hadn't wanted her to marry Frank in the first place. And once Frank left, Ci Ci's pride wouldn't allow her to let her grandmother become privy to just how bad things were going in her life.

Even though she had no proof, she really thought her grandmother was the one who turned her in to social services. And at first she fought like crazy to get her children back. But eventually all the fight left her as she slowly became depressed with all the stressful events of her husband, her children being taken, and her grandmother turning on her. There were days when she moped in her bedroom. When she did get herself together mentally enough to try to get her boys back, it seemed as if the whole world was against her—social services, the court system, her grandmother, and even the church and the so-called holier-than-thou people at the church she sometimes attended.

Then, after two years of fighting, Ci Ci, as she was called back then, gave up on any hopes that she would ever get her boys back. She also gave in to the message that everyone was sending her that she was not fit to be the boys' mother and that they were better off with their new foster parents. She had nothing to give them—no education, no stable shelter, and no means of supporting them financially. And once the boys no longer lived with her, she didn't even have the WIC food vouchers to help supplement the groceries.

Now as she looked at the happy little family, she just wanted to scream. They were probably one in a million, and just as she had figured that she wasn't part of the lucky people, Ci Ci reinvented herself into Morgan Jackson, then later got married to become Morgan Tracy. It was her firm belief that in order for things to happen in a person's life, he or she had to make them happen. Ever since she came to that realization for herself, Morgan had been making things happen, just as she was doing now.

The happy little family finally got up and went on their merry little way. When they did, Morgan inwardly sighed with relief. Their presence really irked her. It bothered her because if only Frank had acted right years before, she too could have had the same wonderful life. The other reason their presence bothered her was because her plans to find another man to be her next husband were not going as well as she wanted them to.

Morgan spent the next hour helping other customers and restocking when the shoe area was slow. Just before she was about to get off for the afternoon, she heard someone call her by her name—her birth name.

"Ci Ci Jackson."

Morgan froze a bit at hearing the name. The only name anyone at work called her was Morgan. And she was proud to be able to now legally go by that name. She dreaded seeing who was calling her name as well, because the last time someone called her out by her real name at the mall, the event was soon followed by her husband getting in a car accident, her being accused of trying to harm her husband, and then she was arrested and put in a correctional facility.

Again she heard the female voice call her name.

"Ci Ci."

She braced herself as she turned to confront whoever it was who knew who and what she really was. When she did she was surprised, and a bit relived at the same time. Standing just a few feet away, holding a pair of hot red high heels in her hand, was Miss Tiny, her newest acquaintance from the correctional facility.

Chapter 11

Morgan regained her composure, acting like the sophisticated woman she'd personified to the management and her coworkers. Instead of addressing Desiree by her nickname she called her by her real name. She hoped that Desiree would take the hint that she was at work and needed to be professional.

"Desiree."

Desiree closed the space between her and Morgan. "What's up, girl?" She then gave Morgan a big hug. "And didn't I tell you about calling me Desiree?" She then slapped Morgan playfully on the shoulder.

Morgan stood back a bit. Although she was actually glad to see her acquaintance, the same acquaintance who had become the closest thing she had to a friend in a long time, Morgan didn't want her bosses or coworkers to know a thing about her personal life. She especially didn't want them to know that she'd done a stint in a correctional facility.

Stepping a bit over to the side, Desiree followed Morgan. She wanted to get the woman out of earshot of anyone who was really anyone in the vicinity.

"Desiree, what are you doing here, girl?" Morgan asked.

Desiree looked quite different in street clothes than she did in her correctional facility uniform. She wore a pair of skin-tight jeans, and a halter top that also looked as if it had been painted on. Her hair was done up in micro-braids that looked pretty fresh. The woman looked nothing like those holier-than-thou women who used to attend her holiness church back in her small hometown. Truthfully, instead of Desiree looking like any of the respectable women in the Bible like Mary, Hannah, or Sarah, she looked more like Jezebel.

"I got out a couple of weeks ago. I came over to the mall to get a pair of shoes to wear to my birthday party." She held the red pumps up. "You like these?"

Morgan looked at them. They were pretty cute. She had actually been eyeing the same pair of shoes when they first set them out on display the week before. "Cute, I like them."

Desiree looked at Morgan's name tag and said, "Morgan?" She said so with question in her voice.

"Long story," Morgan said. "I'll have to tell you about it later."

Desiree pulled her cell phone out. "What's your phone number?"

Without hesitation Morgan gave her the cell phone number. It would be good to catch up with Desiree.

"I'll text you the details for my party. You've gotta come. It is going to be off the chain. I've got a DJ booked and all," Desiree said.

"Text me the information," Morgan said.

Morgan knew she didn't have any intention of attending the party. Overall she felt Desiree was pretty cool, but not cool enough to hang out with in that manner. Plus she was sure there wouldn't be anyone at Desiree's party worth her time or with the possibility of being her next new man and husband. Desiree didn't look like she knew anyone who made close to six figures, not even the woman's lawyer, who was probably hired on a pro bono basis.

"Girl, I gotta go. Call me," Desiree said.

"Will do," Morgan said. Then her friend left.

That evening when Morgan was home she reflected on the events earlier in the day—watching the happy little family and seeing her cellmate from the correctional facility. It seemed as though Desiree was moving along with her life pretty happily and it was now time for Morgan to do the same.

She pulled out her Netbook computer to start searching the Silvermont area to find out who the eligible bachelors might be. It wasn't necessarily easy to find a man, much less one who had things going for him in all the right departments like their looks, their social status, and most importantly their wallet.

Morgan didn't want just any man. That was the way it was when she started her research expedition to find out more about Will in the beginning. And things hadn't changed. Will had pretty much stumbled across her that day at the sporting goods store. It hadn't been hard to find out more about him. She got online that night and did a reverse search on the apartment number and street address. There she found the name William Tracy. Still not sure if the name was actually his, she did a search for all William Tracys in the Silvermont North Carolina area and found there were actually seven listed in the system. From the ages that were listed, she was able to narrow the names down to about three, since the guy looked as if he was about thirty years of age.

With the age and address she did a few more searches cross-referencing the address and age, and she was then able to find an alumni page for Carson State University with the name and picture of the same guy she saw at the sporting goods store. From there she found the guy's Facebook page, which was unprotected. There was a wealth of information in there with pictures, his e-mail address, phone number, the schools he attended as well as the place that he currently worked at.

The Facebook page also had a stream of messages from William Tracy's friends, family, and even coworkers. The information was like a window into the guy's life. She was glad this guy didn't have the restrictions on his page.

In most of the messages people referred him as "Will" instead of William. From there it was easy to find out even more. By knowing the wealth of information she was able to map out where his place of employment was. Then for the next month and a half she figured out his patterns, which were pretty routine.

The guy worked a regular job Monday through Friday from eight to five pretty much. There were some nights when he worked a little later. Once she figured out his day schedule she started figuring out his weekend patterns. He attended church on Sundays at a mid-morning service. He went to the movies a couple of times to the Saturday matinees. It really didn't seem as though the guy had much of a social life.

There were a few times when she was following him that she was tempted to walk up to him and introduce herself. She especially wanted to do so when she felt she was dressed nicely and had her hair and nails done. But she decided to wait for the exact right moment. And that moment came one Sunday at church.

The first Sunday she found out what church Will attended she started going there as well. The pastor there seemed to have some pretty good words to say in his sermons and the choir sang very well, but the main attraction for her was the guy who usually sat in the middle section about three rows back.

It seemed as though Will really got into the whole church thing. He stood when others were standing, clapped his hands during the singing of the choir, and even seemed to be in the Spirit of the Lord. The feeling she got was that the guy was probably saved and pretty straightforward. From what she had been observing she figured when she did set up her so-called chance encounter with him, she would have to come from a holy perspective.

One Sunday morning Morgan decided that particular day would be the day she would at least reveal herself to Will. She got to church a little early, sat in the row where he normally sat, and waited. Like clockwork he came in a few minutes before the service started. Mr. William Tracy walked in smelling of the same cologne he smelled of that first day she saw him at the sporting goods store.

It was all she could do not to speak to him right then and there, but her plan was to wait until the end of the service. That particular Sunday, the pastor talked about having faith and praying for things and having the mustard-seed faith to do so. After service ended and others were leaving the church, Will continued to sit with his head bowed and his eyes closed as he prayed to himself.

The longer Will prayed the closer she stepped toward where he was sitting. By the time he opened his eyes, she was standing right next to him. When he looked up at her she acted as if she was just trying to get past him. Will stared at her for a moment as if he was half surprised and half expecting to actually see her standing there. She remembered their first words to each other like it was yesterday.

"Oh, excuse me. Were you trying to get by?" Will had asked.

"Yes," Morgan said. "I know I could have gone around the other way, but you looked so peaceful as you sat there praying that I just had to watch."

He stood. "Well sorry for delaying you." He moved back so she could pass and she did.

"Don't worry, the delay was a pleasurable one." If Morgan didn't know any better, she'd say he was probably salivating. She knew she looked and smelled good as well.

Now it was time for her to flirt with him so there would be no doubt in his mind that she was interested in him. She winked her eye and then continued on her way down the aisle of seats. The first part of her plan was now in motion. For the next few Sundays she would make sure to make herself visible to him. She'd make herself visible enough for him to eventually make the move to speak to her himself. She knew that it was important for the man to make the first move, or at least think he was making the first move.

For the next few Sundays Morgan made sure she sat close enough to Will so that he would see her. Quite a few times she saw him looking her way, and finally one Sunday after church he approached her in the bookstore located in the church.

It seemed like only yesterday she had been doing her research and got Will hooked. Morgan shook her head to herself. She knew there was no need to dwell in the thoughts of the past. It was time for her to move on. It was obvious that Will would no longer be fooled by her nondisclosure of truthful information anymore. It was time to find a new unsuspecting man with whom she could work her way into his heart.

In the search engine on her computer Morgan started looking though the online version of the local newspaper. She started looking through the community information sections, the social events section, and news highlights for the local community and even the state. With any luck she'd be able to find a few stories with men featured who might fit the profile she was looking for.

Chapter 12

After eight weeks of working hard at her job at the department store and working hard at finding an eligible and desirable bachelor, Morgan had been overall pretty pleased with herself. Morgan found what seemed to be two promising prospects. She was at the point where she was just about to see just how promising.

She turned on water and sprinkled bath salts in her tub. As she laid her clothing out on her bed and waited for the tub to fill, she thought about what her virtual and literally physical searches on the two men yielded. One guy, who was named Richard, owned his own taxi service in the Silvermont area. Richard was just a couple of years older than Morgan, and wasn't too bad on the eyes, although he had a bit lighter complexion than she really liked in a man.

In the visible and physical research of Richard she was able to find out things a computer couldn't tell her. After figuring out where Richard lived and some of his daily patterns, Morgan found out that the guy was too eligible of a bachelor, so much so that he was a big-time player. It seemed as though he had a woman in almost every map quadrant of Silvermont. There was no way Morgan was going to add her name and living quadrant to his map of women.

With him being the player he was, it was obvious to her that the guy was sport fishing, as Steve Harvey would put it. He was in the game just for the game. The last thing on his mind was probably to settle down and be a one-woman man. When it came to doing research on a person, Morgan was glad she had the skills and common sense to do so. If she didn't then she could have possibly become a part of Richard's collection of women.

Morgan shook off the thoughts about the time she wasted on Richard; then she smiled to herself as she thought about the second guy she'd researched. This man owned his own financial services company. She gathered a lot of information and found that the guy's life seemed to be pretty much an open book. Her searches for his first and last name yielded a great deal of information. She even knew that the guy was born on June 11. She didn't know exactly what year yet, but didn't think it would be too hard to find out.

The guy seemed to be very well-rounded. The information she found on him showed that he had attended Silvermont High School, then decided to remain in the Silvermont area, as he attended undergraduate school and graduate school at Carson State University.

With each piece of information she found about the man, she grew more and more interested and excited. He seemed to be the total package. The only thing that gave her a bit of a pause was finding out he was a member of a college fraternity. Will was a member of a fraternity and she wondered if Will might know the guy, especially since both had attended Carson State University. She sighed with a bit of relief when she realized the man was a member of a different fraternity. So her hope was that the men had never met.

This second guy hadn't been so easy to track when it came to physically tracking his moves. He didn't really keep a regular schedule and often times went to places and buildings that put speed bumps in Morgan's ease of being able to trail him. In some ways it was a bit frustrating, but in other ways, it was exhilarating. It gave her a bit of a challenge, and she was up for the challenge.

So far she had found nothing that would give her a reason to stop pursuing the man. As it stood, the more she found the more she wanted to meet him. One day she had even contemplated throwing caution to the wind and she almost walked straight up to him at the gas station he had stopped at. But at the last moment she stopped herself. She wasn't going to waste a thirty-second encounter with him that he'd soon forget in less than five seconds. Her aim was to make a lasting impression on the man whenever they met and parted.

Now her dream was quickly about to become a reality. She was going to continue to play her cards right. In just a few short hours she would be making that first and lasting impression.

In the bathroom she turned the water off in the tub, lit a jasmine-scented candle, and prepared to immerse herself in the hot tub. As she blinked her eyes they felt a little dry. Remembering that her bottle of eye drops for her contacts was in her purse, she left the bathroom to find the purse sitting on the counter in her little kitchen. As she reached for the purse, she knocked over the pile of mail she had let collect over the past few days.

One of the pieces of mail caught her eye. She looked at the standard-sized business envelope, eyeing the name it was addressed to and the name and address where the envelope had originated. In scrawled, feeble-looking letters was her birth name of Cecily C. Jackson. She knew the feeble-looking, scrawled letters. Even without having to look at the name, Morgan would have known who it was from just from the penmanship of the person sending it.

All too quickly the past memories of her little hometown and the life she lived there flooded back to her.
It was probably only her imagination, but she thought
she smelled the slight hint of kerosene on the envelope. Her grandmother often heated the house with a
kerosene heater. She despised that smell. The smell
reminded her of living in a home without central heat
and air, because her grandmother couldn't afford it. As
a child her clothing reeked of the smell and other kids,
especially the snooty kids, picked on her because of the
smell of her clothing.

Her body tensed as she thought about the many
times kids picked on her about one thing or another
thing. She remembered often thinking that if only
her mother would come back and rescue her then she
wouldn't have to endure living with a poor grandmother who wouldn't provide her with not only the
things she wanted, but even some of the things she felt
she needed.

While most people thought of their mothers and
grandmothers in loving ways, Morgan didn't. As far
as Morgan was concerned she didn't have a mother
or a grandmother. A real mother would not have left
her child no matter what the circumstances and a real
grandmother would not have treated Morgan the way
her grandmother had, doing unforgettable, unapolo-
getic things.

Morgan held the envelope by its corner. She had no
idea what the woman wanted that was so important for
her to track her down, but it would have to wait until
the end of time, because she didn't want anything to do
with her. She wanted no part of the past she'd long ago
left behind.

She flung the letter toward the trashcan. She missed
the trashcan completely. It slid on the kitchen counter

instead. Morgan rolled her eyes, not wanting to give the piece of mail any more of the valuable time she needed to get ready for the social event she was about to attend in a few hours. She left it where it was. She'd get it later and decide what to do with it.

Taking a deep, cleansing breath she returned to the bathroom to enjoy the hot bath she'd just run. In the tub she fantasized about how the upcoming night would progress. If luck was on her side, by the time she returned home, she would have the personal contact information of the man she'd been researching for over a week. By night's end not only would she have Mr. Darrin Michael Hobbs's phone number, Mr. Hobbs would also know who she was.

Morgan stepped into the crowded room filled with the A-list movers and shakers of the Silvermont higher echelon. The sound of light jazz filled the room while people mingled, sitting at tables and congregating in mini groups of threes and fours throughout the space. A buffet was set, filled with heavy hors d'oeuvres.

There were a few people she recognized from the community, from the mayor to a few of the people who sat on the city council. There was even a news broadcaster attending this networking business event. Her newly found friend, named Martha, was standing just to the left of a head table, which was set up in the front and center of the room.

Morgan made eye contact with Martha and then headed the woman's way. Martha greeted her with a warm hug like she'd known Morgan all her life, instead of the reality of only becoming acquainted just few days prior.

Mrs. Martha Metcalf was an eccentric-looking African American woman in her late sixties. She seemed to be at the department store where Morgan worked all the time in one section or another. Usually the woman left the store with bags of clothing, shoes, accessories, and items from the home-décor section of the store.

Often Morgan wondered what the woman did with all her purchases. She also wondered just how much the woman spent in the store in a month's or a year's time. By Morgan's calculations, in the three weeks that she'd been observing Martha, the woman must have spent well over $2,000.

Morgan remembered the slow afternoon when she'd let her curiosity get the best of her. She wanted to know more about the lady. Morgan had approached the woman.

"Excuse me, miss. Can I help you with anything?" *Morgan had said to the woman.*

The woman, who had been looking through some silk scarves that were on sale, turned to Morgan and said, "You're new here aren't you?"

This took Morgan by a bit of surprise. First, because the woman hadn't answered with a simple reply to the offering of help, and, secondly, because the woman had barely seemed fully turned toward her when she spoke. It was as if the woman knew Morgan had been watching her.

"Ah, yes. I've been working here a little over seven and a half weeks," Morgan said.

"I figured as much," the woman said. She extended her hand, loaded with clanking metal bangles on her wrist. "I am Mrs. Martha Metcalf."

Morgan extended her own hand to shake Mrs. Metcalf's hand. The bangles continually clanked as they shook hands. "I'm Morgan."

Mrs. Metcalf smiled. "Oh I can see that by your name tag right there." The woman pointed to, and then lightly tapped, Morgan's name tag.

The whole encounter seemed a bit uncomfortable for Morgan, and now she was rethinking her spontaneity about approaching the woman in the first place.

"I've seen you around here." The woman chuckled and gave Morgan a warm smile. "You've probably seen me too."

Morgan had indeed seen the woman. Today she wore an outfit that was almost as loud as the bangles on her wrist. The woman's wardrobe always varied from day to day. Sometimes it was plain, dull, and unassuming, but today was the exact opposite. She wore large round bronze earrings dangling from her ears, and a bright yellow puffy blouse with lime green parachute-looking pants. Morgan knew MC Hammer would be very proud of her choice of pant attire.

"I have seen you in here quite often." Morgan returned a warm smile to Mrs. Metcalf. It seemed as if the other woman's smile was indeed genuine.

Mrs. Metcalf held up a paisley turquoise blue and gray scarf to her cheek. "What do you think about this scarf? Does it go with my skin tone?"

Morgan looked at the scarf against the woman's butternut brown skin tone. Overall she thought the scarf looked great against the woman's skin, but the color of the blouse and pants clashed. "The scarf looks very nice and goes well with your skin tone."

As though the woman could read the bit of apprehension in Morgan's voice, she asked, "It clashes with this outfit, huh?"

Morgan smiled, glad the woman realized her outfit was a bit off.

"You know, when I put this getup on this morning"—the older woman took her right hand and attempted to smooth down the blouse and pants—*"I thought it was a bit much."* She frowned to herself. *"I am really trying to find a style that really suits me."*

Morgan nodded her head as she listened to the older woman speak. Now she felt she was getting a bit of a better understanding about why the woman looked and dressed one way one day and then a different way the next day.

Mrs. Metcalf placed the scarf she was holding back on the table with the stack of other scarves. *"Ever since my husband Harvey died, I find myself with so much time on my hands. I find myself with time I really never had before, and don't know what to do with myself at times."*

The pain the woman felt as she talked about losing her husband was evident on her face. Morgan looked at the creases and wrinkles that formed as Mrs. Metcalf frowned. With an outstretched arm Morgan touched the woman's shoulder as a gesture of caring.

Mrs. Metcalf smiled in appreciation for the caring that Morgan was showing. *"Thank you Morgan for being so kind."*

"You're welcome," Morgan said.

"Don't let me hold you from getting back to work. Somehow or another I'll figure out what fashion style best suits me."

Morgan looked around the immediate area and didn't see another customer in the section. *"It's fine, Mrs. Metcalf,"* Morgan said. *"The store isn't that busy and I'm long overdue for my break anyway. I'd like to help you find some things if you don't mind."*

The woman's face lit up. *"You may call me Martha,"* Martha said.

Over the next few minutes, Morgan helped Martha find two scarves and a blouse that matched both. She also helped Martha find a couple of skirts that would go well with the blouse and both scarves.

Once they finished with picking out the apparel, Morgan led Martha to the accessory table and helped her pick out a pair of earrings and a complementing necklace that wasn't too dull and at the same time not too flashy. Then Morgan asked, "So what do you think about the things we've picked out?"

"I think we did a very good job. I know I wouldn't have picked out the combinations you picked out." Tears welled in Martha's eyes. She continued to speak. "I think the items you helped me find might actually be the style that is best suited for me."

"Oh, Martha, what's wrong?" Morgan asked with concern.

"I sure wish I had a daughter or even a granddaughter like you." The tear fell and Martha wiped it away. "I never had any children." Martha took a deep breath as she tried to regain her composure.

From the time Morgan had spent with the older woman, she had to admit that she'd become pretty fond of her. She too secretly wished she had been able to grow up with a woman in her life as nice as Mrs. Martha Metcalf seemed to be. Morgan felt sure that having someone like Martha in her life would have made her life turn out completely different. In her mind her life would have turned out better.

"You'd think after three husbands, I would have had at least one child. But I guess it just wasn't in the cards that life dealt me," Martha said.

Morgan gawked a bit when she heard that the woman had a history of having three husbands. "You've been married three times?"

"Yep. The first marriage was out of convenience. The second marriage was out of desperation, and the third marriage was actually for love," Martha said.

"Wow," Morgan said.

"That is what a lot of people say." Martha chuckled.

Out of curiosity Morgan asked, "So what happened with your first two marriages?" She didn't want it to seem like she was prying, so she said, "If you don't mind me asking."

"I don't mind at all," Martha said. It looked as if the woman had been really longing for someone to talk to.

"I left my first husband because what seemed so convenient in the beginning began to be a burden. We split due to irreconcilable differences—it seemed we had absolutely nothing in common. Then there was my second marriage of desperation. After about three months, I realized I wasn't really that desperate after all, so I left him. He filed for divorce and I gladly signed the papers.

"My latest husband, Harvey, was the love of my life. After divorcing my second husband it was a good ten years before Harvey and I met. I guess you could say it was love at first sight—that is, in his sight. It took me a few weeks to appreciate my own love for him." Martha laughed out loud.

Morgan laughed with her as she allowed herself to become immersed in the story about Martha's life. "So you didn't fall in love with him quickly?"

"No, no, no. After the bad luck I'd had with my first two marriages, I couldn't have cared less about ever getting married again—it was the very last thing on my mind. Because of this, Harvey thought I was playing hard to get, but I wasn't. I wasn't playing hard to get; I was the real thing—very much hard to get."

With a wistful look in Martha's eyes, she continued to talk. "Harvey wasn't about to let me get away. He told me once after we got married that he knew I was the woman for him, and there was no way on God's green earth that he was going to let me miss out on a good thing."

Martha placed her hand on Morgan's forearm, stating, "That good thing being him of course."

Morgan and Martha both laughed at the last comment.

"Harvey treated me better than both my husbands put together, and even the couple of guys I'd dated before my marriage to Harvey. He was the epitome of a gentleman. He held the door for me when we went places, he held the chair out for me when we went out to dinner, and he took me to only the finest of restaurants.

"Girl, I wish you could have seen me back then. I was used to eating at McDonald's and when I wanted to splurge it up I'd eat at a casual dining restaurant. But none of the places I went would have been considered fine dining. I was like Cinderella changing from a woman just trying her best to make ends meet on an assistant secretary's salary to becoming the wife of a wealthy business owner."

Morgan had been enjoying every minute of hearing about the woman's life but now her ears really perked up. Martha's story was shaping up to be the life and ending she was currently striving for. Morgan had lived the Cinderella life of sorts, or her childhood could have been compared to be more so like Little Orphan Annie. Now here she was talking to someone who personally knew about the plight of scraping to get by.

"Oh my goodness," Martha said, "I have talked you to near death. Your eyes are glossing over."

With alarm in her voice Morgan said, "Oh, no, Martha. That couldn't be further from the truth. Your story actually inspires me, believe it or not."

"Really?" Martha asked in disbelief.

"Yes, really. We seem to have a great deal in common. I come from some pretty humble beginnings and I've been married as well. The marriage didn't work out so well. So now I find myself trying to get my life back on track," Morgan said.

If anyone had told Morgan that morning that by the afternoon she'd be spilling out her own personal information to a complete stranger, she never would have believed it. As it was, she was about to tell Martha even more than she had ever told anyone. She felt that was another aspect she and Martha had in common. Morgan was also lonely in a sense and needed someone to talk to and confide in. Deep down, she also felt that Martha was that someone she could speak in confidence to.

"A nice young lady like you. You're not married?" Martha asked.

"Nope. My husband and I recently called it quits," Morgan said. She couldn't say they had gotten divorced because they hadn't. In order to get a divorce a person had to first be legally married. Opening up about that little bit of her history would lead to an even longer discussion: a discussion about the false pretenses she'd put in place to fool the man she'd called husband for over two years.

"I am sorry to hear that, but that is just the way life can be sometimes." Martha nodded her head. "But I am here to tell you that there are more than just one or two apples on a tree. Heck, there are over seven thousand types of apples out there. Believe me, I know."

Morgan had no idea there were so many kinds of apples in the world.

"A nice young lady such as yourself needs to get on back out there and find another apple," Martha said.

"That's just what I've been thinking," Morgan said. Martha was confirming her thoughts and recent measures she'd taken in trying to find someone new.

"As pretty as you are, you'll find someone in no time I'm sure," Martha said. "You know, you actually remind me of myself when I was younger. I don't want you to do like me and waste some of the best younger years of your life. I let those first two bad apples hinder me from finding a really good man. God smiled down on me and sent me Harvey. I had the best four years of my life with him before the Lord took him on to glory."

Martha's face took on a melancholy hue. Once again Morgan placed her hand on the woman's shoulder, this time with a firmer touch. Then Martha replaced the sadness on her face with a smile. "I refuse to be sad. All I have are happy memories about my life with Harvey and I am going to keep it that way."

Morgan nodded her head in understanding.

"Now back to you. Have you been looking for anyone? Has anyone been looking for you?" Martha asked.

"I've been looking. I've been using the Internet to find prospects," Morgan said.

"The Internet? You mean like on some dating Web site that's supposed to match you with the perfect person?" Martha asked.

"Ah, yeah, something like that," Morgan said. The type of searching she did went way beyond a simple online date matching site. She was able to find out the real deal on men, like specifics about their dates

*of birth and even to each and every place a guy lived,
oftentimes starting with his parents' address.*

*"You need to do it the old-fashioned way. You need
to meet a nice man in person. That way you can look
him in his eyes and tell if he is genuine." Martha shook
her head. "I've heard some not-so-nice things about
the Internet and those dating sites. People lie about
their age, their occupation, and even put up pictures
that are old, and I've even heard of people putting
pictures of other people, pretending that is what they
really look like."*

*Morgan knew about deception and lies. She'd been
deceptive and had told so many lies that even she
started to believe them. "You're right, Martha, but
where can women meet nice men nowadays? In the
library, at the grocery store?"*

*"You can find some nice men in church," Martha
said.*

*"Been there and done that. No, thank you. It didn't
work for me." Morgan had been hurt one too many
times by church folk overall.*

*Martha took a deep breath as if remembering
something. She placed both of her hands on Morgan's.
"I know the perfect place for you to start your search."*

"Really? Where?" Morgan asked.

"Have you heard of the SBA?"

*"The Silvermont Business Alliance," Morgan said.
"Right?"*

"Yes," Martha said.

*Morgan knew about the Silvermont Business Alli-
ance. It was filled with the movers and shakers of the
Silvermont business community.*

*"Well they meet once a month at the town hall with
a laid-back style of networking. The meetings are a bit
swanky. I've been to quite a few because my husband*

was a member. You either have to be a member of the alliance or have an exclusive invitation from an alliance member in order to be able to attend."

"Oh, well. I guess I won't be able to take part of that social meeting opportunity since I'm not a business owner," Morgan said.

"Maybe not, but, my dear friend, you are a friend of a business owner." Martha grinned at Morgan. "And you, my dear, will be my guest for the next meeting."

"Really?" Morgan asked in disbelief.

"Yes, really. They meet on the third Saturday of each month."

Morgan already knew when they met. What she hadn't really fathomed was that she'd ever actually be able to attend a meeting. Now here she was with an invitation to the next gathering, and by the check of her mental calendar, the next meeting was just a few days away.

"Oh my goodness. That is this weekend," Morgan said.

Martha thought about it. "I think you are right."

Morgan touched her hair and then looked at her nails. "I've got to make appointments to get my hair and nails done. What will I wear? I don't really think I have anything swanky enough."

Martha had cut her eyes over toward the dress section of the store clad with mannequins dressed in stunning, swanky-looking dresses. "What more do you need?"

Both Morgan and Martha had laughed as they realized Morgan was already standing in the best place to put together an outfit that would turn any eligible man's head.

Now fast-forward a couple of days and the night of the SBA networking alliance had come. Now she was being approached by Martha, who greeted her with the warmth of a longtime friend. All Morgan needed now was for Mr. Darrin Hobbs to make his own entrance into the room. Then she could see up close and personal what she had only been able to admire from afar, and on a two-dimensional computer screen.

Chapter 13

Martha had been extremely cordial as she walked Morgan around the room, introducing her to person after person. Some faces she recognized, and others she didn't. After a good thirty minutes of meeting and greeting, there had not been any sign of Mr. Hobbs.

On one hand, Morgan was disappointed. But on the other hand, she decided to keep her options open just in case there was another eligible bachelor in the midst who she hadn't known existed. By the time she'd been there for an hour, all hopes of seeing Mr. Hobbs or finding another single and desirable guy faded. It didn't look as if Martha's idea was going to work that particular night.

Resigned to the fact that she should just make the best of it and mingle with people for the next hour, Morgan filled an appetizer plate with finger foods and munched on them. While chewing a savory-tasting mini crab cake, Morgan felt a pat on her upper arm.

"Morgan." It was Martha's unmistakable voice. "There is someone I want you to meet."

Morgan turned toward Martha and almost choked a bit when she saw who was standing next to her. Live and in person, no longer two-dimensional but three-dimensional and close enough to touch, stood Mr. Darrin Michael Hobbs. Up close and personal he looked better than any newspaper article and the picture he had posted on his company's Web site. Although there was a slight resemblance to Jaleel White, Mr. Hobbs definitely didn't look nerdy in the least.

For the first couple of seconds, Morgan was at a loss for words as she fumbled with the napkin she was holding in her hand under the plate. She was all too consciously aware that there might be crumbs on her face and also figured her breath had taken on a crab-like aroma. If she was anyone else, she might have been mortified, but she wasn't just anyone else, and she would do all in her power to regain the composure she had when she first stepped into the room earlier.

Throwing caution to the wind she smiled at Darrin while speaking to Martha. "Martha, who is the handsome-looking gentleman you would like for me to meet?" As she spoke to Martha, she kept constant eye contact with Darrin.

"Morgan, this is Mr. Darrin Hobbs. He owns his own financial planning company," Martha said.

Darrin extended his hand to shake Morgan's. He maintained eye contact with Morgan. "Pleased to meet you," Darrin said.

His voice had a deep, rich baritone quality to it, and his handshake was firm. Morgan liked both attributes about him. Her friend Martha had been right: it was much better to see a person face to face and be able to look them in their eyes to figure out their level of sincerity.

"Hello, Mr. Hobbs. I must say it is a pleasure to meet you as well," Morgan said. She tried to sound self-assured and confident as she spoke, even though she knew her breath might actually be betraying her.

"You two should talk some more," Martha said. "I think you'll find that you both have a common factor that could be mutually eliminated."

At Martha's statement, Morgan finally took her eyes off of Darrin to look at Martha. Martha winked at both Morgan and Darrin. The wink was unmistakably clear. Martha was trying to set the two up and was making sure her meaning was understood.

"Oh, I see someone I need to talk to over there," Martha said. As she spoke she pointed over to the general direction of a group of people gathered and talking to one another in a cluster. "I'll give you both some privacy so you can get better acquainted." Before either Morgan or Darrin could respond, Martha made a beeline straight toward the group of people.

"Well all righty then," Darrin said as he looked down to Morgan. He stood a good seven inches taller than she did.

"My sentiments exactly," Morgan said.

"I think, in a sense, we've just been set up."

"And I agree with you," Morgan replied.

Darrin looked over toward Martha. "Mrs. Martha is something else." Then he turned his attention back to Morgan. "I have a great deal of respect for the woman. So I wouldn't want to let her down by not finding out what our common factor or trait or denominator might be."

Morgan chuckled. "I wouldn't want to let her down either."

Inside Morgan was excitedly having a mental celebration party. She couldn't believe the luck she was having and what good fortune stepping up to Martha at the store was turning out to be.

"So, Morgan, what business are you in? I don't believe I've seen you at any of these functions before," Darrin said.

Okay, the ball was now in her court; she could tell him a lie she could quickly make up, or she could tell the truth. She opted for the truth. She was finding that it was often hard to keep up with the lies she told at times and it might be refreshing to tell the truth for once.

"Actually I don't have a business. I was invited as a guest of Martha's. She thought coming here would give me a chance to meet and greet people and at least do some networking within the Silvermont community."

Telling the truth had not been as uncomfortable as she thought it might be. Besides there was no need to lie about some type of fictitious business or business affiliation she didn't have. Plus she wanted to gauge his reaction to what she was saying about herself.

"Currently I am a supervisor at the mall. In the department store I work in I pretty much oversee operations for each of the departments," Morgan said. "That is how I met Martha." Morgan looked over toward Martha, who was confidently continuing to walk around the room as she greeted and spoke with people. "She is such a sweet lady."

Darrin took a sip from the cup of ginger ale he'd been holding in his hand ever since they had been introduced. "She is a very sweet woman. A bit on the eccentric side, but I like her just the same. Harvey, her former husband, was a shrewd businessman whom I looked up to growing up and as young man trying to make it in the business world."

Morgan set her appetizer plate down on a nearby table. There was no way she was going to continue eating crab cakes and shrimp cocktail while trying to talk. What she needed now was some water to help wash down what she'd eaten and to do a quick rinse of her mouth.

Noticing that Morgan was looking around, Darrin said, "Can I get you anything?"

"Yes, I'd like a bottle of water if they have any."

"I'll get you one. I'll be right back," Darrin said. He headed over toward one of the waiters and spoke with him.

Morgan took a deep breath, still not believing her good fortune. Being able to meet Darrin Hobbs had not ended up having to be the carefully played out minuet that she was going to have to orchestrate. Instead Martha had basically handed the man to her on a silver platter.

The whole scenario made Morgan think about one of her all-time favorite movies and plays called *Fiddler on the Roof*. There was a song that was going through her head as she concentrated on the first line of the song. Under her breath Morgan looked toward Martha and whispered, "'Matchmaker, Matchmaker, make me a match.'"

Martha had found her a handsome find and a good catch. Morgan was just glad she had already done a great deal of homework on her Darrin before this so-called setup and chance meeting. It was sort of like finding out about a company before actually going to an interview. She figured the information she had about the man would help her to further get to know Darrin.

As Darrin exchanged niceties with people as he waited for the water, Morgan wasn't blind to the fact that there were more than a few women in the room eyeing him. From what she could tell, the women weren't attached, especially since none of them were wearing wedding bands. She knew Darrin was single, and now it was obvious that he was also desired by many.

Morgan would need to play her cards right in this situation. She needed to keep this man's attention through her conversation and she also needed to make sure she sparked enough interest in him that Darrin would ask her for her contact information. Every second from that moment on was critical in her quest to seize his full attention. It wouldn't be easy with all the wolves that were circling the room. It would be a challenge but she was up to it.

Darrin returned with two bottles of cold water. He handed one to her and opened the other one for himself. After both taking sips, they continued with their conversation.

"So Martha says you own a financial planning company?" Morgan asked.

"Yes, Excel Financial Planning. I've been in business for myself for over eight years now," Darrin said.

"Impressive. I like a man who knows what he wants and gets it," Morgan said. She wanted to stroke his ego.

Darrin responded by continuing to talk about his business. "I have always wanted to own my own business. I started when I was young with lemonade stands."

Morgan put her hand out to touch his. "You actually had a lemonade stand as a child?"

"Yep, I sure did." He nodded his head. "That venture didn't last long because after doing the math, and calculating what I was spending for overhead, I wasn't making a profit. Then I moved on to other small ventures like collecting aluminum cans and glass bottles for profit, but the profit was minimal compared to the work involved."

Morgan uttered a small laugh.

"Is something funny?" Darrin asked.

"I was just trying to picture you standing on the side of the street with a lemonade stand selling cups of lemonade for twenty-five cents," Morgan said.

"Twenty-five cents? Oh no, my lemonade was a dollar a cup," Darrin said.

"You're joking right?"

Darrin shook his head. "Nope."

"No wonder you didn't make any money."

"My lemonade was gourmet. I wasn't just making a lemonade packet and putting a little sugar in the water. I had fresh-squeezed lemons and a touch of lime juice in my lemonade. I guarantee it was the best in the city," Darrin said.

"I'm sure it was," Morgan said.

As they spoke, Morgan noticed the female news broadcaster staring at them. She figured the woman was probably looking and trying to figure out who Darrin was talking to. For a second she had a fleeting thought as she wondered if the woman might be able to figure out who she was. News broadcasters were in the know, and reported on any number of topics. She didn't think her arrest had made the local news. And with any luck the broadcaster didn't pay any attention to the arrest magazines.

"So, Morgan. Should I be moving on to mingle with some other people? I don't want your man to get the wrong impression about us talking," Darrin said.

"No worries. I don't have a man you need to be concerned about. And, Mr. Hobbs, I could actually say the same for you. It looks as if you have quite a few admirers," Morgan answered.

"Who?" Darrin asked.

"Just look around. Like Miss Courtney Alexander over there." Morgan nodded her head slightly toward the direction Courtney was standing in.

Darrin looked over toward Courtney then back at Morgan. "Ha ha." Darrin laughed. "No need to worry there."

"She has hardly taken her eyes off of you since we've been talking," Morgan said.

"Miss Courtney likes me but my feelings for her are not the same." Darrin took a sip of the water from his water bottle.

Morgan gave him a disbelieving and quizzical look. She'd seen in many movies how people drank water when they were nervous or needed a momentary distraction. "Courtney is a very nice-looking woman with a promising career. Most men would readily respond to the attention she is clearly giving you."

In response Darrin said, "Well, Morgan, I am not most men. But in response to your implied question, Courtney and I have been out on a couple of dates. And I do agree that she is a very nice-looking woman, but there isn't any spark there for me. Courtney is pretty on the outside, but as shallow as they come. She comes from a family with wealth and wouldn't know what hard times were even if she broadcasted a story about it.

"Now I'm not saying having wealth makes a person bad, but Courtney just isn't as in touch with reality as I would like her to be. Plus I know what it means to come from nothing and make it up the ladder of success."

"Okay. Well what about your significant other? Is she more in touch with the real world?"

"She will be when I find her," Darrin said.

"So you're telling me there isn't a Mrs. Hobbs or a potential Mrs. Hobbs in the picture right now?"

"No, there isn't a Mrs. Hobbs or a potential Mrs. Hobbs in the picture right now," Darrin confirmed. "So while we are clarifying things, is there a Mr. Morgan or potential Mr. Morgan in the picture right now?"

Morgan lightheartedly laughed at Darrin's use of humor. "No, no Mr. Morgan."

"Ahhh," Darrin said. "So it looks as if I am single and you are single."

Morgan nodded her head in agreement. "It looks to be that way."

"Okay then. I've figured it out," Darrin said.

"Figured what out?" Morgan asked.

"What the common factor is that you and I have—the one that Martha was talking about earlier."

"We're both single," Morgan said as if she had just thought about the common factor as well. In fact, she knew all along what they had in common, but she was glad Darrin had processed this information for himself.

"Yep," Darrin said. "That Martha really is something else. And if I didn't know any better, I might just think that Martha invited you here to meet me. She knows I am single. She also knows I am a very picky man."

Morgan wondered what in the world Darrin meant about being picky. Even though it looked as if the evening was going way better than she could have ever planned, there might actually be a roadblock or at least a speed bump that was about to slow down the progress she thought was being made.

"You're picky, huh?" Morgan tried to sound as nonchalant as possible.

"Maybe I shouldn't say picky. I am a man who has standards and wants his lady to have standards as well. I don't like women who are fake, and I don't like women who don't carry themselves in a manner becoming of a woman."

"And you don't want a woman who is shallow," Morgan said. She'd show Darrin that she was listening to him and retaining what she was learning.

"Bingo," Darrin said. "I also like a woman who listens to what I am saying." He winked at Morgan conspiratorially.

Morgan smiled, knowing she had scored a point with Darrin.

"I think you are right; having standards and being picky are two separate things. I lean toward the side of having standards as well. So it looks as if we both have that in common," Morgan said.

Morgan thought about how ironic it was that Martha had not only invited her to the networking event, but it was also a bonus that the man she was hoping to at least glimpse at during the event was the same one she had been researching for the past couple of weeks.

She thought about Martha's matchmaking skills and the song from the *Fiddler on the Roof* movie again. Without even really knowing it, Martha had indeed helped Morgan connect with who seemed to be turning out to be a potentially very good catch.

Chapter 14

"You know they say that people should not go on their first dates to the movies right?" Darrin asked.

Morgan reached her hand over toward Darrin's lap, where he held the tub of popcorn. She pulled out a handful. "Yeah, I've heard something like that." She laughed.

Darrin laughed with her.

"So do you want to leave?" Morgan asked.

"Not in a million years. I've been waiting for this next *Mission: Impossible* movie. I usually make it a point to see them as soon as they come out," Darrin said.

"I was just joking. When you told me you loved the *Mission: Impossible* movies on the phone a couple of weeks ago, I immediately thought about this movie coming out," Morgan said.

"You did?"

"Yes, I listen to what you say and I keep mental notes," Morgan said.

It had been a couple of weeks since they'd first met at the Silvermont Business Alliance meeting. Darrin had given Morgan his phone number and she called him, waiting three days before doing so. She wanted him to wonder if she was going to call, and she also wanted to see if he was anticipating her call. She had been pleasantly surprised when she called him and he sounded as if he'd been waiting right by the phone.

They had ended up talking for over an hour that night and the next couple of nights after that. Darrin Hobbs seemed very interested in her and she was very interested in making sure he knew she was just as interested in him. Now a couple of weeks later they were finally going on a date.

"I love that characteristic about you," Darrin said. "I love that you pay attention to the small things."

"You do?" Morgan said. She was glad she'd scored a few more points with Darrin. Her plan was working; the man had continued interest in her.

"Thank you for setting this movie date up. I couldn't have planned it better," Darrin said.

"If your mission is to flatter me to death, then you are on the right track," Morgan said.

"I aim to please, that is for sure," Darrin said.

They both reached into the popcorn bucket at the same time, each pulling out a handful of popcorn.

"This theater is really filling up. I am glad you suggested we get here early to get good seats," Morgan said.

"Sweetheart, when it comes to movie-going and premieres, I don't mess around," Darrin said.

"My goodness, the movie doesn't even start for another twenty-five minutes," Morgan said.

"This will give us a little more time to talk before the movie starts." Darrin placed his hand on Morgan's. "And I know I said it when we met in the lobby, but it is wonderful seeing you in person again. You look more beautiful than you did the first night I saw you."

"Thank you again, Darrin," Morgan said. "It is nice seeing you in person as well. I almost feel a little shy."

"Don't be shy, woman." Darrin looked her up and down. "You have absolutely nothing to be shy about."

Morgan had tried to put as much effort into her dress and appearance as she had the night she'd gone to the meeting of the Silvermont Business Alliance. The difference was that this time she'd chosen to wear a pair of jeans and a nice sweater blouse. And instead of high-heeled pumps, she'd worn a pair of high-heeled boots.

Darrin looked around the theater. "Mark my word, by the time the previews start for upcoming movies, this place will be packed, and I guarantee you there will be groups of three, four, and even five trying to find seats together. It amazes me how people think they can come late with multiples in their group and seriously think they can sit together," Darrin said.

"And they get an attitude when they have to sit in separate places," Morgan said, adding to Darrin's comment.

"I was just joking about the whole first date being bad at the movies. I mean it isn't like we haven't talked on the phone almost daily since the night we first met," Darrin said.

"Very true," Morgan agreed. "It's like I've known you for more like two months, not for just like a couple of weeks."

"I feel the exact same way." With a business-like tone, Darrin said, "I know the night isn't even over yet, but when am I going to see you again?"

"I guess that means you like my company?" Morgan said.

Her phone started to vibrate and play the sound she had chosen for her ring tone. It sounded like what would now be considered an old-fashioned telephone. "Oops," Morgan said.

She'd meant to turn the ringer off as soon as they entered the theater. The caller ID displayed Amber's name. She found the button to mute the phone and the ringing immediately stopped. A few other people pulled their cell phones out and looked as if they were turning their ringers off while a couple of other people glared her way. One of those people was Darrin. He'd tried to replace his glare with a straight face before Morgan could see it, but she caught it nonetheless. She didn't know what everyone's problem was. The movie wasn't anywhere near starting yet.

Acting as if nothing had happened Darrin said, "I like talking with you, and I especially like being around you, and I don't want another couple of weeks to go by before we get a chance to do this again."

Morgan took his cue and didn't say anything about the loud-ringing phone. She was relieved that it hadn't rung later on during the movie. She also shook off the slight chill she felt when she noticed the glare he'd given her. The last thing she needed was to have her cell phone be the thing that messed up their first date together.

"Oh well, let me think about that." Morgan started giving the question some serious thought. On the one hand she needed to try to make up for the look she got when her cell phone rang. On the other hand it was Friday night and she wondered what the rules of etiquette might say about this kind of thing. She should probably wait a few days to let this date marinate in his mind.

Darrin interrupted her contemplating thoughts by saying, "Let me put you out of your misery. How about tomorrow?"

"Tomorrow?"

"Yeah, tomorrow? Do you have to work?"

"No, actually I don't have to work."

"Do you already have plans? I am sure a beautiful single woman like yourself probably already has plans lined up."

"As it stands, I was actually just going to sit home and read a good book. It seems like I've been going nonstop the last couple of months," Morgan said.

"Oh well, I'll understand if you'd rather curl up in your bed, eating bonbons and reading a good Charles Dickens book."

"No disrespect to Mr. Dickens and all, but I like to read more contemporary books," Morgan said. "And besides, the great thing about a book is that a person can pick it up to read it at their convenience."

Darrin poked his bottom lip out and sighed. "Yeah, I'll understand and I'll be all right."

"Please don't do that," Morgan said as she looked at the poked-out lips of Darrin.

With the continual poking out of the bottom lip, Darrin said, "Do what?"

"Please pull your bottom lip back in," Morgan said.

"Give me a reason," Darrin said. His voice sounded dopey and awkward with his lip out.

"Tomorrow sounds great. What would you like to do?" Morgan asked.

Immediately Darrin pulled his bottom lip back in and smiled so that both rows of his white teeth were showing. "You have just made me a very happy man for the second time tonight. First you bring me to see one of my favorite series of movies and now you've agreed to see me again tomorrow."

The lights dimmed slightly as the movie screen lit up to start showing previews of soon-to-be-released movies. Darrin gave Morgan's hand another squeeze. Then both Morgan and Darrin sat back in their seats, ready to enjoy the soon-to-come *Mission: Impossible* movie.

Just before the movie started, four guys walked into the theater together. They walked around and up and down the sides of the theater looking for seats. Darrin nudged Morgan in the arm with his elbow. She nodded her head to indicate that she was seeing the same thing he was seeing.

As they had been talking about earlier, the group had been split. Two of the guys had found a seat in the same place, while the other two guys had to sit alone in completely different places from their friends. Morgan nudged Darrin back and she heard him laugh in a conspiratorial-like snicker.

As the first scene of *Mission: Impossible* started, Morgan noticed that Darrin was completely engrossed. It was as if his eyes had glazed over as he watched. Morgan had seen one *Mission: Impossible* movie before but really had not ever kept up with them.

Because she wasn't as engrossed as Darrin was, she noticed another latecomer enter the movie theater. It looked as if the person was by himself. It was dark but she could tell they guy was tall and of African American descent. The more she watched him as he walked around and looked for a seat, the more Morgan sensed a bit of familiarity. Then it hit her. The guy was so familiar because it was her most recent ex-husband, Will.

Almost subconsciously she shrank down in her seat. It just so happened that at the same moment the music in the movie hit a high crescendo, which would have caused a person to jump in their seat a bit. Darrin must have thought that she'd shrunk down because of the music in the movie, because he patted her hand for a second, then went back to being enthralled by the movie.

For a reason she couldn't really explain, Morgan's heart began to race. Then it started racing even more as she realized that there was an empty seat in the row in front of them just a few chairs down from where Darrin was sitting. She hoped and prayed that Will would find another seat elsewhere, but her prayers had seemed wasted because, before she knew it, Will was making his way down the row of seats whispering for people to please excuse him while he headed to the empty seat.

Morgan was pretty sure Will couldn't see her because of the dimness of the theater and because he was turned toward the screen in the opposite direction as he passed people. But just to be sure, she turned her head to the side and in a downward motion as she reached for the bucket of popcorn Darrin was holding in his lap. She knew it wasn't her imagination, but she thought she could smell the cologne that Will was wearing.

Once Will reached his seat, he seemed to sit back comfortably. When a few minutes passed, Morgan cut her eyes toward where Will was sitting. She reached again for a handful of popcorn. From her vantage point she could not see Will's face, so she was pretty sure he should not be able to see her face either.

She relaxed a bit but not too much because she now realized her heart seemed to be racing. There was no way that she wanted Will to see her out on a date with another man. It had nothing to do with wanting to rekindle anything with Will. It had everything to do with not wanting Will to see Darrin, giving him the possible opportunity to tell Darrin anything about her, especially that they had been married, and that she allegedly tried to kill him.

So now it seemed as if she were in her very own *Mission: Impossible* to figure out how she was going to get out of the theater without Will seeing her with Darrin. She took a sip of her Sprite soda as she ate popcorn and contemplated her dilemma.

Midway through the movie Morgan felt and heard her phone vibrate. She grimaced. It happened to be a scene where the theater was completely quiet and she knew anyone sitting in close vicinity could hear the annoying vibration. She fumbled her hands in her purse to find the button to completely turn off all sounds, even the vibration. Again she saw Darrin glance over her way.

She couldn't really tell if he was glaring this time because she was still all too aware that her ex was sitting in such close proximity. She hoped he hadn't heard the sound and looked her way to see where it was coming from. She shrank back again as far as she could in her seat and stared straight forward at the screen.

The movie was just about to end when she finally came up with a weak but the only possible workable plan she could think of. Her plan was to excuse herself a few minutes before the movie actually ended. She knew she'd miss the ending, but it didn't really matter all that much since she'd barely followed the story line since seeing Will enter the theater.

As the movie seemed to be wrapping up, Morgan excused herself. "Darrin, I've got to go to the bathroom." She shook her soda cup, which sounded of depleted liquid and only ice shaking around in it.

"You're going to miss the ending," Darrin whispered.

"Fill me in on it. I drank a lot of soda," Morgan whispered back.

Darrin nodded his head in understanding.

"I'll meet you out front," Morgan said.

"Okay," Darrin said. He returned his attention to the last scene of the movie.

Morgan stood, bending slightly to excuse herself out of the aisle. She continued to bend as she crept out, hoping two things—she hoped that by bending down she wouldn't look like her regular height in case Will did see her, and she also hoped that Will was just as enthralled by the movie as Darrin had been so he wouldn't have seen her.

Once she was out of the theater she headed directly for the bathroom. She hadn't completely lied, she did have to use it, just not as bad as she had let on to Darrin. She had been able to take a few extra moments in the bathroom to regain her composure. As she looked at herself in the bathroom mirror she could tell that the close encounter had shaken her a bit. Now all she needed to do was get out of the parking lot without encountering her ex.

When she thought the coast might be clear, Morgan exited the bathroom. Looking toward the direction of the theater she'd exited, she saw people coming out. So she waited a few more moments before stepping farther out to look for Darrin. She hadn't wanted to run into Will by mistake.

After a few more moments, she took a deep breath and stepped out. She saw Darrin standing in the lobby, leaning against one of the tables. He had his cell phone out and it looked as if he was checking messages or surfing the Internet. She walked up behind him and tapped his shoulder.

"Hey," Morgan said.

Darrin turned and smiled. "Hey, I was just about to put an All Points Bulletin out for you."

She could have sworn that she still smelled Will's cologne in the air. As discreetly as she possibly could, she looked around in all directions, hoping her ex was nowhere in sight.

"Sorry about that. I was sitting over there on the other side." She pointed in the direction of some seats that were in the vicinity of the theater they had been in. "I must have missed you when you passed by." She hated telling the lie.

Since they had met she had been pretty good about not telling any lies. She had omitted information about herself, but hadn't told many lies. She also didn't volunteer to give more information than was needed about her personal life as she wanted to start anew with Darrin.

"Oh, I'm sorry, I didn't even look anywhere near those seats. I just headed straight toward the front to meet you," Darrin said.

"Well after a few minutes I finally got a clue that I'd probably missed you coming out of the movie. And as soon as I started looking around I saw you over here," Morgan said.

"Is everything okay?" Darrin asked.

"Yeah, why?" She wondered if he sensed something was off in her demeanor.

"Somebody was pretty adamant about trying to get in touch with you," Darrin said.

"Oh, that," Morgan said. She was glad he hadn't sensed her anxiety from her sighting of Will. But she really wished he hadn't brought up the phone inter-ruptions either. "It was just my coworker and friend, Amber."

"Ahhh." Darrin nodded his head.

Thinking about her encounter with Charles at the Bonefish Grill and how often his vibrating phone had gone off during their dinner, she wondered if Darrin was thinking that Morgan had another man she was seeing. Her abrupt exit and short disappearance after the movie was over might have helped him come to some type of wrong conclusion.

"Darrin, I am getting the feeling that you might be thinking that the phone was ringing because of another guy," Morgan said.

"Hey, what you do is what you do. We aren't in a relationship or anything," Darrin said.

Morgan realized what she had been thinking must have been true. Even though they weren't officially in a relationship it was clear that Darrin was concerned and that he was even possibly a bit jealous. "Darrin, let me assure you that that was my friend Amber, both times. There isn't another man on the side I am trying to juggle while seeing you. I guarantee to you that I frown on people playing games with other people's emotions in relationships, and that is the one hundred percent truth if I ever told it."

Darrin nodded his head, taking in what she was saying. "No worries. I just wanted to make sure all was well."

Now that she had put out that small fire, Morgan said, "Okay, you ready?"

"Yeah, give me just a second to finish putting this information into my phone." Darrin typed something into his cell phone and when he was done said, "Okay, I'm ready."

He walked Morgan to her car.

"So, what is on the agenda for the rest of the night?" Darrin asked.

"It's pretty late."

"Would you like to come to my house? We could talk a bit more. Or I could come over to your place," Darrin said.

"Always the go-getter, aren't you?" Morgan asked.

"Yes," Darrin confirmed.

"Mr. Hobbs, thank you for the invite to come to your home, but I must decline, maybe some other night. I'm sorry but I can't give you my address just yet. I am still getting to know you."

Darrin poked his lower lip out again slightly.

"Now, now. You pull that lip back in. We made a deal. We would see each other again tomorrow, and you are supposed to keep that lower lip in," Morgan said.

Darrin pulled his lip back in. "So this is it for to-night?"

"Yep," Morgan said. She looked around to see if she might spot Will.

"Okay, fine then," Darrin said.

"It's not like you aren't going to see me again in the next twenty-four hours," Morgan said.

"I know, I know, but not only am I a go-getter, but I am spoiled as well. I want what I want when I want it," Darrin said.

"And let me guess. You usually get what you want?"

"Yes, I do."

"Well, my friend, I am truly sorry to disappoint you on this evening, but we will need to part ways for now," Morgan said.

Darrin opened her car door. "All right, I know when to give in."

Morgan cranked her car while Darrin closed her door. She rolled her window down to talk to him. "So what are we going to do tomorrow?"

"I'll let you know. I've got something in mind I think you'll like. You've told me a few things about yourself and I've been doing a little mental filing."

Morgan smiled. "Oooh, you've got me curious."

"Good," Darrin said. He winked at her. "Talk to you later. Drive safely."

"Okay and thank you," Morgan said. She pulled out of the parking space, found the nearest exit for the movie theater parking lot, and left as quickly as she could.

Once she felt she was truly out of danger of being spotted by Will, Morgan finally took a breath of relief. Her excitement about finally going out on an actual date with Darrin had almost been messed up by the sight of Will. She had to regroup so that she could take a full assessment of how the night had gone. Her quick assessment told her the night had been absolutely great. The night had been so great that Darrin was already planning another date for them the next night.

She smiled to herself, and if she could have she would have patted herself on her back, but thought better of it while driving on the interstate with Friday night traffic. She tapped her hands on her steering wheel as she drove in anticipation of her scheduled date for the next night and also in anticipation of where her newly found relationship was going.

Chapter 15

As Morgan drove to her apartment complex the tunes from the jazz club she and Darrin had been to earlier that night continued to play over and over in her head. Darrin had treated her to a night on the town with dinner and dancing at a local jazz club. Afterward they had walked to a local park on one of the walking trails as they enjoyed a full moon and pleasant weather. She pressed the accelerator on her Hyundai Accent, making it go faster. She was still giddy as she thought about the progress she was making with him.

A sound interfered with the song she was remembering. It was a police siren and to accompany it was a blue light. Looking in her rearview mirror she saw that she was being pulled over. "Aww, man," she said to herself.

She pulled her car over to the side of the road while still hoping the cop was really looking to pull someone else over instead. To her dismay the police cruiser also pulled up right behind her.

Her heart started to beat fast. She disliked cops very much, ever since she'd been arrested in her home. Placing her hands on the ten o'clock and two o'clock positions on the steering wheel, she waited patiently for the police officer to make his way over to her driver side window.

It had only taken a couple of moments and she saw a flashlight beam coming through her window. The officer tapped the window with the flashlight. "Open your window please, ma'am."

She did as she was asked to do and rolled her window down. "Hi, Officer, what seems to be the problem?"

The officer used his flashlight to beam the light into the rest of her car interior, looking around to see what she did or didn't have. "Ma'am, you were just doing forty-five in a thirty-five mile-per-hour speed zone. Can I see your driver's license and registration?"

Morgan opened up her glove compartment and pulled out her registration. Then she opened up her purse and pulled out her driver's license. "Officer, I am really sorry. I didn't realize I was going that fast. You see I had this jazz tune in my head from a jazz club I went to earlier and I was driving and humming it. I guess I lost track of how fast I was going." Morgan attempted a smile.

The officer's face was stolid; he hadn't even cracked a grin. "Ma'am, I'll be right back." He took Morgan's license and registration back with him to the police cruiser.

As soon as he was gone, Morgan placed her hands back on the safe ten and two o'clock positions so the officer could see them if need be. She closed her eyes and immediately started praying.

"Dear Lord, I need your help and I need it right now. Please, Lord, don't let the officer give me a ticket, and please, Lord, make sure there isn't anything showing up under my name that might not have been properly cleared from all the legal troubles I had recently. Lord, you know I said was going to do better and be better, and I am doing that. All I am trying to do is be a good person, so please grant me leeway in this situation. In Jesus' name I pray. Amen."

When she opened her eyes she saw that the officer was still sitting in his car. She thought he was taking entirely too long in there. A knot formed in the bottom of her stomach. It was not looking good for her in the least. With nervousness she tapped her fingers on the steering wheel.

Finally after what seemed like an eternity, even though it had only actually been about three minutes, the office returned to the car. "Okay, ma'am. I am going to give you a warning for now." He handed her a warning sheet. "Try to watch the speed limit when you are driving and humming music." Finally the officer offered a slight smile.

"You drive safely now, ma'am," the officer said.

Morgan couldn't believe her ears. It was the second time the Lord had answered a prayer for her practically on demand. She knew she wasn't perfect but she was going to continue to try to be better. It seemed to really be paying off for her in the divine department.

"Thank you, Officer, and I'll be sure to drive below the speed limit from now on if I need to."

The officer returned to his police car and Morgan rolled up her window. Then she mouthed a thank-you to the Lord. "Thank you."

When she pulled back on to the road a new song came to her. It was a song her grandmother used to play in her living room as she was growing up. The song was "I'm Still Holding On" by Luther Barnes and if she remembered correctly the song featured his cousin Deborah Barnes as the lead singer. She was still holding on. She had given the Lord her own hand when she was young, and it seemed as though the Lord was still holding on to her as well.

When she reached the stairs to ascend to her apartment her cell phone rang. The caller display showed Darrin's name. She smiled, shaking her head, and answered the call. It seemed as though the man really liked her a lot. They had just parted just a little over thirty minutes ago.

"Hello, Darrin?"

"Did you make it home safely?" Darrin asked Morgan.

"Yes, with the help of a friendly neighborhood officer," Morgan said. Her nerves had finally gotten under control.

"An officer? What happened?" Darrin asked.

She held the cell phone up to her ear with one hand while unlocking her apartment door with her other hand. "I was still a little giddy over this date I had with a fantastic guy. And I was humming that last jazz tune that we danced to in my head."

"Yeah, and?" Darrin asked.

Morgan locked her apartment door behind her, and placed her purse and keys on the counter. "I wasn't paying attention to how fast I was going and I got pulled over."

"Are you serious?"

"Yep." She stepped into her bedroom, not paying attention to what she was doing. She pulled open one of her dresser drawers, looking for her favorite pair of warm socks. The drawer she'd pulled out was one she used for important papers and mail. Instead of feeling socks her hand touched the letter her grandmother had sent her.

There were times when she wished the letter had landed in the trashcan instead of on her counter. For some reason she couldn't bring herself to throw it away, but she didn't want to open it either. So it was as if the letter was taunting her. The first chance she got she was going to put it somewhere else—somewhere she wouldn't have to be reminded of it so easily.

After taking a deep breath she found the socks in the other drawer, pulled her earrings out of her ears, and placed them on the dresser. She then returned to her little living room and sat down on her couch and curled up under a throw.

"How fast were you going?"

"I was going ten over the speed limit. No worries. I got a warning ticket and he let me go on my merry way." Morgan wanted to change the subject. "You know you have great timing. I had just gotten to the stairs of my complex when you called," Morgan said.

"Good, I just want to make sure the special lady in my life is safe," Darrin said.

Morgan liked to hear Darrin refer to her as being special in his life. He had been referring to her that way for over a week now. A month had passed since their first meeting and already they had been out on eleven dates.

"I really had fun tonight," Darrin said.

"So did I," Morgan said.

"It isn't often that I can enjoy a live band and then just walk and talk and enjoy nature. I hope you weren't too bored with the walking and talking."

"Not in the least," Morgan replied.

While walking they talked about their goals, hopes, and dreams. Morgan shared that she wanted to one day go to school and get a bachelor's degree in fashion merchandizing or interior design. Darrin never seemed to act as if he was looking down on her because she only had a high school diploma.

Darrin shared with her how he wanted to expand his business and how he loved taking pictures. One day he wanted to be able to take the time to take photography classes and buy a camera to capture beautiful shots. He had e-mailed her some of the pictures he'd taken over the years and she thought he had a knack for photography.

Morgan had really enjoyed the time she'd spent talking with Darrin. Overall the guy seemed pretty cool. She was a little concerned though, because with all the time they'd been spending together, she hadn't felt a spark of anything that even closely resembled love with the man.

The more she thought about the lack of feelings she had for the man, she realized it shouldn't have been much of a surprise. Ever since her children had been taken away from her by social services years ago, she'd felt numb when it came to showing any kind of real emotion or love toward anyone.

Just like Darrin, Will had been a nice guy. Any other woman would have allowed herself to fall in love with the man—but not Morgan. She put her feelings and heart on ice. She wasn't going to allow herself to have feelings of love. If she could help it, she wasn't going to let anyone else get close to her emotionally.

It seemed as though everything she'd ever loved was eventually gone from her life—first her mother leaving her, then her first husband leaving her as well, and then her three children being taken by social services. Having her children taken away had been the last straw. Because of the lack of emotion she now had for people and things, it wasn't hard to lose either of them anymore.

Losing Will hadn't been an emotional shock, and sadly enough neither had losing her son Isaiah. In a way she was glad she'd guarded her heart, because now their losses were often only an afterthought.

"I won't hold you long. I just wanted to make sure you made it to your apartment safely," Darrin said. "You do know it would be so much easier if you'd just tell me where you live so that I could pick you up, then I could just drop you back off and we could stop wasting all this gas."

"All in due time, my dear," Morgan said.

"Or you could have just come over to my place. I've got plenty of rooms, and I promise I wouldn't have bothered you. You'd have your own guest room with a bathroom," Darrin said as he continued to try to change Morgan's mind.

Morgan hadn't told Darrin where she lived yet, because she didn't want him to think she was easy, but the way things were going she was contemplating letting him know her address soon. She had finally agreed to visit him at his home and had done so a few times. The first time she went, she never let on to him that she already knew his address was 1485 Green Forest Drive, and that she'd already driven by his home when she first started researching him.

"I'm getting closer to telling you. I definitely don't want you thinking I am easy and that I give my number and address out to just anyone," Morgan said.

"Oh, so I'm just anyone, huh?" Darrin said. His voice was playful as he spoke.

"No, you are not just anyone. But I know you will respect my decision."

"In all seriousness, Morgan, I do respect your decision. You've got standards, and I like that. I think there is a difference between your having standards and a woman who is just plain playing hard to get. So I do respect you," Darrin said.

"Thank you, Darrin."

"You're welcome, beautiful."

Morgan smiled, thinking that the man was on top of his game. "You do make it hard for a lady to resist, I'll tell you the truth on that one."

"Well good then, that means all of my hard work isn't for nothing," Darrin said.

She heard him yawn into the phone.

"Did I just hear you yawning?" Morgan said. She looked at the clock on her cell phone.

"Who me? Nah, that wasn't me," Darrin said.

"Lies aren't good, Mr. Hobbs." Morgan took on a playfully authoritative tone.

"Okay, okay, I am in denial," Darrin said.

"No, what you probably are is tired. Man, it is after two o'clock in the morning. We both need some sleep. You've got a company to run tomorrow, and I've got to go to work," Morgan said.

Darrin chuckled, and then said, "You're right. We'll both be zombies tomorrow, running on feelings of euphoria from tonight and the fumes of energy we wish we had.

"The next two days are actually going to be pretty hectic for me. I've got a couple of business meetings and will need to meet a client out of town on Tuesday. So I may not be as engaged as I have been the past few weeks," Darrin said.

"Darrin, I understand. Don't worry about me. I know you are a hardworking and busy man. I've been wondering how you could afford to spend so much time with me these past weeks anyway. I guess the honeymoon is over. You're not as captivated by me as you once were," Morgan said.

"Not true in the least," Darrin said.

"I know, I know. Seriously. Do what you need to do. I'm here, Darrin. I'm not going to disappear just because I don't hear from you for a day or so," Morgan said.

"No worries there either. Just know when we are not together, I am always thinking of you," Darrin said.

"I feel that, Darrin," Morgan said.

"I truly hope you do," Darrin said.

"Good night, Darrin," Morgan said. She felt like yawning herself and wasn't looking forward to waking up early in the morning.

"Good night, my special lady," Darrin said.

Morgan folded and straightened a few sweaters that were out of place on one of the display tables. She was working in the women's department that day. When she thought the table was neatly arranged again, she headed back to the register to locate the returns customer service had given her so they could be put back out onto the sales floor.

As she placed the last jacket on a hanger to hang it back with other similar items, she felt a tap on her shoulder. She turned.

"Hey, Ci Ci," Desiree said.

"Hey, Tiny," Morgan said. She was actually glad to see the woman. She had tried to call her a couple of times, but the phone number she had for her said the customer couldn't be contacted at the time. Morgan knew that had really meant that Desiree's phone was out of service.

Desiree rolled her eyes. "You can call me Desiree now."

"Sorry. What's up with that?" At the correctional facility, Desiree wanted to only be called Tiny; now she wanted to be called Desiree. Morgan was just trying to keep up with it all.

"You should know about wanting to turn over a new leaf and use another name," Desiree said. She pointed to the name on Morgan's name tag. "Right, Morgan?"

Morgan hadn't told Desiree anything about her name change and her reasons for changing her name. She was about to get on the defensive but Desiree spoke again.

"I am a changed woman, so I decided to go ahead and go by the name my mother gave me," Desiree said.

Morgan looked around. Things were going pretty slow in the store and she was due for her break. She stepped over to one of the cash registers. "Hold on a second, Desiree."

Morgan picked up the phone, called the store manager, and let him know she was going on her thirty-minute break.

"Have you eaten yet?" Morgan asked Desiree.

"Yeah, I just ate."

"Well how about some dessert then? Let's walk down to the food court and grab some ice cream or cookies," Morgan said.

Desiree raised both hands in a surrender motion. "We can go down there, but I ain't grabbing anything."

Morgan looked at Desiree like she'd lost her mind. "Girl, come on." Morgan led the way as Desiree caught up with her.

Once they both had cones of ice cream, they found a table and seats in the back of the food court. Morgan couldn't wait to hear what Desiree had on her mind and what was going on with her. She was acting a bit strange with her comments about grabbing things, and her change in lifestyle and use of her first name.

"So what is going on, Ti . . ." Morgan was about to say "Tiny" but caught herself. "What's up, Desiree?"

"Like I said, I've changed."

Morgan knew there was something else about Desiree that was different from the last time she saw her. Desiree had on a pair of brown slacks and a short-sleeved shirt that wasn't a couple sizes too small, and her hair was slicked back with gel. She wasn't wearing any makeup and she wasn't being her loud and boisterous self. The change was noticeable. She looked regular. Plain. She looked nice.

"Now that you mention it, I do see a change in you," Morgan said.

"I've stopped doing wrong. I've stopped lying, and trying to get over on people," Desiree said.

Sitting back in her seat Morgan said, "Say what?"

"I've given my life to the Lord."

With a sigh, Morgan said, "Really?"

All too often Morgan heard stories or saw stories on television about people who went to prison. They got their lives straight, only to get on the outside and go back to doing the things they did that put them in prison in the first place.

"Yes, really," Desiree said.

"So those preachers that came to visit the correctional facility finally got to you, huh?" Morgan said.

"Not just them. My mama has always been a God-fearing woman for as long as I've known her. And the recent events in my life have let me know that the way I was trying to live wasn't in my best interest," Desiree said.

"How so?" Morgan was curious.

"My phone got stolen."

"Really?" Morgan asked.

"It was at my party. That party was probably the last straw in my realizing that I needed the Lord in my life."

Morgan tasted her ice cream, which was starting to melt as she held it.

"I asked some of my so-called friends to come to the party, and they came, and brought some friends of their own. We had the DJ playing music, my auntie had helped me make party food, and everything was going great. Then one of my friends found out one of my other friends was dating the same man."

"They found this out at your party?" Morgan asked to clarify that she was understanding.

"Yep," Desiree said. "And get this, then they figured out they both have babies by this same guy."

"Oh, no," Morgan said.

"Oh, no, is right," Desiree said. "Turns out this guy is supposedly still dating them both, and each wanted to lay claim to him," Desiree said.

"This guy is cheating on both of them, and they still want to argue with each other?"

"Not just argue. These two had a knockdown, drag-out fight."

"No, Desiree." Morgan put her free hand up to her mouth as her jaw dropped wide open.

"Yes, and I do mean knockdown, drag out. They knocked over tables and chairs, broke the door to my hallway closet, and one of them actually started pulling the other one by her hair and literally dragged her to the front door," Desiree said.

"You cannot be serious," Morgan said. She couldn't believe what she was hearing. But then again, she really didn't know what kind of life her former cellmate led.

"I am just glad you weren't there to see it," Desiree said.

"Desiree, I am sorry about that. I wanted to come but—"

Desiree cut her off. "Girl, don't even worry about it a bit."

"So what happened?"

"Most of it happened so fast. First I was trying to figure out why in the world the two were fighting in the first place. Then I was reeling over the fact that they had kids by the same man; then I watched the two fight like they were in a wrestling federation.

"It seems like in no time at all, the police were at my apartment door. And I just knew for sure that I'd some-how be arrested and that I might have violated some kind of probation rule. I prayed from the moment the police got there until the second they left. I promised the Lord that if He helped me out of that situation, I would stop all the nonsense and give my life to Him."

Morgan quickly ate more of her ice cream, which was now starting to drip onto her hands. Desiree did the same thing. They each used a handful of napkins to help catch the dripping mess.

"I went to church that next Sunday and when they opened the doors up to the church for people to give their lives to Christ, I was one of the first ones to approach the altar. You might have seen it."

"I might have seen it? How?" Morgan was confused.

"I am pretty sure the camera was somewhere near me when I walked up there," Desiree said.

"Camera? What church?"

"New Hope Church." Desiree said it as if it were a matter of fact.

New Hope was one of the largest mega churches in Silvermont. Morgan knew the church well, as she was once a member. It was where she had finally set up her so-called chance encounter with Will. Will still attended the church as far as Morgan knew.

"Girl, let me tell you. The pastor was out that Sunday and one of the other ministers led us to salvation. Lord knows I am glad to be saved, but it was a bonus to have that man lead the prayer. He is good looking as I don't know what."

Morgan had a feeling she knew just who Desiree was talking about. "What's his name?"

"I think it was Minister Thompson or something like that."

"Was it Tomlinson?" Morgan asked.

"Yeah, yeah. That's it," Desiree said. Her eyes lit up as she spoke. "Now that is one fine-looking brother."

"Well he is married," Morgan said.

"So you do know about New Hope. Did you see the broadcast from a month ago?"

"I do know about New Hope, but I don't watch any of their services," Morgan said.

All too well she knew about New Hope. She also knew Minister Phillip Tomlinson and his wife, Shelby. The Tomlinsons were very close friends with Will. Will and Phillip were actually best friends.

"You should check out their services, they come on each Sunday. Or better yet, why don't you come to a service with me?" Desiree asked.

Morgan chuckled. There was no way she was going back to New Hope Church anytime soon. "Thanks, but no thanks. You will be forever trying to get me to go to a church service won't you?"

"Now more so than ever," Desiree said.

Morgan cut her eyes at Desiree. Then she rolled her eyes at the dripping ice cream she was holding. "This is a lost cause."

"Do you mean my trying to get you to come to church with me, or the ice cream?" Desiree asked.

As if contemplating, Morgan looked around. "Both," Morgan said.

Desiree chuckled. She tasted her ice cream, and then did her best to wipe her sticky hands again. "I think I am going to agree with you."

Chapter 16

Darrin pushed the button on the elevator for the twelfth floor. "Excel basically takes up half of the twelfth floor."

"You have a pretty good-sized business then?" Morgan said.

"It has grown since I started. We just moved into the building at the end of last year."

The elevator stopped and the doors opened. Both Morgan and Darrin stepped out into a foyer area which had twin reception areas that seemed to mirror each other. One area had a sign that said EXCEL FINANCIAL PLANNING and the other reception area was void of any signage.

"As you can see, my company is over here. The other side is still up for lease. It's sort of nice having the floor to ourselves, to tell you the truth."

It was after business hours and Darrin was taking Morgan on a tour of his office building. While doing her research she had found where his company was located, but had never actually stepped foot into the building. So it was nice to finally have something she was actually genuinely seeing and finding out more about for the first time.

Beyond the reception area were double doors that led to the offices of Excel Financial Planning. There were several cubicles, and a meeting room with an oval table that would seat ten people. Next to the meeting room was a large office with windows and blinds for the occupant's privacy when needed.

Darrin showed her where just about everything was located, down to the bathrooms. Then at the end of his tour he showed her his office.

"And this is my office," Darrin said.

"I figured as much," Morgan said. She stepped in and liked what she saw.

Darrin had a large oak desk and bookshelf that matched the design and the wood of the desk. He also had another small meeting table in his office that would sit four people if need be. His walls were adorned with his academic degrees from college along with certificates and plaques. Throughout the office were various mementos of his fraternity and its purple and gold colors throughout. Everything in his office was neat and looked organized.

Morgan set her purse down on Darrin's office desk. "Impressive, I like."

"Thank you," Darrin said.

Morgan walked over to the window of the office and felt dizzy as she got closer to it. The window extended from floor to ceiling of just glass. It felt as if she got too close she would actually step off the building.

"Be careful," Darrin said.

"Why?"

"You don't want to fall," Darrin said.

"Really?" Morgan said, wondering if the glass window was actually strong enough to keep a person from falling if they were to accidentally, or even purposefully, press against it.

"No, just kidding. Many people do get a touch of dizziness when they approach it."

With tentative steps, Morgan approached the window. She wanted to get close enough to touch it. She wanted to overcome any fear she had about it as well. With each inch she got closer to the window her heart seemed to beat faster and faster. She could not remember the last time she'd been so fearful and excited about something in a long time.

She closed her eyes. The window as a challenge that she had to overcome and after what seemed like an eternity, the tips of her fingers finally touched the glass. It was cool to the touch, but it seemed solid. She inched herself even closer to the glass, until the point that she was able to place both hands with flat palms on the glass. Allowing herself to open her eyes, Morgan stared out over the city of Silvermont.

It felt as if she were suspended in midair. And for a moment she felt a bit weightless. Without even realizing it she took a breath. At some point she had actually stopped breathing.

"Are you okay?" Darrin asked.

For a moment she'd forgotten he was there. It was as if she were alone in the world. For a brief moment, it was as if she didn't have a care in the world. She stepped back, only to find that Darrin was directly behind her. She stiffened a bit.

He placed his arms around her. "Are you okay?"

Even though she wanted to pull away she kept still. "Yeah, I'm fine. I am just a little afraid of heights, that's all."

He placed his chin on the top of her head. The gesture was a bit awkward and she wondered if that was because, after all the time they'd been going out, she hadn't really felt any romantic feelings toward the man. She wondered if the fact that he was a nice guy was going to be enough to sustain her through their budding relationship.

"It's beautiful, isn't it?" Darrin said.

"It is." Morgan admitted she thought the same.

"I love coming over here at night. You should really see it on a night when the moon is full. You talk about picturesque; I wish I could capture it with a camera. But there is no way to capture that kind of godly nature. There aren't flash bulbs large enough to illuminate the night," Darrin said.

He squeezed her a little tighter. Morgan felt the need to move away from him. He was taking too much time up in her personal space. Her cell phone rang.

Saved by the bell, she thought. She stepped to the side and picked up the purse she had laid down on Darrin's office desk. The caller ID displayed Amber's phone number. Usually when Amber called and she was with Darrin she ignored the call, but tonight she welcomed the distraction.

"Hold on one second, Darrin," Morgan said.

"Go ahead." He waved his hand, gesturing for her to answer the call.

As she answered the phone Darrin walked over to his office desk and picked up a stack of sheets that looked like reports from Morgan's vantage point.

"Hello," Morgan said.

"Hey, girl. I sent you a few text messages. Did you see what the president did with Olivia?" Amber said.

"Ahh, no. I'm not home."

"You're never home lately," Amber said.

"I am recording it on my DVR. We can catch up tomorrow at work. So don't spoil it for me," Morgan said.

One of their main common interests was a television show called *Scandal,* starring actress Kerry Washington. They had even gotten so engrossed into the show that they had exchanged cell phone numbers and had started texting one another during the show with various reactions to the scenes being played out among the characters.

But the last few weeks, Morgan had been otherwise engaged with Darrin.

"Oh, gotta go. It's back on. Talk to you tomorrow," Amber said.

She hung up before Morgan could reply. Morgan knew that whatever was going on in the episode was probably good, but she was on a mission, and she couldn't take her eye off the prize, who was sitting at the oak desk just a few feet away from her.

Even though just a couple of seconds before Darrin looked as if he was totally engrossed in looking at the papers on his desk, as soon as she ended the call, he quickly turned his attention to her. She knew he was just trying to find something to fill his time for the moment.

"Missing something good on television?" Darrin asked.

Morgan knew she needed to make sure Darrin knew she wasn't upset about missing a television show, and was more interested in him. "Nothing too big, that's what DVRs are for. Besides, being with you here live and in person is much, much better."

She hoped what she was saying helped to assure Darrin enough that she was very interested in the time they spent together. From what she was looking at around her, and had seen over the past weeks, Darrin had everything going for him, and he just might be in the market for a wife soon. As far as Morgan was concerned, she was in the market for a husband; they just needed to make it to the register at the same time. If she had anything to do with it, and she'd make sure she had everything to do with it, she would be in the line for soon being Mrs. Darrin Hobbs.

Darrin stood. "So I'm better than some show with great ratings?" he asked.

Morgan stepped over to and around the oak desk and took the opportunity to invade his personal space. "Yes, you are way better than a television show." She took both of his hands into hers, looked up into his eyes, and kissed his cheek.

When he tried to turn his head too quickly to get a kiss on the lips, Morgan shifted her head just in time for him to miss her lips. Instead he got a mouthful of her hair for a brief moment.

"Oh, Morgan. You are really serious about this whole not getting too close for comfort thing, aren't you?" Darrin asked.

Morgan could see the disappointment in Darrin's eyes. She stepped back a bit. "Darrin. I know we are both grown adults here, so just know that when I say I am not playing games, I am not. I know what getting too close could lead to. And I care too much about myself to let some heated emotions mess up any positive future we might possibly have."

Darrin cocked his head to the side as if questioning what she meant.

"I mean whatever future. Be it a long-lasting plutonic friendship or a walk down the aisle in a church somewhere with people throwing rice, rose petals, or blowing bubbles at us. Whatever is politically correct these days," Morgan said.

"Okay, I know people used to throw rice in the past, but I think the politically correct thing is now birdseed so the birds can at least benefit from it," Darrin said.

Morgan was a little surprised Darrin was actually rolling with her comment about walking down the aisle. They had only known each other for a short time, and bringing up anything about weddings and marriages was a bit risky and premature to say the least.

"And I've seen people blow bubbles at a few weddings. It is really pretty nice, but I can't say that I've seen people throw rose petals," Darrin said.

"Me either. I've only been to a couple of weddings. But I think it would be pretty," Morgan said.

"Why roses? Why not daisy petals or carnations?" Darrin said.

Morgan smirked. "Now I know you're not being serious. I mean daisies are pretty for some and carnations are okay, but roses are absolutely beautiful. There is nothing like a rose. There is nothing like the way they feel, smell, and how they look, especially when they are closed at first, then open after a day or so after being in a vase of water."

"So I guess you like roses, huh?"

"Yes. Not that I am a rose fanatic or anything. I don't have a rose tattoo, or a rose theme throughout my apartment. It is live roses for which I have an affinity," Morgan said.

Morgan's cell phone rang again. This time she saw that it was Desiree calling. She debated answering it, and decided to go ahead and take the call. She found in the past that if Desiree didn't reach her, she had a tendency to call again within the hour.

"Hold on just a second," Morgan said to Darrin.

It looked as if Morgan saw a flicker of annoyance on Darrin's face for just a moment, but then it was gone. He nodded his head as if in understanding, but Morgan knew by now that one of Darrin's pet peeves was getting interruptions, especially when her phone rang while they were together. He wanted her all to himself. In a way she liked that he was so very much into her, but sometimes she just wanted to take a breather.

For some reason it seemed as though her cell phone only seemed to ring when the two of them were together. When she was in her apartment, she never seemed to get any phone calls. But she figured this may have been because lately she'd been spending most of her time out with Darrin either on a date, at an event, or relaxing at his home.

Morgan answered the phone. "Hello."

"Hey, Ci Ci." Desiree caught and corrected herself. "I mean Morgan. Sorry about that."

"Not a problem. What's up?" Morgan asked.

"I need a huge favor," Desiree said.

Morgan mentally braced herself, wondering what Desiree could want. She wondered if it had to do with money, or something illegal, or even if she wanted Morgan to come with her to a church service. None of the favors she thought about were remotely attractive.

"I need to use you as a reference and wanted to see if it was okay with you." Desiree said.

For the second time that night Morgan began to breathe again. She hadn't remembered exactly when she'd started holding her breath, but figured that it was probably just after Desiree asked for the huge favor.

Relieved that it was something as simple as being a reference, Morgan quickly said, "Yes, of course you can use me as a reference."

"Great. I've got your name and number, but I'll need an address," Desiree said.

"Not a problem. Let me call you back with that information, or I can send it to you in a text. I am out right now and being rude to my host," Morgan said.

"Oh, sorry about that. Just text it to me. I am filling out applications now online for jobs."

"Will do. In just a few minutes," Morgan said.

She was glad that Darrin was only able to hear her side of the conversation. She was sure that he was getting an idea of what they were talking about from Morgan's side of the discussion. She needed to text the address to Desiree because she didn't want to say where she lived out loud with Darrin listening.

"Okay, thanks, Morgan. I really appreciate it," Desiree said.

"You are welcome," Morgan said; then she pressed the button to end the call and turned her attention back to Darrin. "That was Desiree. She needs for me to be a reference for her. She is applying for jobs," Morgan said.

"You sure are a popular lady. Your phone rings off the hook," Darrin said.

"Not popular by any means. I just know a few people," Morgan said.

Morgan had still not yet given Darrin the physical address of her apartment. She wanted to make sure their relationship was close enough but not too close that he became too comfortable or content with her that he started taking her for granted. The course she was taking was working better than she thought it might. She believed this was true simply because she didn't yet have any romantic feelings for the man.

Chapter 17

"Morgan." Amber Westfield was calling her name.

It was unusual for Amber to be on the floor and she wondered why she was there now looking for her. With an unassuming and professional smile Morgan said, "Yes?" Even though the two women had become close and comfortable with one another, Morgan continued to treat the human resources manger as she should, professionally.

"Girl, I had to come down here myself and find you," Amber said.

She didn't know what to make of Amber's lackadaisical way of addressing her on the department floor. Now Morgan's curiosity was really piqued. On the one hand the woman sounded by her tone of voice as if they were girlfriends hanging out in the break room, but sadly enough from past experiences Morgan knew to brace herself for anything.

"You need to come with me up to the office, right this instant." Amber's tone had all of a sudden turned all business.

Morgan's heart began to race. "What's up?" She knew her voice sounded a bit shaky.

She ran through the many possible reasons that she could have been summoned to come to the main office. She hadn't put any false information on her job application. She had left blank the block that asked if she had any felonies, because it was technically true. The charges had been dropped and Will had forgiven her.

Then she started wondering if Will had really forgiven her. She had done a lot of mean and hateful things to the man. Maybe he had waited until that very moment to come to her job and tell the management and anyone else who would listen about how she tried to hurt him. He might have even told them about how he thought she was trying to kill him.

She made up in her mind. Her past had once again caught up with her. She would have to start all over from scratch for what seemed like the umpteenth time. Would security escort her out? Would she be allowed to take her few belongings from her locker? She had a good mind to make a fast turn and just flee from the store. But she couldn't; she needed the keys to her car and apartment.

When they walked into the door of the HR office, Amber led Morgan directly to her office, allowing Morgan to enter first. When she stepped in the first thing she noticed was that the woman's office was filled with vases of roses of all sorts of hues and colors. There were so many flowers that she didn't have a place to sit. She looked at Amber, wondering why in the world she would summon her to a place that they couldn't even sit down and talk civilly in. Morgan had to say that she admired the office full of roses as the floral smell permeated her nostrils. She figured with so many roses, the store must have been gearing up for some new type of decoration theme.

"Is there something you want to tell me?" Amber said.

"Ah, uhh . . ." Morgan's voice trailed off at a loss for words. She wasn't about to divulge any information that the company didn't already know about.

"So who is he?" Amber asked.

"Who is who?" Morgan would play dumb until the end—mainly because she was essentially dumbfounded as to what Amber was talking about.

"You need to give me some advice on how to get a truckload of flowers delivered to me. And does your Mr. Right have a brother?"

"Huh?" Morgan said.

"All these flowers were delivered for you a little while ago."

"Are you serious?" Morgan's disbelief was completely genuine.

Dumbfounded, Amber looked at Morgan. "Does this face look serious or what?"

"Yeah, I'd say so," Morgan said. She stepped over to one of the vases of flowers, which had a big card and envelope attached to it. Unlike the little cards in the little envelopes that usually came pitch-forked into vases of flowers, this card was like a regular greeting card and her name was clearly written on the front. Amber was indeed telling the truth.

She opened the card and read silently to herself:

Dear Morgan,

I went into the florist to buy roses for you and couldn't decide on what color to buy. I learned that the color orange means fascination and desire. You have continually fascinated me since the day I met you. The color light pink means sweetness and I think you are a very sweet woman. The color red represents love, courage, beauty, and respect. The color lavender represents enchantment because you have put a spell on me. Don't pay too much attention to the blue roses as they represent what is impossible or unattainable and I don't feel

like this applies to you, but it is a beautiful color. Pay very very close attention to the yellow roses with the red tip because they represent my feelings of falling in love with you!
   Darrin

   P.S. I had to send these to your job since you wouldn't give me your home address. Looking forward to seeing you tonight! :)

Morgan read the card twice, realizing that all of what he had written would not have fit on a little business-sized card. She smiled at the smiley face he'd written after the post script. It had been two months since their meeting at the SBA networking event. And in that month, Darrin and Morgan spoke to each other daily and over the past three weeks or so, they had seen one another almost daily as well.

Things were going far better than she ever could have hoped. Darrin was all she wanted in a man and more. He was attentive to her needs, he didn't have any qualms about spending money on her, which was even more evident by the dozens of roses that sat in front of her in Amber's office. And he was prime and ready to find a mate—all signs to her that her plan to find a new husband was well on its way to being quickly put into motion. It was as if things were moving in their own automatic motion.

"Humph, humph." Amber cleared her throat.

Morgan turned back to look at her standing in the office doorway.

Amber's hands were splayed out in a questioning motion. "So am I not privy to who this mystery man is?"

Morgan grinned and turned around in a pirouette-like turn that any ballerina would have been proud of. The office smelled wonderfully fresh. The flowers were absolutely beautiful. Morgan sighed with relief, realizing her past wasn't haunting her and with pleasure from the card chock-full of feelings from Darrin. The man had said that he was falling in love with her.

Amber set a vase of flowers to the side and closed her office door. "All right, missy. Tell me what is going on or you will never leave my office."

For a moment Morgan could only continue to grin at Amber. She was at a loss for words. "I don't know what to say."

"How about starting with a name," Amber said.

"Darrin."

In a condescending yet playful tone Amber said, "Now see, that was a good start. It wasn't too hard now was it?"

Morgan handed the card she received from Darrin over to Amber so she could read it.

Once Amber finished reading it, her lower jaw was dropped wide open, and tears were in her eyes. "This is like some kind of fairy tale. Reminds me of something Richard Gere probably would have done in the movie *Pretty Woman*."

Amber touched one of the yellow roses with the red tips. "And homeboy said he is falling in love with you. Whew." Amber fanned herself with the greeting card she was still holding.

Then she suddenly stopped in the midst of her fanning. "Oh, now wait a minute. Is this Mr. Darrin the reason you've had to record *Scandal* for the last three weeks? You've been otherwise occupied?"

Finally Morgan spoke, answering Amber's questions. "Yes, Darrin is the reason I've not been glued to the television for our weekly texting about *Scandal*. I met him about two months ago."

"You met him two months ago and you didn't tell me?" Amber frowned. "I mean I know you and I have only known each other for only about twice that amount of time but, girl, you are like a sister to me. I mean I tell you everything just about."

"Honey, a girl doesn't kiss and tell. And besides, I didn't want to say something too early, just in case things didn't work out. I mean I've been on other dates and didn't say anything to you."

Amber frowned again.

"Okay, okay, sorry. I wanted to tell you a couple of times. I even started to but stopped myself."

"A date or two with a guy here or there, but two months of dating, and an office filled with roses. I'd say it is more than a mere fling."

Morgan couldn't disagree with her friend, and Amber didn't even know the half of it. Darrin attended to as many of her needs as she would allow him to take care of. He did lots of little things to show his thoughtfulness. One day he'd borrowed her car to run an errand while she was at work. It seemed a little strange to her, but she didn't mind. When he returned, her car was full of gas and he'd had it washed and detailed. That was the first gesture of care and thoughtfulness she remembered him doing and from there he continued to do many things for her.

She felt like she was living the life of Martha at times, especially when Darrin took her out to eat. They ate at all types of restaurants, be it fast food, casual dining, or the higher-end swanky restaurants of all types of foods. Darrin liked all types of food except seafood. Morgan realized this when every time she brought up a seafood restaurant to eat at he declined. Eventually she asked him about it and he said he was allergic to it. Mexican was his absolute favorite. Morgan had gained an appreciation for more of the authentic Mexican food, realizing that what she had been accustomed to eating at the local fast food taco place she frequented left a lot to be desired.

Not once had Darrin asked her to pay for or contribute to anything, not their meals, the movies when they went to them, or any of the other activities they enjoyed doing together, like going to the museum, music concerts, and even a trip they took to the state fair in Raleigh, North Carolina.

She had done more with Darrin in the few months that she'd known him than she had done with Will or even her first husband. She also felt that all in all she enjoyed all the fun she and Darrin had together because they were always on the go.

Both of them had even attended another SBA networking meeting, and Morgan had felt comfortable enough to stand pretty much under him to make a statement. She wanted Miss Courtney Alexander and all the other women in the place to know that Darrin was taken. There had been some sour faces when they'd departed together that night. Even her friend Martha had mentioned all the sour faces she'd seen the next week Morgan saw her shopping at the department store.

There was a knock at Amber's office door. She opened it to see who was there.

"Hey, Ms. Westfield," another employee said as she peeked into the office, but stopped when she saw all of the flowers. "Wow, nice."

"Not mine," Amber said. "Wish they were."

"Well they are beautiful," the employee said. Then she continued, "The applicant you are scheduled to interview for the housewares department is here."

"Shoot, I forgot about that interview. Thanks."

The employee departed from the doorway.

Amber looked at Morgan and then at her watch. "Looks like they are fifteen minutes early, that is a good sign." Then she looked around her office. "There is no way I'll be able to interview in here."

Morgan grinned sheepishly.

Amber cut her eyes in Morgan's direction. "Thanks, Morgan."

"Sorry about all this," Morgan said.

"Oh no, you're not, and I wouldn't feel sorry either if I were in your position. I would feel giddy as I don't know what," Amber said.

Morgan gave Amber a high five and said, "I do."

After they finished with their high five, Morgan got a look of dismay on her face. "How on earth am I supposed to be able to get all of these flowers to my apartment?" She'd been thinking and speaking out loud, not really expecting an answer from Amber.

"I can help you with that. You can load what you can in your car, and hopefully the rest will fit into my minivan."

"You'd do that for me?" Morgan asked.

"No problem. That's what friends are for. Even though you didn't think enough of me to tell me about your new boyfriend, and it looks like a possible soon-to-be fiancé."

"Oh, I don't know about all that. We have only been dating a short time."

Amber smirked. "Okay, Miss We've-only-been-dating-a-short-time. This man has sent you dozens of roses and has basically professed his love to you in this greeting card. And I am willing to bet you there is way more to this story that you aren't telling me."

Morgan nodded her head in agreement.

"So just do me one favor," Amber said.

"What is that?" Morgan asked.

"Just don't forget to address at least one of the wedding invitations to me."

Morgan swatted Amber's arm playfully. "You'll be the first one I address a wedding invitation to should it come to that point."

"Oh, it'll come to that point, you mark my word," Amber said.

"We'll see, but my hand looks a little bare if you ask me." Morgan looked down at her left hand's ring finger.

"Won't be for long." Amber looked around the office full of flowers. "So you are going to see him tonight?"

"Yes, we are going out to dinner. We are going to celebrate a deal Darrin has been working to get. He is pretty sure the deal will close soon. The man is so sure that he wants to celebrate early," Morgan said.

"He sounds pretty confident," Amber said.

"Some people would say confident. Others would say that he is cocky. He is probably a bit of both, to tell you the truth. He is a go-getter and strives to get what he wants, and from what I've observed so far, he usually gets what he wants. So this deal of his will probably go through," Morgan said.

Morgan looked at her own watch. "I need to get back on the floor, before Human Resources fires me for not working while on the clock."

"Yes, Ms. Jackson. And I need to interview this new applicant so we'll have another body to help cover housewares."

"When are you leaving today?" Morgan asked.

"I'll be out of here at four o'clock."

"Great. I get off at three-thirty. That will give me time to get as many of these flowers as I can into my little Hyundai Accent, and then meet you so we can start filling your minivan," Morgan said.

"Oh, no. We won't be carting a thing. I'll call my cousin Mickey from automotive to move all of these flowers."

"Mickey is your cousin?"

"Yeah. He's like my fourth cousin or something like that, not too close in relation, but close enough that I don't want the powers that be to know we are related. I don't want to jeopardize my job, and Mickey needs to work to feed those five kids he is trying to support."

Morgan felt as if a weight had been lifted off of her shoulders. She was dreading the thought of having to cart all of the flowers to their vehicles. If it had been one vase, that would have been one thing. But trying to cart all of them would be tiresome at best.

"Well, I can't be but so mad at you," Amber said.

"Why do you say that?"

"Because at least you provide equal treatment for your man and your friends," Amber said.

"Say what?" Morgan asked in confusion.

"It looks as if Mr. Right doesn't know where you live and neither do I. You've never invited me over to your place, and I invite you to mine all the time."

Morgan chuckled. "You're right. I believe in treating all people fairly and equally."

"It looks like I'm getting lucky today finally getting a chance to visit you. Even if it is only because you are in your time of need," Amber said.

"I guess that settles it then," Morgan said.

"Settles what?"

"If you are getting lucky, it only stands to reason that Darrin can become lucky as well. I need to let him know where I live and invite him over."

Amber rolled her eyes. "Very funny."

"Yeah, funny, but I think I will invite him over, especially since I'll have the beautiful flowers to decorate my apartment. All I will need now is a few candles and to have a nice homemade dinner prepared for him in appreciation for all he has done to win my heart over."

"Whooo, girl. It is getting hot in here again. I am scared of you," Amber said.

"Don't be scared. He has taken things up a notch. I should do the same."

"I am right there with you on that one."

Chapter 18

"Whew, girl." Amber wiped her forehead and huffed. "You could have at least told me you lived on the third floor before asking me to help you take all these flowers upstairs."

"First of all, I didn't ask you, you volunteered. While you were trying to be nosey to find out where I live," Morgan said.

"Not true." Amber leaned on the siding just outside of Morgan's front door to her apartment, while Morgan took her keys out for the eighth time to unlock her door. There were some knucklehead teens living in the apartment complex who looked a little untrustworthy. It was a nuisance locking and unlocking the door, but she didn't want to risk finding one of them hiding in her apartment later. Morgan figured she might be just a bit paranoid, probably because she had done quite a few sneaky and underhanded things in her life.

"It is true. And secondly, if I had told you I lived on the third floor, I know for a fact you wouldn't have helped me bring them up here," Morgan said.

"You got that right. I would have asked Mickey to help you with this, too."

Morgan rolled her eyes at Amber. "Well these are the last ones."

They both stepped into the apartment relieved to feel the coolness of the air conditioner on their wet, sweating skin. Both women took a seat on Morgan's rented furniture. Morgan sat on the couch and Amber huffed again as she sat on the loveseat.

"Sorry about that," Morgan said.

"It's all right, girl," Amber said in reply. "This is just a sign to me that I need to get back into the gym. This being out of shape is for the birds."

The two women sat silent for a full minute before Morgan spoke again. She sat up and said, "Do you want some water?"

"Yeah, that would be great. I want lots of ice, too," Amber said.

Morgan stood, went to the kitchen, and filled two Big Gulp–sized North Carolina Tar Heels drinking cups with ice and cold water. She pulled two flexible straws out of a drawer, bent them, and hooked them from the inside of the cups.

"Here you go." She handed one to Amber.

Amber took the cup, sat up, and spilled some of the water on her pant leg.

"Sorry about that," Morgan said.

"It isn't your fault. I am the one who sat up too quickly. No worries," Amber said.

"Be careful with your straw. It is shorter than the cup and if it falls in you'll have to go fishing for it."

Both women took long sips from the straws, drinking almost half of the contents of each cup.

"Now this is some good water," Amber said.

"Right now I think cold prune juice would taste good to us as thirsty as we are." Morgan chuckled.

Amber laughed right along with her, and then took another couple of sips of her water. "Okay, so that settles it. I need to go on a diet, start exercising, and really need to drink more water."

"I am with you on that one," Morgan said.

"You don't need to lose a thing. I wish I was your size. What are you, a size eight?"

"Yep."

"The last time I was a size eight was before my second daughter was born. Now three girls later, I have topped off at a size eighteen," Amber said.

"I'd feel better at a size six," Morgan said. She took another sip of her cold water.

"Well if Mr. Right likes a size eight then, like the old saying goes, if it ain't broke then don't try to fix it."

"He seems to be pleased," Morgan said.

Amber cut her eyes to the left, looking at roses, then to the right, looking at more roses; then she stared directly at Morgan with a smirk. "Oh, honey, I think he is plenty pleased."

Morgan grinned, knowing Amber was right.

"Now stop keeping me in the dark. Tell me more about this Darrin," Amber said.

"More like what?" Morgan was hesitant about sharing the information, because even though Amber was a friend, of sorts, she was a single female. The last thing Morgan wanted was to tell her friend all about her new man and how great he was, because some women had the tendency to want to go after other women's men. Deep down she didn't feel like Amber was the type, but didn't want to find out the hard way either.

Then the more she thought about it she knew that when it came down to it, a man could only be taken if he wanted to be taken. So she opened up to Amber, like she had wanted to do for the past few weeks.

"More like what is his last name, what does he do, and what is his IP address?"

"His IP what?" Morgan said.

"His IP address. You know, the personal signature for his computer?" Amber said.

Morgan had a true quizzical look on her face. "I've learned a lot about the man, but an IP address? Where do you come up with this kind of stuff?"

Then Amber busted out laughing. "Just kidding."

Morgan had to laugh too. Amber could be silly at times.

"His name is Darrin Hobbs and he owns his own financial company. He is single, never been married, and does not have any kids," Morgan said.

"Soooo, what's his deal? Is he a mama's boy? Is he on the sweet side? Is he buck ugly?"

"No, no, no, and no," Morgan said.

"I only asked you three questions. Why four no's?"

"The extra one was for whatever other crazy question you are about to ask me."

As if not wanting to waste another second in finding out more about Darrin, Amber said, "So where'd you meet him?"

"We met through a mutual friend. Our friend knew that we were both single and she set us up."

Amber tilted her cup to suck the last of her water out of her cup. She shook the ice a little and tried to drink any more droplets of water that had slid to the bottom of the cup.

Morgan stood, took Amber's cup, and headed back to the kitchen to refill it with water. As she filled Amber's cup she continued to tell her about Darrin.

"It's really weird in a way." Morgan raised her voice as she spoke from around the corner in the kitchen so that Amber could hear her over the running water.

"How so?"

"Well since we both were single, and both realized why our friend was setting us up, our relationship has pretty much been on fast-forward ever since." She returned to her little living room area.

"You've known him how long?"

"About two months," Morgan said. It had seemed as though the two months were longer than they actually were. She guessed it was because she and Darrin spent so much time together, be it on the phone, corresponding in e-mails or text messages, or in person when they were going out on dates, or just chilling out at his home.

"Only two months and this man is professing his love to you already?" Amber shook her head. "What did you do to him? What did you put in his drink, a love potion or something?"

"I didn't put anything in his drink." Morgan sounded a bit more defensive than she'd meant to.

Amber's eyes widened. "Calm down, girl."

She smiled and tried to soften up her statement. "Silly, there aren't any love potions out there. I wish there were. We've done a lot in two months. To tell the truth it is like we've packed six months' worth of dating into these past eight weeks."

"Is he tall, short, light, dark? Do you have a picture?"

"Actually, I do have a picture, in my phone." Morgan looked around for her cell phone. Then she remembered that she'd left it and her purse in the car as she was so focused on getting the flowers into the house.

"Shoot, I left my phone and purse in the car." She wondered why it had been so quiet in the apartment. Normally Darrin would have called, texted her, or sent her an e-mail by now. He was very attentive to her safety and needs. Often he checked on her when she was traveling back to her apartment from his home. It didn't matter to him if it was in the middle of the afternoon or if it was eleven at night, he made contact to make sure she was safe. She had yet to spend the night at his house and had no plans to do so until she had a "Mrs." in front of her name.

Morgan looked at the clock on her fireplace mantel. "I didn't realize it was so late."

"That's right, you all have a date tonight?"

"Yeah, he is going to take me to that new Brazilian restaurant on Seventh Street."

"Have you ever had Brazilian food?"

"No, this will be a first for me."

"Well if it is anything like the Braza Brazilian Steakhouse in Raleigh, then you are in for a treat."

Morgan stood and located her keys on the kitchen counter.

Amber stood too.

"I need to get my phone. Knowing Darrin he has probably called a couple of times to make sure I got in okay."

"Are you serious? Is this apartment complex that bad? It doesn't look that bad."

"No, he's just like a papa bear trying to protect his wife and cubs."

"Oh, how sweet. What a cute comparison."

Morgan thought it was sweet, and knew the man cared about her, but sometimes his care and concern got on her nerves. She shrugged her shoulders.

"Sounds like love at first sight to me," Amber said.

"Maybe," Morgan said.

"That man is in love with you and probably started the day you met." Pointedly, Amber asked, "Are you in love with him yet?"

"That's a pretty direct and straightforward and personal question," Morgan said. She was taken aback by not only Amber's directness but also the question itself.

Morgan had been so focused on finding the right man with the three qualities that mattered the most—his looks, social status, and his wallet—that she'd forgotten about any kind of love aspect. That aspect had been the furthest from her mind.

"Well?" Amber asked with expectation in her voice.

Morgan led Amber out of the door; then they walked down the steps together toward their cars, which were parked side by side.

"Truth be told, things have moved quickly. I can truly say that I am charmed by him, but my feelings are not moving as quickly as his feelings are."

"Charmed. Now that is an interesting choice of words," Amber said.

"Who wouldn't be after receiving dozens of rainbow-colored roses?" Morgan said.

"I guess you're right. With all he is doing, I'd think you wouldn't find it hard to love the one you're with," Amber said.

"In due time I am sure," Morgan said. She used her key fob and pressed the button to open her automatic doors. She saw her phone and purse sitting in plain sight on the passenger seat of the car.

"I'll see you on Monday," Amber said.

"Monday?"

"Yeah. I am off the next two days and you know I don't work weekends."

"Oh, yeah, that's right." Morgan stepped over to Amber and gave her a hug. "Thanks for all your help."

Morgan unlocked her phone to check if there were any messages.

"You are more than welcome." Amber got in her car and started the engine. She rolled her window down as she pulled off. "Have fun tonight."

"That's the plan," Morgan said with more enthusiasm than she actually felt. Her lack of enthusiasm had to do with her phone screen. The phone's screen indicated that she had five text messages, two voice mails, and an e-mail. She knew without checking any of the virtual forms of communication that all were from Darrin. His concern often seemed overbearing and a bit in the extreme at times.

Chapter 19

"You cannot be serious," Amber said. The disbelief in her voice was also evident by the astonished look on her face.

"Can I have my hand back now?" Morgan asked.

"Girl, with a rock like that somebody might try to take that finger to get it off of you."

Morgan took her left hand back. "It is beautiful isn't it?" She tilted her hand this way and that, looking at the glittering diamond ring on her left finger.

It was Monday morning and they were back at work in Amber's office. It had been the first opportunity Morgan had gotten a chance to see Amber in person to show and tell her about the ring, the proposal, and the celebration dinner thereafter.

"So he closed the deal, huh?" Amber asked.

"Huh?"

"Weren't you all supposed to be celebrating some deal Darrin was trying to close?"

"Oh, yeah, but . . ." Morgan's voice trailed off as she thought about what Amber was saying. And the more she thought about it the more it made sense. She felt like hitting her forehead with the heel of her hand.

"Girl, I hadn't even thought twice about the supposed deal Darrin was trying to close." Morgan got a sneaky look on her face as she thought about the engagement night's events. "I think you are right about that open deal that needed to be closed, because he never mentioned anything else."

Morgan nodded her head. "I am going to get him. He pulled one over on me." Then she smiled. "It isn't easy to fool me and Darrin succeeded."

"I guess you could say I am surprised, but not really surprised. Because at the rate that man was going, I knew he was going to ask you sometime soon," Amber said.

"Well I am glad you weren't surprised, because I actually was. I thought he might ask me but maybe in a few months, when we got to know each other a bit better—or to at least have more time elapse since we met."

"You know what they say don't you?" Amber asked.

"No, what do they say?"

"They say that women fall in love and want to get married, but men decide they want to get married, then allow themselves to fall in love."

Morgan tilted her head to the side as she thought about what was being said. It did look as if Darrin was prime and ready to find a mate. And in his eyes, that mate was her, and it was okay for him to profess his love for her in the quest to make Morgan his wife. "You might be right about that."

"So tell me, how did he propose?" Amber asked.

"The man is creative. I'll give him that one. And for the most part he is romantic, except when he is giving me velvet fake roses from the gas station."

Amber sat back in her office chair. "I've got to hear this."

"Okay, we went out to dinner like I told you. You were absolutely right about the food at that Brazilian restaurant. It was scrumptious."

Amber cut in. "I told you it was." Then she sat straight up. "Now go on."

Morgan rolled her eyes. "I will if you stop interrupting me."

Amber made a motion as if she was zipping her lips shut and ready to listen.

"So we went to the buffet area, loaded plates, then we sat back at the table and waited for the meat to come out." Morgan interrupted herself. "You didn't tell me they were going to come out with meat on humongous skewers and cut it right onto your plate."

Without saying a word, Amber made the motion of zipping her lips again to remind her that she wasn't saying a word.

"Let me cut to the chase. So when we turned our rocks over from green indicating we wanted more food, then over to red to let them know we wanted them to stop serving us more meat, Darrin pulled out another rose."

"He pulled out another rose? What color was it?" Amber said before she could stop herself. With a sheepish look she said, "Oops."

Morgan smiled. She knew her friend couldn't help herself.

"Yes. He pulled out a red rose made of velvet with a pipe-cleaner stem." Morgan paused to see what Amber's reaction was going to be.

As her head and mouth dropped in disbelief and confusion, Amber said, "Say what?"

"You heard me. The man spends hundreds of dollars on real roses and then he hands me a fake rose at dinner," Morgan said.

Morgan paused again to see what other kind of reaction she might get from her friend, but Amber was too smart for the bait. It was obvious that Amber knew the night had turned out fine as evidenced by the rock glistening on her left hand ring finger.

She continued to speak. "So he hands me this rose and tells me to smell it. I didn't want to smell it, I didn't want it anywhere near my nose, but I humored him anyway. I took a quick sniff and pulled it away from my nose."

"Without cracking a smile Darrin asked me how it smelled. I hadn't smelled a thing. He pleaded with me to take another sniff. So I did. I took a longer sniff, but truly didn't smell a thing," Morgan said.

"Stands to reason, fake roses don't usually smell like anything unless they've been sprayed with something," Amber said.

"With the straightest face ever, Darrin asked me to try to sniff it again. He told me to open up the fake petals because the scent might be within them." Again Morgan interrupted her own story. "Now, let me tell you, by that point, I was full, tired, and ready to go home to smell my real flowers in the living room."

"I know that's right," Amber said.

"I opened up the petals on the rose and saw something on the inside start to glint from the light."

Amber gasped in a breath of air and with a mouth wide open she covered it with one of her hands as she smiled, anticipating the next part of the story.

"I opened it up even more and saw the ring, which was being held in place by a piece of the pipe cleaner." Morgan grinned.

Tears of emotion and excitement started to well up in Amber's eyes. She pulled a tissue from the box that was sitting on her desk and dabbed at the corners of her eyes.

"Darrin took the rose from me, pulled the pipe cleaner from the ring; then he walked around the table to kneel on one knee in front of me. With his pearly white teeth showing, with a grin he spoke, asking me to be his wife, to have and to hold from that day forward."

Amber dabbed more at her face as a couple of tears made their way down her cheeks. "Oh, my goodness. That is so romantic." She sniffed.

"It was very romantic. And I didn't spoil the moment for one second. I immediately accepted his proposal," Morgan said.

"That is the most beautiful story I have ever heard. I mean you hear about stories like this in books, on television, and see them in movies, but you are the first person to have what I'd call a *Pretty Woman*–type of proposal," Amber said.

The tears coming from Amber's eyes were touching. But not touching enough for Morgan to feel anywhere near crying herself. If she was honest with herself she honestly felt numb about the whole situation. Things really were happening at a pretty fast speed. And in her wildest dreams, she would have never imagined, or planned it out so wonderfully.

Amber moved the mouse on her desk to activate her computer screen. "Congratulations, my friend. Now you've got a lot to plan and do. Did you set a date yet? Don't worry about setting up your bridal registry account because we can start it right now." Amber clicked icons on her quest to start the needed wedding planning wheels in motion.

Morgan held up her hands. "Whoa, whoa. Slow down there."

Amber's fingers froze on the keyboard. She looked at her friend. "What's up?"

"Darrin has a houseful of stuff, and I've got an apartment full of stuff as well. We probably will not be registering anywhere."

It wasn't any of Amber's business that many of the items that were in her apartment were rented. She also didn't want to explain to Amber why she really had no desire to register anywhere. She'd been married once, and also had her second pseudo marriage to Will. All she really wanted to do was get the deed over with.

"That is nonsense. I am sure there are still things you'll need," Amber said.

"That might be true, but there isn't time to register anyway."

"What do you mean?" Amber asked.

"We are getting married the week after next."

"Say what?" Amber's mouth dropped wide open. "Why so quick?"

"Darrin and I both think we shouldn't waste any time. I don't have a large family and Darrin doesn't either. We don't want a big wedding. We just want to have a ceremony and celebrate our union together—privately."

"Okay. . . ." Amber let her voice trail off as she removed her hands from the computer keyboard.

"We will be doing a destination wedding in Kapalua Bay Beach, Maui."

"As in Hawaii?"

"Yep."

"How in the world . . . Why . . ."

"We want to do a destination wedding, and we looked at a lot of locations but since I don't have a passport, tropical locations are limited. So we looked at Hawaii," Morgan said.

Amber seemed astonished. "That was quick, when did you have time to plan all this?"

"We got together on Saturday, went over to his travel agent, and booked everything. He paid for it and we were out of the door."

Amber sat back. She was visibly and audibly speechless.

"I know it all seems like things are moving fast, but who really has time to waste? I am going with the flow," Morgan said.

Amber shook a chill off. She then said, "Well all righty then. I guess you two have it all figured out."

"I think we do." Morgan smiled. She was pleased with the progress she and Darrin had made on their wedding planning. It had taken away the stress of planning for a big wedding. It also hadn't hurt a bit that Darrin had the means to financially take care of the wedding expenses.

"This afternoon we are going to look for a wedding band that will complement my engagement ring," Morgan said.

Amber took a deep breath before she spoke. "Morgan. I am really happy for you if you are happy."

"Thank you," Morgan said.

"Now don't get mad at me when I say this."

"Say what?" Morgan asked.

"Do you think you need to slow it down and assess things a bit? I mean you've known this man for barely two months. You can't really *know him* know him."

"Amber. I hear the care and concern in your voice. And I do understand what you are saying. But the same could be said for me. Darrin doesn't really know me either. I am just going on faith that things will work out between us. Believe me I am not completely making a blind decision. I've done a little background checking on the man and he isn't a criminal or anything. He really seems to be a good guy. He has a lot going for him. And one of the next steps that he wants to make is to find a mate and get married and he has fallen in love with me. Just so happens I want the same things he wants and he would be a great mate."

The look of concern on Amber's face was replaced by a look of relief. "You know you are a grown woman, and of course you know what you are doing. Who am I to stand in the way of you two lovebirds?"

Morgan replayed in her head all she'd just said to Amber. She couldn't remember saying a thing about actually loving Darrin. She liked Darren, liked what he could do for her, and felt he was a good man overall. It might be possible for her to eventually fall in love with the man, but she wasn't going to hold out too much hope for that aspect of her upcoming marriage.

Amber pulled her away from her thoughts. "So I guess the real reason you came in here is to ask for some time off the week after next."

Morgan laughed, because that was indeed the secondary reason she'd come to see Amber. "Amber, girl, you can see right through me."

"You know I can." Amber laughed as well.

Chapter 20

"Mr. Darrin Michael Hobbs, do you take Cecily Morgan Jackson to be your lawfully wedded wife? To have and to hold, from this day forward?" the island minister asked.

They stood on the beach, listening to the gentle sound of tiny waves as they hit the nearby shore. The earthy smell of sea salt filled the warm and tropical air. The smell of fresh flowers permeated their noses as well due to the Hawaiian leis made with fresh flowers. Morgan, Darrin, and their guests wore around their necks the leis made with live flowers.

Darrin gazed lovingly into Morgan's eyes and said, "I do."

"Please place the ring on Morgan's finger," the minister said.

"And do you, Cecily Morgan Jackson, take Darrin Michael Hobbs to be your lawfully wedded husband? To have and to hold from this day forward?" the island minister asked Morgan.

"I do," Morgan said as she stared back into the excited and thrilled eyes of Darrin. She squeezed his hand and tried to mirror his enthusiasm but was sure she fell short. She was enthusiastic but for reasons far different from Darrin was experiencing.

"Now will you please place the ring on Darrin's finger?" the minister said to Morgan.

"Everyone, this is a blessed occasion as these two are now wedded in holy matrimony. I now pronounce you husband and wife," the minister said. "You may now kiss your bride, Mr. Hobbs."

Morgan smiled and looked at Darrin as he placed both his hands on her cheeks and then kissed her. Morgan had kissed Darrin quite a few times, and thought the man was a great kisser. This particular kiss to seal their matrimony lasted longer than any kiss she could ever remember.

She heard oohs and ahhs from the few witnesses they had present at their tiny little wedding. The minister and wedding guests, and even the photographer, clapped their hands with joy and excitement in honor of the wedding celebration. "And now, ladies and gentleman, I present to you Mr. and Mrs. Darrin Michael Hobbs," said the minister.

Darrin kissed Morgan again. "I love you, Mrs. Morgan Hobbs."

"I love you too, Mr. Hobbs," Morgan said in return.

Music from speakers unseen piped in Hawaiian music with an upbeat, celebratory tempo. They were standing on the beautiful Kapalua Bay Beach in Maui in Hawaii. It was the most picturesque and romantic moment that Morgan had ever experienced. The sun was just starting to set on the horizon behind them. She would have never dreamed that one day she'd be on a tropical beach, miles from North Carolina, getting married. Morgan knew she would never forget this moment for the rest of her life.

Darrin and Morgan turned around and faced their guests. Standing as guest and witness for both Morgan Darrin was Martha Metcalf, and the other witness was a childhood friend of Darrin's who lived on the island of Oahu, which was a nearby island. The friend named Dave had gladly agreed to come over to Maui along with his own wife named Lalani. Lalani was a native of Hawaii and had grown up in Maui.

Darrin squeezed Morgan's hand as they stood in their white attire. Morgan wore a white ankle-length lace designer dress, which flowed in the gentle island breeze. In her hair she wore a beautiful red rose and held a bouquet of rainbow-colored roses in her hand. Darrin wore a pair of white linen loose-fitting pants along with a white short-sleeved button-down shirt.

Their feet were bare, as were the feet of their guests. This was a short and informal wedding. The whole ceremony from start to finish was complete in less than five minutes. The ceremony was so short that there weren't any chairs. The guests stood throughout. All that was intended and expected was for the bride and groom as well as their guests to be comfortable, relax, and enjoy the event. As far as Morgan could tell, all was going according to plan.

"I'd like to thank you all for coming to witness and be a part of our wedding," Darrin said. "I couldn't imagine having this wedding without such great friends as you all. It is indeed a blessing to have you all here with us."

"Yes, thank you so much. We both thank you for being a part of our special day," Morgan said.

Each person along with the minister congratulated the couple. Then the photographer took photos of them as he tried to capture the beauty of the sunset in the distance. Because the wedding was so informal, Morgan and Darrin had taken some pictures earlier in the day with the photographer in order to get as many day and evening shots as possible.

"Everyone, we are going to head back over to the hotel now to continue this celebration with dinner and music," Darrin said.

They all headed back to the hotel, which was only a short walk from the beach on which the ceremony was held. After washing sand off of their feet, the guests put their shoes on and they congregated in a small private room that Darrin had reserved for their small wedding party and guests.

Morgan felt as if she were dreaming. She wanted to pinch herself. Everything since her proposal had seemed to happen so quickly she was still trying to get her bearings. She could not believe that her plan to find an eligible and desirable man who had money had happened so quickly. As she looked at the engagement ring and wedding band on her hand she gave them a squeeze, which was the next best thing to pinching herself.

The private room had a table that sat six. Morgan, Darrin, and their three guests sat down at a table that was brimming with food. It was like a mini luau with baked sweet potato, poi, Huli-huli Chicken, long rice, rolls, papaya slices, pineapple chunks, mangos, coconuts, roast pork, and ambrosia.

There were other items that Morgan couldn't name or pronounce, and the only reason she knew the few foods she did currently recognize was because she and Darrin had done some searches on the Internet when booking the hotel for the wedding to figure out what types of food they wanted at their wedding reception.

"Darrin and Morgan, everything is absolutely beautiful," Martha said.

"Thank you, Martha," Morgan said. "And thank you so much for coming. It is such a surprise seeing you." Morgan saw Martha just about every week at the department store. She had even seen Martha just a few days ago. Morgan told Martha about their wedding plans.

Little did she know, Darrin had already been in cahoots with Martha, secretly planning her arrival as a surprise. Martha had the money, means, and time to travel anywhere she wanted, whenever she wanted. Morgan was honored that Martha chose to come to Maui for them.

"Honey, I would not have missed this for the world," Martha said. She had worn a pastel-colored layered silk dress. Morgan had seen the dress on display in the women's department of the store and thought Martha had done a wonderful job picking it out. The dress looked gorgeous on Martha. "I'll be right back. I need to locate the ladies' room."

Dave and his wife stepped up to Darrin and Morgan.

"Morgan, how did you get this man to finally settle down?" Dave said.

Darrin glared at his friend and playfully hit him in the arm. "Now, Dave, we're not the same as we were in college, now, are we? Do you want me to tell Lalani here about your crazy days in college?"

"Do tell, Darrin. I'd love to hear about you two and your college days," Lalani said.

Pretending as if he were scared and reading from a script, in a robotic-sounding voice Dave said, "Morgan, Darrin was a complete angel in college, he never did anything wrong. As a matter of fact he never ever even dated any women before you."

Darrin hit his friend in the arm again. "You always have been a jokester."

With a change in demeanor and a more serious tone Dave said, "No, seriously, Morgan. Darrin is a great guy, and he's always been so focused on building his business, I didn't ever think he'd settle down."

Morgan would have loved to have had Amber and Desiree come to witness their wedding, but knew that wasn't possible. Amber wasn't able to come because she didn't have the means and Desiree was still on parole and couldn't get the permission to leave the state. This was one of the times she wished she had more friends, but those types of times were few and far between.

It seemed as though Darrin wasn't too disappointed in the two women not coming; he almost seemed relieved. Morgan had been starting to get the feeling that Darrin didn't really like her friends very much. He had met Amber once and the meeting hadn't gone well. He had yet to meet Desiree but every time Morgan tried to arrange a time for them to meet Darrin always had a weak excuse, so Morgan just stopped trying.

With tropical Hawaiian music being piped into the room, the wedding party dug into the mini mountain of foods before them. At the end of the dinner service, Morgan and Darrin took the opportunity to dance to one of the slower songs and considered it their first dance as husband and wife.

When they were finished, waiters brought out cupcakes. The top of the cupcakes were decorated with beautiful red roses that were actually made of edible frosting. After everyone got their cupcake fill, Darrin and Morgan said their good-byes. "Lalani, it was nice meeting you," Morgan said.

"Yes, it was nice to meet you, Lalani," Darrin said.

"Thank you. You must come back and visit us sometime," Lalani said.

"We would invite you over this trip, but I am sure you will be preoccupied with honeymoon business," Dave said.

Darrin took Morgan into his arms and said, "Yes, sir, there is much on our list of things to do, all pertaining to being newlyweds and honeymooners."

They gave Dave and Lalani hugs; then the couple parted.

"I am going to call it a night as well," Martha said. "I'll see you two lovebirds back on the mainland in North Carolina when you get back home."

"Are you sure you'll be okay here for the next few days by yourself?" Morgan asked.

"Honey, Ms. Martha will be just fine, I'm sure," Darrin said.

Martha laughed. "Don't worry about me, Morgan. I have seen a few things in the brochures that I'd like to check out. But the main thing I want to do is find a nice umbrella to set in the sand at the beach. I just want to enjoy this Maui sun at the beach."

"See, Ms. Martha will be just fine," Darrin said.

Morgan knew the only thing on her new husband's mind was continuing their honeymoon privately in their hotel room. She gave Martha a heartfelt hug. Having Martha there had been like having the mother she'd never had in her life.

"Congratulations again," Martha said. Then she gave Darrin a hug as well and left.

"Sweetheart, my darling, my love," Darrin said.

"Yes, my husband." Morgan liked saying it. She was legally able to say it.

"Are you ready to retire to our room?" Darrin said.

"Retire to our room? What's up with all the formalities?" Morgan asked.

"I don't know how to better say, 'Let's go to our room and be a married couple,' without it sounding tactless" Darrin said.

Morgan took her index finger and placed it on Darrin's lips to indicate that she wanted him to stop talking. "Shhhhh," she said. "Darrin, I know what you want, and how long you've wanted it. Not another word," Morgan said.

Darrin complied as Morgan took his hand in hers and led them both to their hotel suite.

Chapter 21

"How many bathing suits did you bring?" Darrin asked.

"Seven," Morgan said.

With camera in hand Darrin took a couple of pictures of Morgan as she posed in one of her bathing suits in front of him as they relaxed on the beach.

"One bathing suit for each day," Darrin said.

"Yep," Morgan said.

"Too bad you won't get a chance to wear them all," Darrin said.

"And whose fault is that, Darrin?"

"It was all your fault."

Morgan put her hands on her hips. "How in the heck was it my fault?"

He walked over to her and kissed her on the lips. "Because, my dear, if you weren't so tempting, then I wouldn't have kept you in our honeymoon suite for the first two full days."

"I started to honestly think we were going to spend our whole seven-day honeymoon in the hotel suite, only seeing our room service attendant," Morgan said.

"You are right, we would have, but you tricked me into letting you out," Darrin said.

"Really now, I mean really? All I said was can we go sightseeing and you hopped out of the bed before I could get the sentence out all the way," Morgan said.

"That was all it took, besides the fact that I felt like I was getting cabin fever," Darrin said.

"And the other fact," Morgan said.

"What's that?"

"The fact that you love to take pictures and you know this place is too scenic not to be out and about taking pictures," Morgan said.

"I am taking a picture of the most beautiful thing this whole island has to offer," Darrin said.

"Darrin, flattery will get you everywhere," Morgan said.

Darrin pulled a purple island flower out of a flower arrangement that sat on a table not too far from where they were taking pictures. "I know roses are your favorite, but humor me please and put this in your hair on the side. It matches your bathing suit."

Morgan did as she was asked.

"Perfect," Darrin said.

He took a few pictures. She posed for him, looking at the camera, then to the left and to the right. In some pictures she smiled and in others her face was peaceful, as if she was enjoying and taking in the nature all around her.

"You are really photogenic," Darrin said.

"Thank you. No one has ever told me that before."

"Come here," Darrin said.

She walked over to Darrin. He turned the back of the camera to her so she could see what he was talking about. Clicking the button that would allow him to view any previous pictures taken, he showed Morgan the last twenty frames he had shot.

"They do look pretty nice."

She had to admit that except for one picture out of all the ones she'd seen, they all looked like a professional photographer had taken them. And truth be told it looked as if she could pass for a professional model.

"I think it is a combination of things, and the main thing is you and your camera," Morgan said.

"Ahhh, in the words of my new wife, 'flattery will get you everywhere,'" Darrin said.

It was now day six of their honeymoon in Maui. The couple had been on just about every excursion the island had to offer. They had been snorkeling, para-sailing, scuba diving, jet skiing, sightseeing, and zip lining. Morgan had even learned how to surf. With it being their last full day, they decided to take advantage of the spa. Both Morgan and Darrin had the full spa treatment. She'd had a massage before at a spa in Silvermont, but she'd never had the level of treatment that she had in Maui.

The massage along with everything else about their wedding and honeymoon would be something she would remember for the rest of her life. Morgan felt giddy because she knew that the best was yet to come. If the past six days had been any indication of how her life was going to be, she couldn't wait to get back home.

Morgan was very pleased with herself. Her life was finally going just the way she planned. She thought she had it with her first marriage and then with Will, but now she realized her life with Darrin would give her not only what she needed but also what she wanted. She deserved the finer things in life and Darrin was the one who was going to give her the avenue to be able to afford the life she wanted.

"Are you enjoying yourself?" Darrin asked.

They were sitting in white robes in lounge chairs, waiting to be called for their massages. So far they had already had facials. Now they were about to get the deluxe treatment for their massages. They sipped on tropical smoothies.

Morgan sighed. "I most certainly am," Morgan said.

"So why are you sighing?" Darrin asked.

Morgan took a sip of her smoothie. "By this time tomorrow we will be on a flight back to the real world."

"We will and I'm looking forward to picking you up and carrying you into the threshold of our home," Darrin said.

"Our home," Morgan said.

"Yes, Mrs. Hobbs, our home. And I can't wait for you to finally spend the first night there."

"It will be nice not to have to leave late at night and in the wee hours of the morning. It will be nice to not have to get out in the cold, sleet, wind, and rain anymore either."

Darrin cut his eyes over to Morgan. "What are you the mailman now? I don't remember one night of cold, snow, or sleet. Maybe a couple of drops of rain now and then."

"Okay, okay, you're right about the snow and sleet, but don't you remember that rainstorm we had three and a half weeks ago? I got soaked by the time I got in my door," Morgan said.

"Well, my dear. You don't have to worry about that anymore. When you come home, all you have to do is drive right up into the garage."

Morgan could see herself driving up into the garage in her car. Then another thought came to her head. Now that she was officially the Mrs. Hobbs, it was time she started looking for a new car. Darrin had a nice Lexus and she had been eyeing the red Mercedes-Benz the store manager was driving.

She smiled to herself. She was pleased with herself because she was on the brink of getting everything she ever wanted. Getting Darrin to fall in love with her had been easy. It had been a whole lot easier than she thought it was going to be. She wondered if there had been some divine intervention playing a role in her love life, but quickly decided this was not the case.

She was the one who had put the wheels in motion, and it was just dumb luck that she had walked up to Martha that day in the store. Meeting Martha, she decided, was the pivotal point. There was no way in her mind that she would have gotten as far as she had with Darrin so quickly had it not been for the fact that the woman personally knew Darrin and that he trusted Martha. So if anything instead of being thankful to the Lord for her new husband she thanked Martha.

Morgan held her glass up to Darrin. "Let's toast."

"What do you want to toast to?" Darrin asked.

"To us," Morgan said.

Darrin held his glass up and toasted Morgan. "To us."

He then leaned over toward her to kiss, and taking his cue, Morgan leaned over as well and kissed him.

"I love you so very much, Morgan. You have made me the happiest man in the world."

Morgan kissed Darrin again. "You, my husband, have made me the happiest woman in the world." She kissed him again, this time a little harder and longer.

"Mr. and Mrs. Hobbs," they heard someone say. Looking up they saw two of the massage therapists calling them. "We are ready for you."

They both stood with their smoothies in hand and followed the therapists. Morgan was glad they were called because it seemed like lately Darrin was getting too mushy for her. It seemed like every time she looked around he was trying to hold her hand and telling her how much he loved her. She figured it was because they had been right up underneath one another for almost a solid week and she was ready for a breather.

The other reason she was glad for the interruption was because she hoped Darrin had not realized that she hadn't said "I love you" back to him after the toast. Even though she had been hoping she would eventually fall in love with him, the feelings just weren't there. She liked the guy enough, but love was something strong—something she hadn't felt in years.

But there was no way she was going to let a little thing like not being in love with the guy keep her from having everything else she wanted. He had far too many other things going for him. So she figured she would tell him she loved him just enough to appease him. And as far as she was concerned her quota for telling him she loved him had already been reached for the day.

It was as if he wanted her to say she loved him all day like he was saying it and it was getting on her nerves as well. By her count she'd told him she loved him five times that day already: in the morning before their showers, again after breakfast, then right before they boarded their tour bus to go sightseeing. Again she told him she loved him when they were about to eat lunch, then again after lunch when they were about to get on the elevator to go to their suite.

After their massages Morgan and Darrin returned to their hotel suite. Darrin had hinted that he wanted to go back to the room for some one-on-one rest and relaxation. Morgan let him know that she definitely wanted to get some rest. She felt like the last few days of going on excursions nonstop was finally catching up with her.

"You first, my dear," Darrin said as he gestured for Morgan to enter the suite in front of him.

Morgan stepped inside and slipped her sandals off. The bed was calling her. She really wanted to rest. She felt relaxed from the massage and just wanted to continue relaxing. Darrin closed the door behind her.

"Where do you want to go for dinner tonight?" Darrin asked.

"I don't know. To tell you the truth, I don't really want to go out tonight. Maybe we can just order room service," Morgan said. She sat down on the side of their bed.

Darrin seemed to get a glint in his eye. Morgan knew that meant he thought she had some other ideas as well for their night inside the hotel suite.

"I see that look in your eye and I know what it means."

"Good, I am glad you and I have an unspoken understanding," Darrin said.

Morgan smiled weakly. "Do you see this look in my eye?"

"Yeah, I see it and it isn't matching mine. What's up? Are you tired?" Darrin asked.

"Actually I am. We've been running nonstop the last few days," Morgan said.

"Hold that thought," Darrin said. He stepped inside the bathroom and closed the door.

Morgan took the opportunity to pull an extra blanket out of the closet and lie down on the bed. She pulled the blanket up to her ears. By the time Darrin came out of the bathroom she was almost asleep.

She heard him whispering, "Morgan, are you asleep? I can't believe you fell asleep that fast."

In her sleepy state she was thinking the same thing. She had been even more tired than she thought. She felt the cover being pulled up a little more, and then felt a kiss on her forehead.

"I love you," Darrin whispered.

Morgan stirred a little. Her last thought before she slept was that she wasn't going to say "I love you" back.

Chapter 22

Morgan awoke as she thought she was seeing the first rays of sun peeking through the blinds in their master bedroom. She stretched where she lay. Next to her Darrin was snoring loudly. She looked over at the clock and realized it was noon. At first she couldn't believe she'd slept that late but then realized her body was still on Hawaiian time with a five-hour time difference.

She stepped out of the bed, trying not to disturb Darrin. He would need all the rest he could get before returning to work the next day. She wasn't scheduled to return to the store for another two days. Her stomach grumbled as she was usually accustomed to rising and ordering breakfast from room service in the mornings.

Wondering what they had in the house to eat she descended the stairs and headed to the kitchen to check it out. In all the times she had visited Darrin she had never allowed herself to get too comfortable or to let him think she was too comfortable in his home. She didn't want their relationship to go on a path where he became satisfied with having her as a long-term girlfriend instead of a wife.

Her thinking was that if he got too accustomed to her and she did all of the wifely things that wives did, like cook, and clean, and engage in premarital romantic relations, then he would start to take her for granted. To some it might have sounded crazy, but to her she truly felt that the two rings on her left ring finger signified the fruit of her labor.

Opening the refrigerator, Morgan saw that Darrin didn't have much. It looked much like that of a true bachelor. It looked different from the refrigerator she had first seen at Will's apartment when she met him. Of course Will was frugal and liked to cook. He went out on special occasions but for the most part ate his meals at home and even made his lunch for work.

Morgan hunched her shoulders and let out a huff. She wasn't really sure why she allowed any thoughts about her ex into her brain. So instead she stared into the refrigerator and made a mental note of what was there. There were a few bottles of water, a bottle of outdated orange juice, and condiment bottles like ketchup, soy sauce, lemon juice, mustard, and even a jar of something called Bone Suckin' Sauce, which was also outdated. She threw the orange juice and Bone Suckin' Sauce away.

Closing the refrigerator she decided to check out the cabinets. Even though there was a little more in his cabinets they too were also pretty much bare. In one set of cabinets he had regular-sized containers of salt and pepper, a bottle of hot sauce, and an assortment of spices and seasonings.

The amount of spices and seasonings he had seemed extremely odd. He had chili powder, chicken rub seasoning, hamburger grilling seasoning, sage, basil, parsley, and rosemary. There was also every type of seasoning Mrs. Dash made along with garlic salt and lemon pepper seasoning. As if Darrin cooked pies all the time, she found cinnamon, ginger, nutmeg, and even an old bag of expired brown sugar. She threw the rock-solid bag of expired sugar away.

In his lower cabinets she found pieces of cookware and bake ware that looked used. She wondered if Darrin had tried his hand at cooking at one time or another.

She was going to have to ask him about all the condiments he had. Once her assessment of the kitchen was done she knew it was obvious she was going to have to go grocery shopping. There wasn't anything she saw that she could really work with for fixing them a nice breakfast, lunch, or even dinner later on.

Returning to her bedroom she opened up her suitcase and pulled out a jogging suit. She dressed and grabbed her purse and keys off of the chest of drawers located in their walk-in closet. In all the time she was dressing and preparing to go to the grocery store, Darrin hadn't moved at all. He just continued to snore as if he was getting some of the best sleep in his life.

In her car she carefully pulled out of the garage and closed it with the garage opener Darrin had given her a month after they had started dating. She was always mindful and respectful of his home and only used it when he knew she was coming over. Now today after she returned from the grocery store she wasn't going to have to call first to let him know she was on the way. It was a great feeling.

The closest grocery store that she knew about was just a couple of miles away. She wasn't as familiar with that side of Silvermont as she was with the one she lived in with Will or the area where she had her apartment. So one day she was going to take the time to better familiarize herself with the area.

As soon as Morgan got out of her car and reached the doors of the grocery store, her cell phone rang. She pulled it from her purse. The display showed Darrin's cell phone number. She smiled, thinking the man had an uncanny sense of timing.

"Hello," Morgan said.

"Hey, where are you?" Darrin asked. His voice was gruff, sounding as if he was still coming out of a groggy sleep.

"I see you're at it again," Morgan said. She laughed.

"At what?"

"That intuition or whatever it is you possess that always knows when I am going somewhere. Or that I have arrived somewhere."

"What do you mean?" Darrin asked.

"I just got to the grocery store. I was just about to walk in. It seemed like you were pretty good with timing whenever I would leave your house or we would part from our dates. You had that same sense of intuition, always seeming to sense when I had arrived home safely," Morgan said.

"Oh, that. I guess deep down my senses just want to know that my lady is safe, that's all. Now that you are my wife, my senses are probably in overdrive." Darrin laughed a bit himself.

"Well, anyway. I am at the grocery store. You were really living the bachelor lifestyle weren't you? You don't have much of anything in the kitchen to eat."

"No, I don't. You know me, I don't cook. That is why I eat out so much," Darrin said.

"Did you try to in the past?"

"Huh? What do you mean?"

"I saw where you have a multitude of spices and seasonings, and cookware and bake ware in the kitchen. Most of the items looked used."

"Oh, that. Yeah, remember when I told you I dated this girl for a few months?"

"Yeah."

"Well she used to love to cook. I bought all that stuff for her to cook," Darrin said. "When we broke up I never even used any of it."

"Oh, that explains it all then."

"All of what?"

"The old, expired Bone Suckin' Sauce and that hard bag of brown sugar. They expired awhile back. I threw them away."

"You threw my sauce away?"

"Yeah, expired a year ago."

"Man, that was something I was actually still using. I use it on my hamburgers and roast beef sandwiches sometimes, sort of like other people use mayonnaise and ketchup," Darrin said.

"Oh, sorry about that. I'll pick up some more while I am here at the store," Morgan said.

"Thanks. What else are you getting?"

"I am going to pick up some breakfast items, and some stuff to make sandwiches. You know I don't really cook that much either, especially dinner, but I can make the basics, spaghetti with meatballs, and baked chicken. I saw you had some chicken rub seasoning. Maybe I'll actually cook us some dinner tonight," Morgan said.

"Okay, that sounds good. So when do you think you'll be home?"

Morgan felt a bit annoyed by the question. She had just gotten to the store and had no idea how long it was going to take her to buy a house worth of groceries. "I don't know, why?"

She wanted to know why he was so curious about when she would be home, especially since they had just spent the past seven days together nonstop. She figured he would probably be welcoming the time by himself by now.

"I just wanted to make sure I was up and ready to help you bring the groceries in," Darrin said.

Morgan felt as if she had a rock in the bottom of her stomach. Now she felt bad about the negative feelings she had about Darrin asking her about her estimated time of arrival home.

"Oh, I really don't know how long it will take since I didn't make a list. I just figured I would go down each aisle and see what we might need."

"Well, why don't you call me when you enter the neighborhood? Then I'll meet you in the garage," Darrin said.

"Sounds like a plan," Morgan said.

"See you soon," Darrin said. "I love you."

"See you, babe, love you," Morgan said and then ended the call.

Chapter 23

The next morning, Morgan awoke at a more sensible time. She saw that Darrin had already left for work. The evening before had been uneventful and quiet. They had both taken the time to unpack all of their belongings from the trip and washed several loads of clothes. Working together they had been able to clean everything and put their items and clothing in their respective places.

The respective place for Morgan's personal and beauty items had been in the half of the bathroom that was deemed the "her's" side of a his-and-hers style design. It was the same with her clothing; she now had half of a his-and-hers closet. Within the walk-in closet were dressers and chests of drawers. The items she had came nowhere near being able to fill up her side of the closet, unlike Darrin's side.

She didn't worry too much about her lack of clothing, because her plan was to fill up the space as soon as she got the chance. She would fill it up with the styles and type of clothing she had always wanted to buy but never had the luxury of freely doing so.

At night's end she had cooked baked chicken with a salad, white rice, and rolls. She had also purchased some powdered lemonade while at the store and had made a pitcher of it for them to drink.

She had set the table for their dinner and turned on some jazz music for them to listen to while eating. Darrin had seemed to be satisfied with the meal and ate it in record time. He'd told her the meal was tasty just before he left the table, giving her a kiss on the forehead. Then he excused himself, telling her he was headed to bed to get some rest before heading back to work the next day.

As she sat there the night before, finishing her meal alone, she was actually glad to finally have some peace and quiet to herself. She wasn't too happy about doing the dishes by herself, but understood that Darrin needed to be fully rested in order to return to his company the next morning.

Now she could finally do what she'd wanted to do since the first day she'd seen the inside of Darrin's house. With him at work she had the whole day to explore. Now that she was Mrs. Hobbs she wanted to see everything she now possessed. He had taken her on a tour of the home upon the first time she'd visited, but she wanted to now see what all the closets held as well as the other bedrooms. She also wanted to check out the attic space he had to see what she might find in there.

She felt like a kid on an expedition. The first place she looked was in the other three bedrooms of the house. Each bedroom had beds, and some type of other bedroom furniture. The smallest bedroom had a twin bed a small dresser and a fake ficus tree in the corner. The closet was full of boxes. Inside the boxes, Morgan found papers that looked like they were from Darrin's business.

In the next bedroom, Morgan found much of the same. This room had a full-sized bed and a dresser, as well as a nightstand with a lamp on it. The dresser drawers and nightstand drawers were empty. The closet of this room had an old printer, a couple of plastic TV trays, and a bookshelf filled with old cassette tapes, VCR tapes, and music CDs.

She closed the door to that room and then opened the door to the last bedroom. In this bedroom, the bed had been taken down and the chest of drawers was pushed up against a back wall. The rest of the room was full of Morgan's items. Darrin had arranged for all of her items to be packed by movers and brought over to his home before they left for Hawaii. He had said he wanted to surprise her and have it done while they were in Hawaii, but couldn't figure out a way to get her key without her knowing.

So he'd had to tell her his plans. While she thought the act to be generous and thoughtful, she was glad he had told her. It gave her a chance to hide any personal belongings that she really didn't want him to see, like the letter her grandmother had sent her. There was no way she wanted Darrin to read whatever her grandmother had written. She still hadn't decided to read the letter herself, although she still couldn't get rid of it. So she packed the letter among other personal papers in a file box. Now as she looked at the boxes and items sitting in the middle of the floor of that room, she was extremely glad she hadn't had to pack it all herself. Within the next few weeks she'd take the time to go through it all and determine what would be kept and what she wouldn't need and would be discarded.

She liked her new home. It was spacious, and had been designed in a way that made it feel like a comfortable home. Their master bedroom was situated upstairs, taking up the front half of the home. They had a sitting area, in addition to the walk-in closet, as well as a bathroom large enough for them to both have their own sink. Their bathroom also had a shower, which was separate from the garden bathtub, and Darrin had also installed a flat-screen television in the bathroom. Now she could watch her favorite television shows while enjoying a hot bath.

By the time she finally made it to the attic it was lunchtime. She debated on eating lunch before checking it out, or waiting until after. Her search of the home thus far had not yielded much of anything interesting. Not sure just how much was or wasn't in there she first decided to at least take a peek. After pulling down the stairs, she ascended them. Seeing a pull string for the light she pulled it to turn on the light bulb. Once the attic was illuminated she saw that there were five boxes.

Not looking forward to going back down the ladder and coming back up, she decided to check the contents of the boxes out while she was already up in the attic. The attic was unfinished; with her bare feet she watched her step, just in case the builder had happened to have left a nail or two lying around.

She opened the flaps of the first box. It was a pretty good-sized box. In it she found Christmas decorations. And in another box sitting on the other side of this box was a long, rectangular box, which she hadn't seen when she first looked. In the long, rectangular box was a Christmas tree. Morgan figured the other three boxes that she'd seen from first glance probably had more Christmas decorations. So she decided to end her expedition and get lunch instead.

As she stepped toward the opening for the ladder she bumped one of the other boxes with her foot by accident. The box started to vibrate and from the inside of the box came a loud laughing sound similar to the sound of the *Sesame Street* character named Elmo. The loud laughing had scared her, causing her to grab her chest with her hand. Her heartbeat seemed to be going a million miles a minute.

The laughing continued and wouldn't stop. Not wanting it to continue much longer she opened the flaps of the box to find out what was making the incessant noise. The box was filled with toys. She pulled them out, tossing them to the side, until she found the red jiggling, laughing Elmo toy.

The toy continued laughing and jiggling in her hand. She felt around the toy's body and looked for an on/off switch. When she found it she quickly switched it off. Taking a deep breath, she willed her heartbeat to return to normal. She wondered if her being startled was strictly from the loud laughing and vibrating box, or if it was because she felt like she was being a snoop in her own home.

She figured it was the latter. It did feel like she was being secretive and snooping in her own home. Old habits were indeed hard to break. She didn't have to sneak around anymore as if she were on some type of secret mission. She had the prize she had been seeking—a man who wasn't bad on the eyes, and had the financial backing to be able to make her happy. She hadn't found love but as far as she was concerned that was okay, because she knew that was overrated.

Once her heartbeat returned normal, Morgan looked back down at the box and the items she had strewn on the attic floor. She had thrown out a football, a soccer ball, and a Frisbee. Inside the box there were a couple of Tonka trucks, a gallon-sized zip-type freezer bag of Lego toys, and pieces to a little racetrack.

She placed the Elmo doll and the other items she'd thrown out back into the box, wondering why Darrin had a box of what looked like a little boy's toys. Seeing the contents of that box helped to pique her curiosity as she now wondered what was in the other boxes.

Opening another box she saw that it held clothing. It was packed full of shorts, pants, socks, shirts, and underclothing. It looked like a little boy's clothing. But upon closer inspection she saw two distinct sizes in the clothing. There were some clothes that were 3T, a size for a toddler, and other clothing that was 5T, more of a size for an older boy. Some of the shirts and shorts she saw were the exact same but just in two different sizes.

One of the smaller T-shirts in the box had the name TLC DAYCARE on the front with the full name TENDER LOVING CARE DAYCARE CENTER on the back and the address of the daycare. Another T-shirt, which was a little bigger, said KINDERGARTEN ROCKS on the front and TRINITY PARK ELEMENTARY SCHOOL on the back. Morgan thought she had heard of the daycare before, but was sure she had passed by the elementary school at some point or another. It was one of the elementary schools in the Silvermont City School District.

Totally dumbfounded, Morgan opened another box. There she found more clothing, but the clothing in this box wasn't for a child or children. It was women's clothing. This box was full of clothing. There were pants, blouses, T-shirts, and dresses, along with socks and even women's undergarments. She had no idea whose clothing was in the box, but she did know the woman didn't have much fashion sense and she didn't shop at any higher-end stores.

Closing that box, she checked the last box. This box was filled with shoes. It looked like the shoes of the child or children and the woman, whose clothes and toys she had just found in the other boxes. Morgan was perplexed.

"Why in the world would Darrin have an attic full of other people's clothing and belongings?" she said out loud to herself.

Her curiosity was up. She searched her memory trying to remember if Darrin had ever said anything to her about any woman and kids. He was an only child and had a cousin who lived in Missouri, but she thought that cousin was a male, not a female. Then she searched her memory for any mention of other cousins and couldn't remember.

When they had talked about family, she had done her best to gloss over her family history. She'd told him that she was an only child raised by her grandmother and that her mother left her at a very young age. She also told him that she had been married once years earlier and had three children, but when she and her husband parted they both agreed it best that the children, both boys, go with their father.

She also told him about a longer-term relationship that she had a year or so prior that had not ended very well. Although she had glossed over the information about her first marriage with him, she could not bring herself to tell Darrin all of the details about her fake marriage to Will. Although it was hard to try to explain, she told Darrin she had a son by the guy in the most recent relationship, but she lied about how their relationship ended. She told Darrin that her ex used to abuse her and threatened to hurt her if she ever tried to get her son from him, so she'd cut her losses, left him, and moved to Silvermont.

She tried her very best not to completely lie to Darrin, but in this instance she had to stretch the truth. The truth had to be stretched just enough that if Darrin did ever meet Will, he wouldn't be completely in the dark. She hoped and even prayed that the two men would never meet. And if they did she would just have to make sure the two never talked enough in order for Darrin to find out the truth about her relationship with Will.

She had given Darrin way more information than she had ever given Will. This was mainly because she did not want her past to completely come back to haunt her like it had with Will. Because of her omission of information and because she really didn't want him to delve too much into the information about her past, Morgan didn't ask too much about his family and past. Now looking at all the boxes in the attic, she wished she asked more, or at least wished she had listened more to what he was saying when he was talking about his life before meeting her.

After descending the stairs of the attic, she folded and pushed them closed, and closed the attic opening. When she got a chance she would ask Darrin about the items in the attic. But she had to time it just right. There was no way she was going to ask him the next time she spoke to him. She didn't want him to think that she had been snooping around the house the first moment she got a chance to, although that was exactly what she had done. She shook it all off and put the questions in the back of her mind for later retrieval.

Overall, she loved everything about the layout of the house, but could not say the same for Darrin's decorating style. He had no style whatsoever. Just like the bedroom with the fake ficus, small dresser, and twin bed, there wasn't much rhyme or reason to the furniture and items Darrin had purchased for his home, other than buying things for functionality. Morgan was going to change all that.

Chapter 24

"'Back to life, back to reality,'" Amber sang.

"I remember that song," Morgan said. "It is by that old group called Soul II Soul right?"

"Yep. How does it feel to be back on the mainland?"

Morgan had just stepped into Amber's office. She closed the door behind her. "In some ways I wish I was still basking in the sun in Hawaii, and in other ways I am glad to be back home."

"Here," Morgan said. She handed Amber a coffee mug, a key chain, a T-shirt, and a lei necklace, all souvenirs from Hawaii. She placed the flowers around Amber's neck.

"Thank you," Amber said. "How do I look?"

"Like you are a native of Hawaii." Morgan handed her another gift. This one was wrapped in tissue paper. "I also got you this."

"What's this?" Amber asked.

"Well open it up and find out," Morgan said.

Amber unwrapped the tissue paper. "Too cute." Amber proceeded to take the little hula Hawaiian girl out of the paper and set it on her desk.

"If you push her little head like this"—Morgan pushed the hula girl's head down—"she will dance and play the ukulele for you."

Just as Morgan had said, the little figurine started moving its little body back and forth. Pre-recorded music sounded from the inside sounding like someone playing a ukulele.

"She is too cute," Amber said.

"Thought I'd bring you back a little bit of Hawaii," Morgan said.

"So did you get all of your stuff moved out of your apartment?" Amber asked.

"Yep, Darrin had movers come and move it for me."

Amber looked at Morgan in disbelief. "Really? He set up the move for your apartment?"

"He set it all up. I didn't have to lift a finger or pay for a thing," Morgan said.

"Really?" Amber looked skeptical.

"What's that look for?"

"That guy is really in to you isn't he?" Amber said.

"Ah yeah, I'd say so." Morgan held up her hand showing her left hand ring finger.

Amber shook her head.

"Seriously, Amber. What is that all for?" Morgan said. She was wondering why the woman she had come to know as a friend was acting as if she had a problem with what her new husband was doing for her. "Is there a problem?"

"Morgan, please don't take this the wrong way, but there is something on my mind. Actually it has been on my mind for a while now, and I am just going to say it," Amber said.

"Go ahead, say it then." Morgan was curious to know just what Amber's problem was.

"I just think you moved way too fast with Darrin," Amber said.

Morgan waited for Amber to say more. "And, is that it?"

"Yeah, in a nutshell."

"What is bringing this all on? And if this has been on your mind for so long then why didn't you say something before now?"

"I didn't want to spoil anything for you. You seem so happy, and I was happy for you," Amber said.

"Yeah, I remember how happy you were. If I remember correctly, you even wanted to know if the man had a brother."

"That's because I was caught up in the moment right along with you. I mean an office full of roses can have a woman seeing the world through rose-colored glasses," Amber said.

Morgan couldn't believe what Amber was saying. It was obvious to her that Amber was just jealous and wasn't really the friend she thought she was. "I see what is going on here. You're just jealous and you don't like the fact that I am so happy."

"Believe me, Morgan, if I weren't your friend I wouldn't be saying any of this to you. I just really think your relationship with this Darrin Hobbs developed really quickly," Amber said.

"Oh, you don't like the fact that Darrin doesn't really care for you," Morgan said.

The one time Darrin had met Amber it hadn't gone well. Darrin had come to the store one afternoon to take Morgan to the food court for lunch. Amber happened to be on the floor talking with Morgan when Darrin had walked up.

Morgan had introduced Amber to Darrin. Amber had been cordial to him, complimenting him on the beautiful roses he'd sent Morgan. But he had treated Amber like she wasn't even standing there, barely saying two words to her.

"Okay, yes, there's that point as well. The feelings are mutual, there's just something about him I don't like. But it's not the main reason. It's as if this guy can snap his fingers and you basically go along with whatever he is saying or doing. I mean I know it's nice to have your stuff in your apartment moved and not have to lift a finger to do it, but didn't you have any personal items that needed to be taken care of? I mean you can't trust just anyone with your stuff, especially movers."

"Not that I have to explain any of this to you, but it's not like he just went behind my back and moved my things. Yes, I did handle my most personal items. So when I said I didn't have to lift a finger, I meant figuratively not literally," Morgan said.

Amber put her hands up in defeat. "Look, let's just drop this," Amber said.

"Yes, let's," Morgan said. She didn't want to continue the conversation, because if it continued she didn't know what she might say. "I think we need to, before I say something I might possibly regret later."

Morgan balled up the tissue paper she was holding in her hand, and threw it in the trash. Then she swung Amber's office door open and left. She figured the couple of people who were working in customer service had probably heard the loud arguing coming from Amber's office and that before the hour was over every employee in the store would be whispering about it.

She wished she could say she didn't care, but she did. Besides Desiree, Amber had been the only person she could call a friend in a very long time. Even though she hated the direction her relationship with Amber was going in, she wasn't going to worry about it for too long. As far as she was concerned, Amber was one in a list of many people who had let her down. She had bounced back from relationship loss in the past, and she had no doubt she would bounce back again. It was just going to be awkward working with the woman day in and day out.

Morgan's mood was foul. She was in no mood to work or greet customers. She called Amber and told her she wasn't feeling well and needed to go home. Amber told her she hoped she felt better soon and she understood.

As she drove home, the more she thought about it, the more she didn't want to go in to a job each day where she had to work with someone she really didn't like or care for. She wondered if she brought the prospect of quitting her job up to Darrin, how he would take it. Maybe he would be agreeable, especially if she told him about her disagreement with Amber. She decided to talk to him when he got home that night.

"Hey, honey," Darrin said as he walked through the front door.

"Hey." Morgan sat up and looked at the clock over the fireplace. She was sitting on the couch in the living room, watching a movie on the Lifetime channel. "You're home early."

She wondered why he was coming through the front door instead of through the garage. Then she saw the mail in his hand and figured he must have checked it and come through the front instead of walking back around to the garage.

"Yeah, still feeling a little jetlag from our trip," Darrin said.

"We have something in common then. I left work early today also," Morgan said.

"Oh really? Is everything okay?" Darrin asked.

Morgan saw this as her opportunity to talk to him about her problems at work. "Well, now that you mention it, no, everything is not okay."

Darrin stopped looking at the mail and directed his attention to Morgan. He walked over to the sofa and sat next to her. "What's wrong?"

"Amber and I had a disagreement today. I think she is jealous of my relationship with you," Morgan said.

Darrin shook his head. "I told you I didn't like that woman. She seems like the jealous type."

"But she is my friend, or at least I thought she was my friend," Morgan said.

"You said it right the second time. You thought she was your friend. I don't know what it is about some women. When they see their friends happy or when they see them in a great relationship they want to act jealous and try to break up a good relationship. Shoot, half the time they only do it to try to get the man for themselves," Darrin said.

"You think Amber wants to try to take you from me?" Morgan said.

"Probably, you never know. I mean, you said you've only known the woman a short time right?"

"Yeah," Morgan said. She thought about how ironic it was that Amber had basically just said the same thing to her earlier about only knowing Darrin for a short time.

"Well, obviously she isn't the friend you thought she was. I would steer away from her if I were you."

"That could be hard since I have to work with the woman," Morgan said.

"No, you don't," Darrin said.

"Huh?"

"You don't have to work with her," Darrin said. "Quit."

"Huh?" Morgan said again. She wondered if Darrin was somehow reading her mind.

"I understand you were working there before because you had to make ends meet for yourself. Well, I'm here now. You don't have to go into someplace for work where you feel like you're not wanted. Go in tomorrow and tell them you are resigning effective immediately," Darrin said.

Morgan couldn't believe Darrin had gone along with her plans to leave the job before she had even brought up the prospect herself. It was as if he and she were in perfect sync.

"Do you know what you are saying?"

"I know exactly what I am saying, Morgan. No wife of mine has to feel as if she is demeaned at work."

"You do know that means that I'll be at home, not bringing a paycheck in," Morgan said.

Darrin put both his hands on Morgan's cheeks. "Sweetheart, I didn't marry you for your paycheck. I can well take care of us and this household."

She knew this fact to be true, it was one of the reasons she had married him.

He kissed her forehead and released her cheeks. "So if you want to go out and find another job you can, if you want to sit home you can do that to. I know you wanted to go back to school. You can enroll at Carson State University and take some classes. Whatever will make you happy, my dear."

Morgan sat with her bottom lip dropped. She could not believe what she was hearing. Darrin had just said the words that were answers to her dreams. Choosing him had been the right choice. He was more than able and willing to give her the life she thought she always deserved.

"So go in there tomorrow and let them know you're quitting," Darrin said. "Oh and here." Darrin stood and pulled his wallet out of his pocket. He pulled out his American Express black card and handed it to her. Looking around the living room he said, "This house could use a little sprucing up. It needs woman's touch, do you think you can help me out with that?"

Morgan screamed, jumped up, and hugged Darrin tighter than she had ever hugged anyone else in her life. "I love you!"

Chapter 25

Morgan thought it was crazy that the first time she had ever told Darrin she loved him and actually meant it had been the evening before. She thought about the saying that went something like "money can't buy you love" and figured whoever said it obviously had not had enough money.

She pulled her car into a parking space, and entered the store through the employee entrance just as she always did. Her destination was Amber's office. Just as she hoped, Amber was sitting at her desk. Morgan knocked on the office door with two quick taps.

Amber looked up. "Hey, Morgan."

"Hey, Amber," Morgan said. She had no desire to be cordial or stay long.

"Morgan, I really want to apologize for the way I acted yesterday and what I said. I shouldn't have said anything to you about my thoughts. If you are happy then I am happy."

"That's just it, Amber. I'm not happy. Yesterday you showed me your true colors. So thank you for your apology, but no, thank you," Morgan said.

Amber's mouth dropped wide open.

"I am here to tell you that I am resigning, effective immediately," Morgan said.

"Morgan, what . . . Why . . . Don't . . ." Amber kept starting sentences but couldn't complete them.

"That's all. I wish you the best, Amber, and I hope you are a true friend to whoever you befriend next."

Morgan left the office, not wanting to talk any further. She thought she'd handled the situation very well. She was calm, civil, and kept her voice down. There wasn't anyone who would be able to say they heard a loud argument coming from Amber's office after she left this time.

With the American Express black card Darrin had given her to use, there was only one regret she had about quitting her job. Now that she'd quit, she didn't want to linger further in the store. There were quite a few items she would have loved to have bought from the housewares department but her pride wouldn't let her. She would have to settle for her second-favorite store, which was located right there in the mall: Macy's. As quickly as her feet would take her, Morgan headed toward the three-story Macy's, ready to check out all three floors.

Morgan carefully backed her car into the garage. The trunk, back seat, and passenger side front seat were all full of packages. She'd had the shopping spree of her life as she envisioned all the changes she wanted to make in her new home. As soon as she picked up the first new item for the house, Morgan forgot about Amber and the job she'd just quit.

Although she was pleased with the purchases she'd made, she was disappointed that her little Hyundai Accent wasn't big enough to contain everything she had wanted to buy. She pulled her first few purchases out of the car.

So far she had purchased a new bedroom ensemble for the master bedroom, which was painted light brown so she decided to use red and purple for the accent colors. Red was her favorite color, and Darrin loved the purple and gold of his fraternity colors. When she placed the red and purple cloth swatches together in the store and compared them to the bedding she liked it matched perfectly.

She purchased a complete Ralph Lauren bedding set with the accent pillows and duvet covers. To accompany the bedding set she purchased three sets of 800-thread-count deep-pocket sheets, one in red, another in purple, and the last one in light brown. When she saw the perfect lamps for their matching nightstands, she'd scooped them up and placed them in her shopping cart as well. Eventually she wanted to look for an area rug for the master bathroom and, at the rate she was going, "eventually" was bound to be sooner than she thought.

For the bathroom she found a set of rugs that were textured and had memory foam that would match the turquoise and white and burnt orange colors she was using as a theme in the bathroom. The bathroom's color scheme was inspired by a hand towel that was embellished with an embroidered colorful bird. Everything in the bathroom seemed brown or bronze, from the floor to the countertops and even the faucets. The colors would bring out the dark brown interior of the master bathroom.

She couldn't wait to put her new bedding set on her bed and decorate the bathroom with its new accessories. That would have to wait, because she needed to make another trip to her car to pull out the window treatments she'd bought for the windows in the master bedroom, the living room, and the bonus room. By the time she finished unloading the car her feet hurt so much she had to take her shoes off to rub her feet. She'd seen a foot massager at the store and put it on her mental list of items to purchase when she went back to the store the next day.

**

The doorbell rang. Morgan placed the plate of finger sandwiches she'd made down on the island in her kitchen. Usually no one ever came to visit, not even Martha, who seemed to be busy most of the time. Martha had such a good time on her trip to Hawaii that she had taken to traveling somewhere every other month or so. This was one of her months, and the last e-mail Martha had sent said she was in San Francisco, California.

She padded to the door in her house slippers, and opened the door without even looking out to see who was there. Today she was expecting Desiree. Morgan had finally finished putting the finishing touches on the house. Her redecorating project was complete. She had wanted to show someone the fruits of her labor.

Calling Amber had been out of the question. They still were not on speaking terms. She figured Amber probably wouldn't mind talking to her, especially since she apologized to her that day she'd quit her job, but as far as Morgan was concerned, there was nothing left for the two of them to talk about. She was finished with Amber, and was mad at herself for even thinking the woman's name when it came to sharing her decorating celebration. So she called Desiree, knowing she would appreciate all Morgan had done, especially once she showed Desiree the before pictures.

She opened the door, and there smiling was her buddy Desiree, who was holding a bottle of sparkling apple cider.

"This is for you," Desiree said. She handed it to Morgan.

"You didn't have to bring anything. I told you that over the phone," Morgan said.

"Girl, you ain't going to invite me over to your swanky house in this swanky neighborhood and expect me not to bring a housewarming gift."

"Come on in here, you crazy woman. This isn't a housewarming," Morgan said.

Desiree stepped in. Morgan closed the door behind her.

"It might as well be a housewarming. It's your new house and it's my first time coming to visit you."

"Come on in," Morgan said. "Oh, but leave your shoes at the door."

Desiree slipped her shoes off. "See I told you it was swanky around here."

"Girl, shut up," Morgan said in a playful tone. "Come in the kitchen."

Desiree followed Morgan to the kitchen. Desiree ran her fingers across the smooth granite tabletop. "Whooo weee. This place is nice." She took a seat on one of the stools next to the island.

"I feel like I've died and gone to heaven." Desiree sniffed the air. "What's that smell? It smells like you're baking something."

"I hate to disappoint, but I barely cook and I don't bake. It's a sugar cookie candle," Morgan said.

"Oh."

"No worries. I've got some finger sandwiches for us to eat, and I bought a cheese Danish from the grocery store earlier," Morgan said.

"Sandwiches and cheese Danish works for me," Desiree said.

"Okay." Morgan clapped her hands excitedly. "I am so excited. I have something for you to look at." Morgan pulled out the picture portfolio she had compiled from the before and after pictures Darrin had taken for her. He'd thought of the idea of her starting a portfolio for school. She handed the portfolio to Desiree.

"What's this?"

"It is a portfolio of the before and after pictures of the designing I did here at the house. I want you to tell me what you think. Then after I'll take you on a tour to see the work I did in person."

Desiree started flipping through the pictures. "Oooh. Ahhh." She pointed to a couple of pictures and again said, "Oooh. Ahhh."

After about the third time Desiree had said, "Oooh," and "Ahhh,' Morgan had thought the woman was making a joke.

"Are you trying to be funny?" Morgan asked.

"No, not in the least," Desiree said without looking up at Morgan. She continued flipping through pictures. "Nice. Great," Desiree said.

When she finished looking at the pictures Desiree said. "This is all so really nice." She looked around Morgan's kitchen. "Miss Centerfold has finally made it to the big time."

Morgan gave Desiree a stern look. "Enough, Desiree."

"Sorry, I was wrong for that. Will you accept my apology?"

"Yes, just don't do it again," Morgan said.

"I won't, I won't," Desire promised.

"Okay, so you've seen the before and after. What do you honestly think?" Morgan asked.

"I honestly think that if I had any money I'd hire you to design my apartment. You've got a gift for what you are doing. Not everybody does."

"Do you think so?" Morgan asked.

"Yes, I know so. The Lord is looking out for you. He has given you this great talent, and He has obviously blessed you."

"Life is good," Morgan said.

"Girl, give credit where credit is due. God is good," Desiree said. "Go ahead and say it, you know I'm right."

"God is good," Morgan said with less zeal than Desiree had. She had to admit the Lord had come through for her right during the times that she needed Him. But she often still wondered why He couldn't have come through for her years ago to have helped her in her marriage to Frank, and to have helped her keep her children, and most of all to have made it so that she would not have been so bitter for years. Her heart had been cold as ice and it seemed like it was just starting to thaw.

"Let me show you around; then we can come back and eat some sandwiches and relax," Morgan said.

She showed Desiree all of the changes she'd made and the other changes she wanted to make. While she was showing her around she also told her about wanting to get registered for college soon.

After the tour was over the two women sat in the kitchen and ate the finger sandwiches Morgan had prepared, and they sipped on the sparkling apple cider Desiree had brought as a housewarming gift. Then Morgan warmed up the cheese Danish in the microwave for a few seconds and they each ate a piece.

"Desiree, it's been great talking to you and catching up. I really miss being able to talk to friends," Morgan said. She hadn't really felt comfortable calling Desiree before now. For some reason, she still got the feeling that Darrin didn't care for any of her friends. And when she tried to make more friends he seemed to frown at that prospect as well.

Over the last few weeks, Darrin had been a workaholic. He left early in the mornings and came home late at night. They had hardly gone out anymore. The one time they had gone out, it was to a community function and Morgan had felt more like a trophy piece the whole night as Darrin treated her like that was what she actually was.

At first she really hadn't minded because she was so engrossed in her interior design project. But after that slowed down, she really started to notice his lack of attention and time toward her. When she'd mentioned something about their not spending as much time together, Darrin had explained to her that he needed to work to make sure they had all the luxuries she was so comfortable with having. She understood this well enough, but still something just didn't set right with her.

Desiree took her last bite of her cheese Danish. "You miss being able to talk to friends? What do you mean? You can call me anytime."

"I know, but—" As soon as she started the sentence her cell phone rang. The caller ID displayed Darrin's name.

Without consciously thinking, Morgan signaled for Desiree to keep quiet in the background by putting her finger up to her mouth.

"Hello," Morgan said.

"Hey, babe."

"Hey, Darrin," Morgan replied. "What's up?" She hoped she didn't sound too conspicuous like she was trying to hide something, when she was indeed trying to hide the fact that Desiree was there visiting.

"You know how you've been telling me you want to spend some time together and go somewhere?" Darrin asked.

"Uh, yeah."

"I want you to know I've been listening, and you're right. We haven't been out in a while. So I am on my way home now. Pick any restaurant you want for dinner and we'll go there tonight."

For a reason she couldn't really explain, her heart started to beat faster. She glanced over at Desiree. "You're on your way home now?"

Desiree perked up as if excited to be finally meeting Morgan's new husband.

"Yep, I should be there in about ten minutes. Why?" Darrin asked. "Are you busy?"

"No, no, I'm not busy. I was just about to step in the shower. I went for a walk a little while ago and am sweaty. I just wanted to know. I will probably be in the shower when you get here, that's all." Morgan knew she wasn't making much sense. But her senses told her it would be in her best interest to have Desiree out of the house before Darrin got home.

"Okay. I'll see you when I get home," Darrin said.

"Okay, see you when you get here," Morgan said.

"Oh, yeah, Morgan," Darrin said.

"Yeah?"

"I love you."

Morgan replied, "Love you too."

Morgan hung up the phone. There was something about the way and tone in which he'd told Morgan he loved her. It was like he was up to something, in a bad way, not a good way.

"Is something wrong?" Desiree asked.

"Why do you ask?"

"Girl, you look like a nervous wreck. You were just fine before your husband called. Not to mention that you didn't tell him I was here visiting and you flat-out lied about going for a walk. You are sweaty looking with those beads of sweat popping out all over your forehead," Desiree said.

"Honestly, Desiree, I wish I could tell you. I wish I could put my finger on it but I can't," Morgan said.

"Put your finger on what? What can't you tell me?" Desiree put her hands on her hips; then she flat out asked, "Is that man beating you?"

"No, no, Desiree, it's nothing like that," Morgan said.

"It better not be. I think I know you well enough to know that you wouldn't let a man put two fingers on you," Desiree said.

"No, that isn't something I'd put up with," Morgan said. She took a couple of deep breaths. "Okay, let me think. I need to think."

The two women were quiet for a few moments.

Morgan stood. She went to a drawer and pulled out a zip plastic bag and a paper towel. In a louder-than-usual and a more jovial voice than she really felt like speaking in Morgan said, "Desiree, it's been great. Girl, we'll have to do this again sometime. Maybe in a few months after I've had a chance to start school and all." Morgan prayed Desiree would take the hint that she was trying to get her out of the house.

Desiree stood.

Morgan cut a piece of cheese Danish, wrapped it in a paper towel, then pulled the aluminum foil box out of a drawer. With her head held down she tugged at the foil as if she was having trouble getting it off of the roll and having problems wrapping the cheese Danish.

She tried to whisper over the noise, hoping Desiree could hear her. "He doesn't really like my friends. And to tell you the truth, I don't think he wants me to have any friends. I also have a feeling he is somehow keeping track of my every move. So without complicating things more please go along with what I am doing."

Desiree gave Morgan a nod to indicate she'd heard her.

As if she had finally gotten the foil straight, back in the louder, jovial voice Morgan said, "Here is a piece of Danish for you to take with you."

Desiree said, "Thank you." She stood. Mimicking what Morgan was doing, she then said, "Girl, look at the time. I really need to be getting out of here. It has been great and maybe we can do this again sometime in the future."

Morgan walked Desiree to the door.

Desiree whispered, "You call me when you can. I don't like any of this one bit. Something ain't right with this situation."

Morgan looked up and down the street. In a loud voice she waved and said, "Okay, you take care now."

Desiree left down the stairs, got in her car, and drove off. As soon as Morgan was sure Desiree was out of sight, she closed the door and headed to her bathroom. Once she was in the bathroom she closed the door and locked it. She turned the shower on and let it run while she sat on the edge of the tub.

Her friend hadn't lied when she said that Morgan looked as if she had actually been out walking and sweating in the sun. Something wasn't right. There were things in the back of Morgan's mind that she'd been ignoring. One thing was the fact that Darrin really hadn't wanted her to have any friends. It was evident by the way she'd acted when he had called. She felt as if she had to lie to him about her company being there. Her conscious mind hadn't registered that information, but her subconscious mind had.

There was something else that was bothering her even more. From their first date, Morgan had been having a sense that Darrin had a sixth sense; it was like he had some kind of intuition when it came to her. She couldn't count the number of times he'd called her when she got home to her apartment after they'd had a date, or even a lot of times when she got off work.

It was true that back when they were dating the distance between his home to her apartment was about twenty-two minutes, give or take a minute or so. She had told him that once, but not in the beginning. The phone calls he'd been making to check and make sure his special lady was safe had started before her conversation about distance. There was another thing that she started to think about as well. There were a few occasions when she had stopped for gas, or at the grocery store to pick up items on her way to her apartment as well, and he always seemed to have that uncanny perfect timing; even on that night she had gotten stopped for speeding, he had called as soon as she reached her apartment. She started to think the timing was way too perfect—no one could be that clairvoyant.

Then she shuddered. His uncanny timing had heightened even more after they got married. She realized that just about every time she left home, Darrin called her and it seemed to be when reached her destination or very soon after. The first time he had done the very same thing the day after they got back from their honeymoon. She had just arrived at the grocery store. Other memories continued to come to light in her mind.

She had no idea how much time had passed since she'd locked herself in the bathroom. Darrin would probably be home at any moment. She quickly went ahead and got into the shower, so that her story from earlier might seem plausible. But deep down she had a feeling Darrin already knew what the real story was. He seemed to have perfect timing with that phone call as well.

If she wasn't mistaken, Desiree had just taken her last bite of cheese Danish when her cell phone rang. Even though the shower was steaming hot, Morgan got a chill that ran directly down her spine.

Chapter 26

Morgan sat on the couch in her living room, flipping channels on the television. It had been three hours since Darrin had called to tell her he'd be home in ten minutes. Finally she heard the garage door opening.

Her body was feeling an abundance of emotions. She was angry, worried, anxious, steamed, and scared all at the same time. She was angry because Darrin was three hours late getting home and hadn't called to tell her where he was. Morgan had called Darrin's cell phone. He wasn't answering so she had left several messages on his voice mail. She was worried, wondering what had happened to him.

She was also anxious because she had a strong nagging feeling that her husband was somehow keeping tabs on her. In the same instance she was highly steamed because her husband might be keeping tabs on her. Overall, for the first time in her life, she was scared.

The garage door opened and then shut.

"Honey, I'm home," she heard Darrin call out. He rounded the corner of the living room. "Did you get my message?"

She turned the volume on the television down with the remote control. "No, what message?" Morgan asked.

"I had to turn around and go back to work. I tried to call you but it went straight to your voice mail."

Morgan picked up her cell phone. There weren't any missed calls. There weren't any voice mails either. "I don't see a missed call or a message from you."

"Oh, man, I am sorry about that," Darrin said. He leaned over and gave her a kiss on her forehead. "Have you eaten yet?

For some reason Morgan started to wonder if Darrin had been on his way home in the first place. She felt she had to be cautious in anything she said to him. "Yeah, I made some sandwiches earlier and ate some of those."

"Good. Maybe we can try to go out tomorrow night. I am beat," Darrin said.

"There are some more sandwiches in there if you want some," Morgan said.

"Ah, no, that's okay. I actually grabbed a bite when I had to make that U-turn to return to the office. That is part of what I told you on the message I left. But you didn't get it." Darrin chuckled. "Modern technology is something else isn't it? Sometimes it can be a man's best friend and other times it can let you down."

Morgan chuckled. She hadn't made the sound because she was amused. She wasn't amused in the least. She'd made the sound because right then and there she felt as if she was having an out-of-body experience; it was like she was floating above the room and watching the actions of the two people in the room play out. She wanted to tell the woman sitting on the couch to run. Like in the Hasbro company's game of Monopoly she needed to pass "Go" and do so very quickly.

Darrin sat on the loveseat adjacent to the sofa. "So how was your day?" he asked. His tone sounded light and refreshed, showed no sign of the tiredness he said he was feeling just a few minutes before.

Morgan shifted the remote control from hand to hand. "Pretty uneventful," Morgan said. Something in her own intuition told her she needed to go ahead and tell him that Desiree had come by earlier.

"Nothing happened today?" Darrin asked.

Morgan felt like she was being baited and knew her intuition was correct. Somehow and someway Darrin already knew about Desiree coming over to the house earlier.

"Nothing big. My friend Desiree came over. I showed her the portfolio." There, she'd told him.

Darrin sat back as if satisfied with her answer. "Have I met her?"

"No, not yet. She's pretty busy and I'll be pretty busy here soon with school and all. So I don't know when you two will get a chance to meet," Morgan said.

"Oh, well, that's too bad," Darrin said as if satisfied that Morgan wouldn't be seeing her friend anytime soon.

Morgan stood. "Here, do you want the remote?" She extended it to him.

Darrin took the remote control.

She started to leave the room.

"Hey, where are you going? I just got home. I thought we were talking," Darrin said.

"Sorry. I am headed to the office to look up the information for Carson State University's fashion merchandising and interior design programs. I also want to see what I need to do to register," Morgan said. At that moment she wanted to be as far away from Darrin as she could be. Something was very wrong and it wasn't all in her mind. She started to walk out.

Darrin hit his forehead like he had forgotten something. "I forgot to tell you about the program I checked out for you."

Morgan turned around. "What program?"

"I checked out a very good online program. They have a school of design and the best part is you can take most of the classes right here from home. I think the guy in admissions said you'll have to go to their campus once or twice to do some onsite training," Darrin said. "I thought I told you about it."

Morgan couldn't believe what she was hearing. Darrin had been making calls on her behalf for college. Had he done this a couple of days before, she would have thought the gesture thoughtful on his part. He was just being the ever supportive husband. Now was different because she saw his actions in an entirely different light.

"You took time out of your busy schedule to look up schools for me?" Morgan asked. "Did you check out Carson State?"

"Nah, I think going online would be the best. You don't want to have to go over to campus five or six times a week. Going to school online will be so much more convenient for you," Darrin said.

She was starting to believe that going to school online would be far more convenient for him. The realization hit her that he didn't want her to go anywhere, he wanted to know her every move, and he didn't want her socializing with anyone else but him. She had no true friends to speak of except for Desiree and Martha. She had alienated Amber all because of the concerns Amber had about Darrin.

It was all too clear that Darrin didn't want her seeing Desiree anymore, and she wondered just how long it would take for Darrin to find a reason for her not to talk to Martha anymore. For a brief moment Morgan second-guessed herself. For a brief moment she thought about all that was happening and seeming to come to light and she wondered if it was really as big as she was

making it in her mind. She had done some crazy things
to Will when they were together, making him second-
guess himself. Karma was a funny thing; sometimes it
came back to bite a person. What went around often
came back around.

"Do we have anything sweet in the kitchen to eat?
I've got a taste for something sweet," Darrin said.

That settled it. None of what was happening was
strictly in Morgan's mind. Darrin knew that Desiree
had come to visit that day. He also somehow knew
she and Desiree had cheese Danish with their lunch.
She wasn't sure if it was some sort of sound recording
device, or some type of video recording device, but she
knew he had something.

Morgan herself had done some dirt in the past, but
now she had changed. Because of the dirt she had done
in the past, she knew that Darrin wasn't on the up and
up. She really didn't want to go back to her old ways.
She hadn't really liked herself back then. The old Morgan from a year ago would have fought fire with fire.
The new Morgan had lost that type of fight. She just
wanted things simple and to move smoothly. She was
starting to realize the single life she'd had just before
meeting Darrin hadn't been all that bad.

To Will she had portrayed herself as being pure and
close to being perfect, but she had been nobody's angel.
Now that she was seeing Darrin in a whole new light,
she would be darned if she would let him get the best
of her. He was running some type of sick game. She
wasn't into playing games and Darrin would soon find
out she was nobody's fool.

Chapter 27

Morgan hadn't slept a wink the whole night. Darrin, on the other hand, slept like a newborn baby. All she could think about were the events from the previous day and events prior that now seemed to be like red flags in the sand trying to warn her about Darrin. Reality was slapping her in the face and the karma was now openly taunting her.

She'd seen a Lifetime movie once about a woman whose husband was full of jealousy and didn't want her to associate with anyone else. He didn't want her to get a job, leave the house, socialize with others, or even go out into the yard. Eventually the man took her to a cabin in the woods and locked her up.

Morgan didn't think Darrin was sick enough to try to lock her up in some cabin in the woods, but knew she couldn't put it past him, because she really didn't know him. Amber had been right about that point. What had she really known about the man? She knew he made at least six figures; she also knew he would give her almost anything she wanted. He dated her, wined and dined her, and the superficial part of her bought it all; hook, line, and sinker.

Then he proceeded to alienate her from the world: people at work, her friends, and he probably would have alienated her from her family as well if she had any contact with them. She had been 100 percent stupid, letting her lust for the finer things in life overshadow any good sense she had. In the Lifetime movie the woman ended up going to a support group for battered women. Even though the husband hadn't abused her physically, he had abused her in an economical way. It was something about getting the victim to be totally financially dependent on a person.

It made Morgan think about her own situation. Was she totally dependent on Darrin? The answer was yes. She didn't have any income that she could call her own. In a way, that was Darrin's fault, but it was also her fault. When he offered her the chance to quit her job, she had basically jumped at it. Again the superficial side of her was happier with going shopping than thinking about her own wellbeing. What did it matter if she had all the finest things in the world if she couldn't really share them? What did it matter if she had beautiful and expensive clothes to wear if she could only wear them in the house? And what good would it do if Darrin bought her a new Mercedes-Benz if it was only going to be parked in the garage? It was no good at all.

That morning after Darrin got up and went to work, Morgan also went to work. She got a notepad and found a felt-tip fine-point marker. She sat at the desk in the office and pretended to be looking at the Carson State University Web site and other online schools. Because the computer held a history of Web sites visited she hadn't wanted Darrin to know what she was really up to.

She had no idea what kind of full extent Darrin was up to when it came to monitoring her movements. For all she knew he might have a computer program that told him what she was doing on the computer in real time. He could be looking at the same sites she was looking at.

One thing she did know was that the camera on a computer could record a person without them really realizing it. This had been a lesson she'd learned the hard way. So she was very careful about what she did and how she did it in front of the computer.

As she surfed the Internet, looking at school Web sites, she wrote a list on her notepad. She used the felt-tip pen because it wouldn't leave an impression on the paper after she tore the top sheet off. She couldn't put anything past Darrin. He might pick up the pad and try to see what she wrote through the impression left on the page. Her activities equaled those of a paranoid person, but something told her that in her situation, paranoia was just what she needed.

On the notepad she jotted notes. She had to get her thoughts out on paper. She had an idea about Darrin's seemingly on-point intuition about her whereabouts. One thing she wanted to check out was if there was such a thing as a vehicle tracking system. She'd seen them in high-impact movies, but wondered if the average, everyday person could actually buy a system and put it on someone's car to track them. It would have been easy to look the information up on the computer about car tracking devices, right then and there, but then she would run the risk of Darrin checking the computer's history of Web sites visited.

The next thing she jotted down was the name of a cab company that she often saw driving around the streets of Silvermont. When she was outside and out of any kind of video recording devices' recording range, her plan was to call them. She had a theory and she was going to test that theory today. She was going to take a few trips, four to be exact. Two of the trips would be by car and the other two trips would be by taxicab. One of her trips was going to be to the library so that she could get on the Internet to research car tracking devices and video and audio recording devices.

At eight thirty-five she turned on the television, just like she did most mornings. Not sure if there was just an audio recording device or if there was also a video recording device, she took her chances and walked around the border of her living room, then through her dining room, and outside to her back deck. If Darrin was indeed recording her, she hoped it was with a simple audio device. If that were the case he'd hear the television and merely think she was watching it.

If she was quick and the taxicab came in a timely manner, she'd be back in the house within the hour. The closest library was only two miles away. If she'd had the luxury of time then she could have simply walked there and back. Time was not a luxury, not today. She walked two blocks down from her home and called the taxi to meet her at the corner of her street and the block's cross street.

Within five minutes the taxi was there, and within another five minutes she was at the library. The taxi driver had looked at her strange, probably because of how short the distance was between where she had been picked up and the library. What did it matter? She paid him the fare and made a beeline for the library's front door.

There was hardly anyone in the library using the computers, so she was able to immediately get on one. When she logged in the computer let her know the session would be thirty minutes. She could probably do what she needed to do in thirty minutes.

Her search for car tracking devices yielded the information she was seeking. Sure enough, it was possible for a person to have an aftermarket car tracking device put on a car. There were many types and they were not cheap. The only way for her to possibly know for sure was to do a full search of the car to see if there was some type of foreign-looking device on it. The only problem was, she didn't know much about cars and except for the engine, everything else looked foreign. With her luck she might accidentally pull her alternator or carburetor out by accident.

Next she searched video and audio recording devices. At first she found home video recording devices, which had cameras she was accustomed to seeing in places of business and also in some people's homes for their security systems. Darrin didn't have any of these systems. So she did another search this time, typing in the key words Hidden Video Cameras. Her head started to swim when she checked out a Web site that sold equipment that was mainly for the purpose of providing hidden cameras.

There were over a hundred products that looked like everyday common appliances that people used all the time. There were alarm clocks and wall clocks with hidden cameras, coat hooks, wall outlets, air purifiers and fans, lamps, smoke detectors, a thermostat cover, a fake plant, and even a fake rock. There was a nanny teddy cam, which was a teddy bear with a hidden camera in it and computer flash drive with a camera. But the thing that blew her away the most was the smart phone dock station that had not only a hidden camera but also a DVR.

They had that very same docking station at home sitting on the kitchen counter. She used the station to charge her cell phone all the time. Morgan was completely floored.

A window popped up on the computer, letting her know she had only five minutes left. The window also let her know that if she wanted to add an additional fif-

teen minutes she could do so. So she did. She came to
the realization that there were at least ten very similar
everyday household items throughout their home.

The items ranged in price from a key chain being the lowest at $29.95 to the highest of $649 for a
fully functioning, everyday-looking garden hose reel/
holder. "Wow," Morgan said out loud and to no one in
particular.

This same site also had real-time GPS trackers that
could be used for an automobile, or for a computer.
There were also cell phone and computer monitoring
devices. Morgan thought her investigative skills were
good, but anybody with this type of equipment would
clearly be at expert status. If she'd had this kind of stuff
back in the day, then she would have really been dan-
gerous.

Her extended time was up, and she needed to get
back home. Just as she thought, she had not received
a phone call from Darrin. But she was willing to bet
when she went out on her second outing she would get
a call from him like clockwork.

By the time four o'clock came around, Morgan's sus-
picions were confirmed. When she took her two trips
out of the house by taxicab, Darrin didn't call her. As
soon as she ventured out and got to the grocery store,
her cell phone rang before she even got a chance to lock
her car door with her key fob.

What baffled her was trying to figure out when he
would have had a chance to place such a device on
her car. Then for some reason she remembered the
first act of thoughtfulness he'd done for her. It was the
time he'd borrowed her car and then filled it with gas
and had it detailed. It seemed strange at the time, and
now she thought she knew why. He'd had it detailed all
right. He had detailed it with a GPS system.

Chapter 28

Her last trip out in her car had been to pick up Japanese food. She ordered a Japanese dish called yakisoba, which consisted of fried ramen-style noodles, cabbage, onions, and carrots. There was also a yakisoba sauce on it and she'd asked the restaurant to add pork.

By the time Darrin came home she'd had time to process much of the information that she'd learned today about hidden recording devices and car tracking. She was also able to process the fact that Darrin wanted to keep her under his thumb—he wanted to control her each and every move. It was something she wasn't agreeable to. Now she just had to figure out how to get out of the mess she'd gotten herself into.

She set the table in the dining room for dinner. For now she would act as if she really missed him and wanted them to spend more quality time together. If his goal was for her to only want to spend time with him, then she would do just that.

It wasn't about playing games; it was about being smart. She would watch his every move, trying to figure out if she could detect any clues as to when, where, and how he was monitoring her. Morgan looked at each and everything in her house in a whole new light now; almost anything could have a camera in it.

There was something to be said about keeping friends close, but keeping enemies even closer. She needed Darrin to think she was clueless about the sneaky things he'd been doing to keep tabs on her and his vision about how their marriage should operate. Hopefully playing clueless would give her time to figure out how to handle the whole situation. Right then she had no idea.

Then as if a light clicked on in her head, Morgan knew exactly what to do. She didn't have to rack her brain; she would use her brain instead. Darrin would be home soon, so she didn't have much time. Morgan ascended the stairs, heading straight to her master bathroom. The toilet in the master bathroom was closed off in its own little room to which the door could be closed.

The only things in that room was a picture she'd purchased herself, the toilet paper with its holder, and the light switch. This was the only room in the house in which Morgan thought there wasn't any kind of surveillance-type equipment. She closed the lid on the toilet, sat down, and switched the light off, just in case she'd missed something. The paranoia she was experiencing was nerve-racking.

Morgan leaned over, clasped her hands together, and bowed her head, before praying in silence. *Dear Lord. Dear, dear Lord. I have really gotten myself into a mess this time. Of course you already know this. I think everybody already knew but me. I got myself into this and I know I should be the one to get myself out of it, but I really don't know how.*

It seems complicated, but it's not. I guess the easy thing to do would be to just cut my losses and leave, but somehow I don't think Darrin would go for that so easily. He might try to give me some resistance. And at one time in my life, Lord, you know I would have done my best to resist him as well, fighting toe to toe.

I don't want to fight anymore, Lord. I just want some peace. I want the kind of peace that doesn't come with headaches. Please keep me safe, Lord. Please give me the answers I'll need to take care of this mess I'm in.

I have all trust in you that you will see me through this, so I thank you in advance. Thank you, Lord. In Jesus' name I pray. Amen.

Morgan stood and reached for the light switch. When she did, a scripture and song with parts of the scripture's words came to mind. She thought, *no weapon formed against me shall prosper.* She made it back into the kitchen at the same time Darrin was coming through the door.

"Hey, honey," Darrin said.

"Hey," Morgan said. "How was your day?"

"Great, absolutely great. Very productive."

"My day was productive as well," Morgan said. "I picked up the items we needed from the grocery store and I picked up dinner for us. It is ready and on the table."

Darrin looked at the dining room table. "Smells great. What is it?"

"Japanese yakisoba. It's sort of like Chinese Lo mein noodles. It's got vegetables, and pork," Morgan said. "It might have gotten a little cold. I'll warm it."

"You do that, I need to run upstairs and get out of this tie," Darrin said. He headed for the stairs.

"Okay, you do that. I'll have it warmed up by the time you come back down."

"I'll be right back," Darrin said.

By the time Darrin returned, Morgan had the food on their plates. They held hands, bowed their heads, and said grace. Then they both dug into their plates of food. With all the running around Morgan had done that day she hadn't had a thing to eat.

Darrin was eating like he hadn't had a bite to eat all day either. She wondered what he had been doing to make him so hungry. Then she realized, he had probably been engrossed in trying to keep up with her.

"So did anything eventful happen at the office today?" Morgan asked, trying to make light conversation.

"Nothing too . . ." Darrin's voice trailed off. He started scratching his throat area. He took a sip from the glass of water Morgan had placed on the table. In addition to scratching his throat, he started scratching his chest and arms. "What did you say was in this Japanese food?"

"Fried noodles, vegetables, and pork," Morgan said. "Why?"

Darrin clutched at his throat. He picked the water glass back up and tried to drink some more water. "Is there seafood in this?"

"No, there shouldn't be. Well I don't think there is. They didn't say there was," Morgan said.

She felt like she was talking a mile a minute as she was starting to understand what was going on. Darrin was having an allergic reaction to something.

Darrin stood. He started wheezing. "I need to get to the hospital."

Morgan dropped her fork, stood, and went into the kitchen to grab her purse and keys. Luckily she hadn't taken them upstairs. They both headed to the garage, and Morgan yelled for Darrin to get into her car. She hadn't wanted to fumble with her keys and adjust Darrin's seats in his car. They needed to get to the hospital.

With her hazard lights flashing she drove as fast as she could, being careful to not get in an accident or cause an accident. Eleven minutes after they left home they arrived at the emergency room door. She swung her car door open and helped Darrin open his car door, since he was fumbling with the door.

After helping him get out of the car, she also helped Darrin walk into the building. "Help, somebody help me, please. My husband is having some kind of allergic reaction."

By now Darrin's lips and face had started to swell. Everything was happening fast; someone had led Darrin to a wheelchair and they wheeled him to the back of the emergency room.

"Ma'am, can you stay here while we get some information from you?" the woman at the reception area said.

"Yes." Morgan looked toward the doors which Darrin had just been taken through. "Is he going to be okay?" Morgan asked. "Is he going to die?" She was near frantic.

The main thought going through Morgan's mind was that Darrin might die from the allergic reaction he was having. She thought about the irony of the whole situation when it came to the history of allegations about her trying to kill Will.

"Just be calm, Mrs. Hobbs. He is in the best place that he could be right now: in the hands of those nurses and doctors back there," the reception area lady said. "What is your husband's name?"

"Darrin. Darrin Hobbs," Morgan said.

Morgan thought about the irony of what was happening. The old her would have been glad that Darrin might not be okay. The old Morgan might have deliberately put a little something extra into his food to cause him to have an allergic reaction. But the new her wouldn't do that. The new her had sped him to the hospital without a moment's hesitation. She had prayed for the Lord to help her, but she hadn't meant for that kind of help.

"Morgan?"

Morgan heard someone say her name. She turned around to see who it was and felt as if her stomach had dropped. It was the second-to-last person she wanted to see right then, especially under the circumstances.

"Shelby," Morgan said, in a tone of confirmation, more so than it being in a tone of greeting.

"What are you doing here?" Shelby asked.

Morgan had forgotten that Shelby worked in the emergency room of the hospital. Shelby was married to Minister Phillip Tomlinson, Will's best friend. Morgan and Shelby had never gotten along. Their aversion to each other was mainly Morgan's fault.

"Mrs. Hobbs," the reception lady said, "they just called and said you can come back there. Your husband is going to be just fine. He isn't going to die from the allergic reaction." The woman sounded as if she was trying to be reassuring.

Morgan looked first at the reception lady; then she looked at Shelby. Shelby also looked at the reception lady and then she looked at Morgan. Morgan knew how it all must look. She was sure that Shelby thought Morgan was up to her old tricks again and now trying to kill another husband.

Shelby stepped back a step, ready to turn. Morgan reached out and touched her arm, willing her to stop.

"Shelby, please don't go," Morgan said.

Maybe it was something in her eyes, or maybe it was the way Morgan had spoken to Shelby. Her pleading voice had been void of spite, and jealousy. Any time she and Shelby had ever seen each other before, the only thing Morgan had for the woman was dislike and it always showed. Not today; today was different and Shelby must have sensed it.

Although Morgan could still see distrust in Shelby's eyes, the woman remained standing in the spot she was in.

"Shelby, this isn't what it looks like," Morgan said.

"What does it look like, Morgan? Like you've gotten married and are trying to kill your new husband? Because that is exactly what it looks like to me. I am so glad Will finally saw you for the woman you really are," Shelby said.

"Shelby, I know this all looks bad, but I assure you I didn't do a thing to hurt him." Sincere tears welled up in Morgan's eyes. "I know I've been awful in the past, and I don't know how to say this, but . . ." This was going to be one of the hardest things she'd had to say. "Shelby, I need your help."

Chapter 29

Morgan was starting to marvel over the mysterious ways the Lord worked. She was beginning to realize that He didn't always come when a person wanted Him, but He was on time—His time. It had been three days since the night she'd had to rush Darrin to the hospital. It was determined that he had indeed had an allergic reaction to fish. The Japanese restaurant had given her the wrong yakisoba. They made a version with and without seafood, giving her the one with seafood by mistake.

A quick call to the restaurant that night to find out all of the ingredients they used in the dish cleared everything up. The lady who had rung up her order remembered her. She told her about the mix-up. Once Shelby was sure that Morgan wasn't up to her old tricks and trying to harm another husband, she was more agreeable talking to Morgan.

By the time Shelby had softened enough to listen to her, it was about time for Darrin to be released. Morgan tried to explain to Shelby that she really wanted to talk to her but would have to do so another day. She asked if she could call her in a day or so.

The day before she took another trip by taxi to a local dollar store; she hoped to find a prepaid wireless disposable phone there. The store had three types. She purchased the cheapest one and immediately called Shelby. Shelby had agreed to meet with her that day.

At one o' clock that afternoon she was going to drive to the Starbucks located in a Target store that was central to each of their homes. When Darrin called her to ask her whereabouts, she would simply tell them that she needed to pick up some things from Target. It was a believable explanation.

For three days she'd been almost a nervous wreck trying to operate as if everything was absolutely great in her superficial world. It hurt each time she had to crack a smile at Darrin, acting as if she was actually happy. Most of her nervousness came from the uncertainty she felt. She still had no idea how she was going to get out of her situation.

When she stepped into the Starbucks she immediately saw Shelby sitting at a table just beyond the counter. She was sitting at a table that looked like it was meant for two, but there were four chairs around it, and three of the four chairs were occupied. Sitting beside Shelby was Phillip, Shelby's husband. And sitting across from Shelby was Will, Morgan's ex.

Morgan hadn't expected this kind of reception and started feeling a bit self-conscious. But she continued toward the table anyway. Not one of the people at the table had ever done anything wrong to her; it was the other way around.

Both Will and Phillip stood when they saw her approaching. Will pulled out Morgan's seat for her; then he and Phillip sat back down. "Morgan, I hope you don't mind. When I told Phillip I was coming to meet and talk to you he insisted on coming," Shelby said.

"I understand. I mean with my track record, I don't blame you for bringing Phillip with you," Morgan said.

She saw the three of them glance at one another.

"When Shelby told me she saw you and she said you wanted to talk, she also told me how scared you looked when you asked for help from her," Phillip said.

Morgan put her head down. She didn't want pity from them.

"Morgan." It was Will who spoke now.

Morgan looked up at him.

"You know Phil is my best friend. When he told me about the meeting and how Shelby said you were acting and how you looked that night at the hospital, my heart truly went out to you. I asked them if I could come to this meeting. If you don't want me to be here, I'll leave."

It was evident that each of these people cared about what was going on with her. She couldn't fully understand why, but she felt their compassion in her heart. They cared. They weren't pitying her. They were here because they wanted to help her.

"Thank you all. Please stay, Will. I might need all the ears I can get," Morgan said.

She was quiet for a moment, not really knowing how to start the conversation. It wasn't every day that a person told people that their spouse meant them ill will, although this had been the exact situation she had put Will in just a year and a half earlier.

"I don't know where to start," Morgan said. She thought about getting some coffee because she knew they might be there for a while.

"Start wherever you want," Phillip said. "We'll take it from there."

"Okay. I got married a few months ago to a man named Darrin Hobbs. You might have seen him in the news, or in the newspapers. He owns a financial planning company," Morgan said. She felt she needed to lay the groundwork of the story before talking about the sick things Darrin was doing.

"Yeah, I know him," Will said.

"You know of him?" Morgan asked Will. Then she asked Phillip and Shelby, "Do you all know of him too?"

"I think he went to Carson State. But he would have been a few years older than me," Shelby said.

"Yeah, he did go to Carson State," Morgan said.

"I don't know of him," Will said, correcting what Morgan was saying. "I know him. We went to Carson State together. Darrin and I had a couple of classes together. We even served on the student counsel at the same time one year."

Morgan's eyes got wide with disbelief. "Are you serious? You know him."

"You know him too, Phillip. Remember the guy who used to start some of the food fights in the cafeteria?"

"Did he wear purple and gold all the time after he pledged?" Phillip asked.

"Yep, that's the guy," Will said.

"Darrin Hobbs. I knew his face but never knew his name. Or at least I didn't think I knew his name. That name is familiar for some reason. Maybe I have seen him on television or in the papers or something." Phillip shook his head as he tried to remember just why the name sounded so familiar.

"Yeah. You see, this is so strange," Will said to Morgan.

"This is strange. Wow, all three of you know him," Morgan said.

"No, I mean it is strange because I thought you already knew that I knew him," Will said.

"Huh?" Phillip, Shelby, and Morgan all said in unison. They looked at Will for an explanation about what he was talking about.

"I knew you two were dating, and he even told me you all got married. You flew down to Hawaii right?" Will asked.

Morgan's mouth dropped wide open.

"How do you know all of this?" Shelby asked.

Both Morgan and Phillip looked at Will. They wanted to know the answer as well.

"I saw you two out on a date one night. It was the premier of the *Mission: Impossible* movie. You had gotten up at the end of the movie. When I saw you walking out I realized it was you. Once the movie ended I saw Darrin in the lobby. He said he was waiting for his date named Morgan. So I put two and two together," Will said.

"He and I exchanged numbers. I told him that you and I had been in a relationship but it hadn't worked out. To tell you the truth, I warned him to watch his back with you, but I didn't go into detail since Darrin and I weren't that tight. I was surprised when I heard you two had gotten married," Will said.

Morgan could not believe what she was hearing, and it was obvious that Phillip and Shelby couldn't believe it either.

"But, Will, you said you thought Morgan knew you and Darrin had reconnected?"

"Yeah, Darrin sends me texts messages every now and then. Mostly his messages have to do with financial planning tips. He really wants me to check his company out, but some of the messages pertain to you," Will said to Morgan.

"Me?"

"Yeah, like the first one was the night of the movie. It was something about how you hated that you had just missed me at the movie and that you said hi. I thought it was strange. I didn't respond," Will said. "Then like I said every now and then he will send me a text message. Like the wedding. He sent me a picture with you two smiling in your wedding attire. Now that was really strange. I remember the message that accompanied the picture. It said 'Greetings from Hawaii—Mr. and Mrs. Hobbs,'" Will said.

"Are you serious?" Shelby asked.

Will nodded his head. "Yep."

"I never said anything like that. I never even mentioned your name to Darrin. I had no idea he was in contact with you and definitely didn't know a thing about him sending you a wedding picture of us from Hawaii," Morgan said. "Why didn't you contact me?"

"Why would I?" Will countered. "You and I weren't on speaking terms. You wanted nothing to do with me, so I left you alone."

"Darrin Hobbs. Darrin Hobbs." Phillip said the name under his breath. "Why does that name sound so familiar?"

"Plus you two looked happy enough," Will said.

The information Will had just told her felt as if it had landed on her like a ton of bricks. This new information took what she was going through to a whole new level. It was a level she wasn't even sure she could really begin to comprehend. It looked as if they were all trying to comprehend what was going on.

"What you've just told me will only compound what I was about to tell you all. Why I asked Shelby for help in the first place," Morgan said.

"Talk to us, Morgan," Phillip said.

"Okay. I think Darrin is crazy," Morgan said.

All three of them stared at her.

"Would you care to elaborate?" Shelby asked.

So Morgan elaborated. She started with telling them about how Darrin treated her while they were dating, with lavish dates and gifts, and his thoughtful concern, always checking on her and making sure she made it to her destination safely. Then she told them about the evolution she was only recently starting to recognize as being more than just thoughtful concern.

In as much detail as she could she told the group about the events of the last five days. By the time she finished all their heads were nodding as if they understood her concern and why she needed help figuring out how to get out of the relationship in a safe manner.

"You said Darrin Hobbs right?" Phillip said.

"Yeah," Morgan said.

Phillip snapped his fingers. "I remember exactly why that name sounds familiar now. That man is strange that's for sure. You need to get away from him and get away from him fast."

"Why, what do you mean?" Morgan asked.

"Yeah," Shelby asked, "what do you mean? What do you know about him?"

Will looked at Phillip with expectancy, wanting to hear what Phillip had to say as well.

"Shelby, you remember Travis and Beryl right?"

"Yeah, from the couples retreat on Redemption Lake. I mean on Lake Turner."

"Yes. Well Beryl used to date a guy named Darrin and if I am remembering correctly his last name was Hobbs."

"What happened?" Morgan asked.

"Long story short is Travis told me Beryl and her two boys basically had to leave the man, only taking the shirts on their backs," Phillip said.

Morgan's thoughts flashed back to the day she'd gone up into the attic. She thought about the boxes with the toys and clothing. "Is Beryl about a size twelve?"

Will and Phillip looked at Shelby for confirmation. "Yeah, she is about a size twelve."

"And the two boys, are they about three and five years old?" Morgan asked.

"They would have been back then. But that was like two years ago," Phillip said.

Morgan put her hand over her mouth and said, "Oh, my goodness."

"What?" Shelby asked.

"Darrin has boxes full of that woman's and her children's clothing, shoes, and even the boys' toys. I found them one morning when I was checking the house out. I thought it was very odd, but I never asked Darrin about it. To be honest I forgot about the things," Morgan said.

"I'm sold," Shelby said. "It is obvious Morgan needs to get away from the guy. The question is, how can she do it?"

"She may have to cut her losses as well. Find a good lawyer and try to move on with your life," Phillip said.

"I agree," Shelby said.

"This is all way too strange," Will said.

Morgan wanted her things, She didn't have much but she still wanted her personal belongings. "I can't just up and leave. I want my things. I don't want them to collect dust in an attic."

"I suggest you cut your losses and never look back," Phillip said.

"But where will I go? What will I do?" Morgan had no idea.

For a split second Phillip and Shelby looked over at Will. He ignored them and looked the other way. Morgan had seen the whole display. She didn't expect for them to give her a place to stay, and she was thankful that she at least had someone to talk to about the situation.

"I can give you some money for a hotel. I am at least willing to do that," Will said.

"Will, you are much too good of a person. Thank you," Morgan said. "I do have a little money in my savings account, but I would like to use it to hire some movers and a storage unit."

"Morgan, didn't you just explain to us that your husband probably has video recording devices out of the wazoo at your house? How do you think he will react when he sees a moving company moving furniture from the house? Don't you think he might be just the least bit upset?"

"I think he would probably pop a blood vessel. I only plan to take what I came into the marriage with. And all of my things are still packed in one of the guest rooms. I am thinking the movers would only be at the house for an hour or so at the most. I've got an idea about how I can distract him while the movers are there," Morgan said.

"Whatever it is you are planning, it sounds risky," Shelby said.

"It probably is risky, but there is no way I am going to let Darrin get the total best of me. He has already manipulated my life too much and it is time for that to stop," Morgan said.

"At this point, I will only ask one thing of you all. I just need for you to send up as many prayers as you can for me. I am going to need them," Morgan said.

"I can do that and something else as well," Phillip said.

"What's that?" Morgan asked.

"When we leave here, I want you to drive your car over to my car dealership. I am going to have my mechanics go over your car with a fine-tooth comb if need be to see if they can find anything that looks like a tracking GPS or anything that looks remotely suspicious," Phillip said.

As humbly as she could she said, "Thank you, Phillip. Thank you all. I don't know how to thank you enough."

Chapter 30

"Surprise," Morgan said. She knocked on Darrin's office door.

Darrin looked up from a report he was reading at his office desk. He looked startled for a moment and took a quick glance at his computer screen. Morgan couldn't see what was on the screen, but she was willing to bet it was the information for the GPS tracking device he'd had planted on her car.

What Darrin didn't know was that she had left the device in the garage at home. The only thing his screen would have showed was that her car was supposedly at home. She knew that as soon as she parted from him that afternoon, he'd be calling the tracking company to find out what the glitch in the system was.

"Morgan, honey, what a pleasant surprise."

"I am glad it is pleasant. Some people don't like surprises," Morgan said.

"What brings you here, my dear?" Darrin asked.

"I have come to take you out to lunch. I can't remember the last time you and I had lunch together. Remember I told you I wanted to spend more time with you, and if I can't get you to come home earlier to do so, then I thought I'd bring myself to you."

"I, ahhh—" Darrin started to say something, but Morgan cut him off.

"I, ahhh, nothing. Come on. Get your wallet. We don't need your keys, I'm driving. Don't worry, I won't hog all of your time, I know you'll need to get back to work in a timely manner."

Darrin hadn't budged from his spot. She needed him to move from his spot. The movers should be arriving at her house any second now.

"Darrin, I am not taking no for an answer." She walked over to his desk. "If you don't come with me then I'll just hang out here the rest of the day." She touched the mouse on his desk and shook it back and forth as if she were trying to get on his computer.

"Whoa, be careful. If you click the wrong key you could cause some major financial damage," Darrin said.

Finally he stood and Morgan took a deep breath of relief.

Two solid hours later, Morgan returned to Darrin's office building. She dropped him off at the front door. The movers had completed their mission and she was now free to go. She would never be returning to the house at 1485 Green Forest Drive. She now needed to oversee the moving company's placement of her items into the storage unit she'd rented.

She wondered how long it would take for Darrin to give her a call. There wasn't a need to wonder very long. Darrin called her forty-five minutes after she'd dropped him off.

Bracing herself she answered the phone. It was now or never. "Hello," Morgan said.

"Morgan," Darrin said, his voice sounded strained as if he was trying to hold his temper at bay.

"Hey, yeah, what's up?"

"Where are you?" Darrin said.

"Home," Morgan said.

"No." He paused. "You're not," Darrin said. It sounded as if he was actually gritting his teeth as he spoke.

She could tell he was angry.

"How do you know I'm not at the house? Are you actually there or are you looking at the GPS tracker information?" Morgan asked.

Darrin chuckled.

"Is something funny? If there is I missed it," Morgan said.

"You found the GPS tracker, huh? That is what is funny," Darrin said.

"I am glad you think so."

"Don't get so uptight about it. I just put a tracker on your car in case it got stolen. I was just looking out for you, sweetheart."

"Stop, Darrin. Save your breath. I don't know what kind of game you are playing but I'm out. Find someone else to play with."

"You are right. I'm not home, but I can come home. Let's talk about all of this tonight when I get home. Maybe by then you will have calmed down some," Darrin said.

"The only person you'll be talking to at the house will be yourself. I won't be there," Morgan said.

"Oh, my goodness. Are you really that mad? Okay, okay, fine, blow off some steam. I'll call a hotel and make a reservation for you to have a night away. Where do you want to stay?"

"As far away from you as I possibly can. Darrin, I am leaving you. I am not coming back to your home," Morgan said.

"Say what?" Darrin just about yelled into the phone.

"You heard me right. I am not coming back to that house," Morgan said.

"If you don't return home tonight then don't ever come back, and forget about getting any of your things."

"Why don't you let me worry about that? What are you going to do, box my things up like you did to that other woman and her kids?"

There was silence on the other end of the phone. She was sure he was trying to figure out how she knew about the woman named Beryl and her children. He was probably wondering just how much she knew.

"So anyway, don't expect me to come back because I'm not," Morgan said.

"Morgan, you don't want to do this," Darrin said.

"Darrin, it's done." She hung up the phone.

She wished she had her own hidden camera to see the look on his face right now, and she really wished she had access to the video feed of the hidden cameras he had in his home for when he got home. She was pretty sure she had found most if not all of the hidden cameras he'd had strategically placed throughout the house.

The same Web site that she'd found with the hidden camera devices and car tracking devices also had a device to detect hidden cameras. She had ordered one and had it overnighted to the house. It was been risky, but Darrin pretty much kept the same schedule and he was never home during the day.

She ran the detector through the house before leaving to pick Darrin up for his distraction lunch, the same distraction lunch she'd used to get him away from his computer while the movers moved her items from the guest room. Darrin would be absolutely livid when he found out all of her things were gone from the guest room. He would also be furious to find that his surveillance devices were gone. He could report them stolen, but how was he going to explain secretly recording his wife? Morgan had no idea if his recording activities were legal or illegal, but she was sure Darrin would not want personal business about his home to get out into the community.

She pulled a box of clothes and her file box of personal papers out of the storage unit, locked it up and headed to the hotel Will had so graciously paid for her to stay in for a week. For once she was really thankful Will was such a good man. She was remorseful for the way she had treated him. She had tried to hurt the man in all the places that counted: his pocket, his psychological wellbeing, and even his belief in the Lord. She made a mental note to call him. She needed to apologize to him for all the wrong she'd done to him in the past.

While she was making mental notes to apologize to people, she thought about Amber. Amber had only been trying to be a good friend. But all Morgan could seem to see was a jealousy that didn't exist. Amber was owed an apology as well.

Once she got settled in at her hotel room, Morgan took a shower and dressed in her pajamas. It had been a long day and she was drained. There was one more thing she wanted to do before she turned in for the night. The letter from her grandmother was starting to weigh heavy on her mind. It was time she opened it to find out what her grandmother had to say.

She opened the file box of personal papers in which she was pretty sure she had placed the envelope. After rifling through some old bills and junk mail she located the envelope with the unmistakable handwriting. Her hands became shaky as she tore off the end of the envelope and slipped out the single sheet of lined paper. She opened it and read:

Dear Cecily,

I hope this letter finds you doing well. I wondered for years how you were and what you were doing. I was happy and sad to see the man who came to my door looking for information about you. Happy because finally I had word that you were alive and well. But I was sad, because the man didn't look like he was pleased to see me. I didn't know what to think. I know I am probably rambling. I am trying to find the right words. I just pray this letter makes it to you. I just pray that you are safe and sound.

Cecily, I know you think I had something to do with that business about your children being taken by the social services people. I know you didn't believe me when I told you I didn't have anything to do with it. I just hope you'll listen to me now. Things were so confusing and I thought I was helping the situation when I went to talk to them on your behalf. Those people turned my words around and used them against you. I am sorry for that.

I hope you can find it in your heart to forgive me for not acting sooner to help you. Please find it in your heart to forgive me for handling things wrong when I did try to reach out for help for you. And lastly, if you can find it in your heart to call me, please do. The phone number is still the same.

Cecily, please know that I love you still and always. My love for you has never changed over the years.

Love, Mama Geraldine

Morgan read the letter twice before setting it down beside her on the bed. Her grandmother said that she hadn't been the one to deliberately have the children taken from her. Her grandmother was actually asking for forgiveness. And just as importantly, her grandmother still loved her.

For the first time in a long time, Morgan started to feel the hard outer shell of ice she'd formed around herself start to melt a bit. It was melting just enough to cause her to reach for her cell phone. According to the clock it was a little past six o'clock in the evening. She dialed the 910 area code exchange and the last seven digits she had committed to memory.

When the person on the other end picked and said, "Hello," Morgan's body loosened up a bit.

"Hello, Mama Geraldine," Morgan said.

"Cecily. That you?" Morgan's Grandmother Geraldine said. The voice on the other end sounded feeble. To Morgan it sounded as if her grandmother had aged tremendously.

"Yes, Mama Geraldine. This is Cecily," Morgan said, using her first name.

"Oh, Lord, have mercy. Thank you, Lord. Thank you, Lord. Thank you, Lord," Mama Geraldine said into the phone. "God does answer prayers." Then she started to cry.

Epilogue

It seemed like over the past few days, Morgan had been apologizing to people left and right. She started with Amber, and shared the ordeal she'd been through with Darrin. Instead of Amber rubbing it in her face, she had given Morgan a warm hug. Then she offered to hire Morgan back if she wanted her old position back. Morgan had quickly taken her up on the offer.

She had also called Desiree to apologize to her about dismissing her so quickly and not being a better friend. Now she was going to take the opportunity to apologize to Will. He was the one she needed to apologize to the most.

"Thanks for meeting me, Will," Morgan said. "And thanks for agreeing to do this." They were sitting on a bench located outside of their son Isaiah's daycare. Isaiah had gone on a trip with the preschool and was scheduled to come back at any moment.

"You're welcome. I am actually glad you suggested it. Every child deserves to have both their parents in their life," Will said.

"Every child does deserve to have a relationship with both of their parents. I only wish I'd had one with my parents," Morgan said.

Will looked at her quizzically.

Morgan had never really told him anything about her family that was actually truthful. "I know most of the information you know about my family came from you finding it out yourself, especially since I lied about my parents being deceased."

Will nodded his head.

"Truth is, I don't know who my father is, and the woman you keep calling my mother is actually my grandmother. My mother left me when I was very young."

"I thought that lady Ms. Geraldine was your mother," Will said.

"She raised me, so she might as well have been my mother. Some people in town thought she was my mother." Morgan waved her hand. "Anyway. I think having my mother leave me, then my first husband leave me and then having my children taken away, turned on a cold switch in the bottom of my heart. At least that is what I think."

Will listened intently as Morgan was finally telling him the truth about her childhood and life.

"Hopefully what I am telling you will give you some insight into why I acted the way I did during our so-called marriage."

"You said your kids were taken from you?" Will asked.

"Yes, I couldn't take care of them. I asked my grandmother for help, social services, and even the church, but no one helped me. I tried so keep a roof over our heads and food on the table but I just didn't have the means. Social services came one day and said I was neglecting my children. For a long time, I really believed my grandmother called social services to take my kids." Morgan spoke in a voice softer than Will had probably ever heard her speak in.

"I did the best I could to try to fight and get them back, but in the end I gave up. I realized the people at social services were right. I didn't have any means to take care of the kids and after a while I started thinking they were better off wherever they were."

Morgan continued to speak and get everything off of her chest. "After losing my mom, my husband, and then my kids, who I loved dearly, I let my heart go cold, vowing to never let anything or anyone touch it again. I ended up turning my back on the church and on God." Morgan sighed.

"As timing would have it, ironically I just found out my grandmother never had any ill will toward me. She wrote me a letter asking me to call her. I have no idea how she got my address. I don't know why, but I picked up my cell phone and did as she asked. I hadn't spoken to the woman in years because I just couldn't forgive her for what she'd done to me," Morgan said.

"I know how she got your address. I actually gave it to her," Will said.

Instead of asking Will a number of questions about how he'd gotten her address and why he gave it out, she said, "Thank you for doing that."

Will sat back, surprised by her response.

"When I talked to her, it was as if the years melted away and I was a little girl again. My grandmother cried when she heard my voice on the phone, and something just told me that she would never do a thing to intentionally hurt me. As it turns out, she did talk to social services on my behalf, but they took what she said and twisted it until they made a case against me. It was all a big misunderstanding and for all those years I despised my grandmother.

"By the time we ended our phone conversation I was crying as well," Morgan said.

"Wow, that explains a lot," Will said.

"Because of all the pain I felt about my children, I never planned to have any more children. Getting pregnant with Isaiah threw me for a loop."

"You never wanted any more children?" Will asked. Morgan could see the hurt in his eyes. Will loved children and wanted a houseful of them.

"No. Sorry. If it had been up to me I wouldn't have had a baby. I didn't want to risk loving again and then loosing again," Morgan said.

"Wow."

"I know this is a lot of information to process at one time. I know it will take time to explain it all. But the main thing I want to say is that I'm sorry for the way I treated you and sorry for the way I've treated Isaiah. I was awful and I was wrong," Morgan said.

"Sometimes, hurt people want to hurt other people. Well, I was one of those hurt people. It doesn't make it right, and I know this will sound crazy, but I can better understand where you were coming from now," Will said.

"Back at the correctional facility, you said you forgave me. Did you really forgive me?" Morgan asked.

"Yes, Morgan. I forgave you. Now you have to forgive yourself. Don't look backward, look forward instead," Will said.

"Thank you for forgiving me even though I hadn't even had the sense at the time to ask you for your forgiveness. I think the Lord has forgiven me as well. I've had to turn to Him often over the past few months, and He has come through for me each and every time. I won't let Him down. I won't stray away again."

Morgan shifted her body, turning toward Will. "I've started going to church again; not New Hope, but another church," Morgan said.

"I am glad to hear that," Will said.

The activity bus for the daycare pulled up to the curb. Both Morgan and Will turned their attention to the bus. Within a couple of minutes three- and four-year-olds filed out of the bus in a line following their teacher. As soon as Isaiah saw his father he broke from the line and ran over to the bench.

Will picked up his son and gave him a hug. "Speaking of moving forward. Morgan, I would like to reintroduce you to your son."

Morgan looked at the little boy she had given birth to. He was over a year older now. His face had changed and he no longer looked like a baby; he now looked like a tiny version of his father.

Isaiah smiled at her, put his arms out as if he wanted Morgan to hold him. She opened up her arms and took the boy in her arms. As she held him close it felt like a piece of ice had chipped off of her heart.

Discussion Questions

1. How do you think the story would have changed if Morgan had gone ahead and opened up the letter from her grandmother when she received it instead of months later?

2. Do you think Morgan's rekindled connection with the Lord is genuine? Why?

3. What was the first red flag you noticed about Darrin that might indicate he wasn't such a fabulous catch?

4. What were some of the other red flags that Morgan might have noticed sooner if she hadn't been so money hungry?

5. What was your opinion of Morgan in the beginning of the book?

6. What was your opinion of Morgan at the end of the book?

7. What did you like most about this story?

8. If you could write a next chapter for Morgan, what would it be about?

9. Did you know that Morgan and Will's story started in Monique Miller's novel titled *Quiet As It's Kept?*

10. Did you know that Darrin is a character from Monique Miller's novel titled *The Marrying Kind?*

About the Author

Monique Miller is a native of North Carolina and is a graduate of North Carolina Central University in Durham, North Carolina. She is a member of the Divine Literary Tour (DLT) a non-profit organization that brings together Black Greek authors from across the nation for a cross-country tour to promote literacy.

Monique's creative writing landed her a placement in the 2003 Black Expressions Book Club's Annual Fiction Writing Contest. Monique's novels include *Nobody's Angel*, *The Marrying Kind*, *Quiet As It's Kept*, *Redemption Lake*, *Soul Confessions*, and *Secret Sisterhood*. Currently, Monique resides in North Carolina with her family.

Web site:	www.moniquemiller.com
Twitter:	@BooksByMonique
E-mail:	moniquemillerauthor@gmail.com
Facebook:	Author Monique Miller

Notes